W9-AJP-156

THE HARD BOUNCE

The Debut Novel from the Creator of *Thuglit*

Todd Robinson

F+W Media, Inc.

Published by
TYRUS BOOKS, an imprint of F+W Media, Inc.
10151 Carver Road, Suite 200, Blue Ash, Ohio 45242. U.S.A.
www.tyrusbooks.com

Hardcover ISBN 10: 1-4405-5892-2
Hardcover ISBN 13: 978-1-4405-5892-4
Trade Paperback ISBN 10: 1-4405-5767-5
Trade Paperback ISBN 13: 978-1-4405-5767-5
eISBN 10: 1-4405-5768-3
eISBN 13: 978-1-4405-5768-2

Printed in the United States of America.

10 9 8 7 6 5 4 3 2 1

Praise for *The Hard Bounce*

"Schooled by retro pulp and a workingman's gritty self-preservation, Todd Robinson's prose cuts with a rusty blade and we can't tear our eyes away. No glib talkers here, no high-handed lessons, just the kind of noir you'll recognize if you ever had to pick between frying pan and fire."

—Sophie Littlefield, author of *A Bad Day for Pretty*

"Todd Robinson's debut is tough and gritty, but what makes *The Hard Bounce* such a standout is its sly humor and surprising poignancy. The razor-sharp dialogue will have Elmore Leonard watching his back."

—Hilary Davidson, author of *The Damage Done* and *The Next One to Fall*

"Todd Robinson is an immense talent, writing modern crime fiction with a toughness, realism, humor, and smooth prose that few match."

—Dave Zeltserman, author of *Outsourced*

"A brilliant novel—smart, funny, and deeply moving."

—Ken Bruen, Barry and Shamus Award–winning author of *The Devil*

"Staccato-like dialogue and action start to finish; this author has writing chops and reminds us of it throughout this hardboiled yet poignant story of a dark past, the loss of humanity, and the difficult road to finding it again in places most dare not look."

—Charlie Stella, author of *Johnny Porno*

Praise for *The Hard Bounce*

"*The Hard Bounce* is a big, proud, bruiser of a novel—packed with humor, guts, and heavyweight grace. Robinson's the best hardboiled crime writer I've come across in years."

—Benjamin Whitmer, author of *Pike*

"The team of Boo and Junior are two of the best, most entertaining characters to invade hardboiled fiction in a long time. Todd Robinson's *The Hard Bounce* follows this dynamic duo through the underbelly of Boston as they get bruised, beaten, battered, shocked, and shot. Being a bouncer is an even tougher gig than you thought. A kick in the nutsack with a surprising amount of heart."

—Victor Gischler, Edgar- and Anthony-nominated author of *Go-Go Girls of the Apocalypse*

"*The Hard Bounce* is one of those rare debuts that roars its intentions from the first page and that keeps you reading with the power and force of its darkly witty voice. Robinson's bringing crime back to the mean, working streets where it's always belonged with this deeply affecting, startlingly affecting novel. Boo Malone is one of the most intriguing, compelling, and empathetic protagonists I've encountered in a while, and you'll be thinking about the secrets of his past for a long time after you've finished that last page."

—Russel D. McLean, author of *The Lost Sister*

Twenty-Three Years Ago

The Boy was eight years old when he learned how to hate.

It's still difficult, even today, for him to remember the events in their right order. He knows where they should go, but hard as he tries, they drift through his mind like glitterflakes in a snow globe.

The screaming and the blood followed the first explosion. That much he's sure of. So much blood.

The second explosion. Running at him. Throwing himself at a grown man like a rabid animal unaware that it doesn't stand a chance. He was big for his age. He still didn't stand a chance.

Bang. He was gone. Just like that. Tumbling in and out of consciousness with no idea where he was. What time it was. Who or where he is.

Bang. He was back. A priest. He can't understand him. The inside of an ambulance, feeling it hurtle through the Boston traffic, the doctor unable to control his tears as he tries to stem the tide of blood that won't stop pouring out of him. The Boy didn't know there was that much blood inside of him. He knew he would run out soon. He was terrified.

Bang. On a gurney. Lots of people yelling. He bites somebody's hand. A sharp pinprick in his arm. *Where is she?*

Bang. Another priest. He's saying the same unintelligible words as the first.

Months in a hospital. Pain like an eight-year-old should never know exists in this world. Parades of doctors—first for his ruined body, the second for his damaged mind.

He has an anger management problem, they say.

Anger management. It's a nice term for people who can afford it.

Psychologists in two-hundred-dollar sweaters and condescending smiles, telling him:

You need to let it go.

Think about the rest of your life.

Think about how lucky you are.

The world is a beautiful place.

The world is not a beautiful place. Not to The Boy, who's going to need two more operations before he can piss without a tube and spigot.

They ask him why he's such an angry person, what he's so angry at.

Think about how lucky you are.

Chapter One

I can't tolerate a bully, even when my job is to be the biggest swinging dick on the block.

Somebody in the booking office for The Cellar thought that all-ages punk shows on the weekends was a bright idea. Maybe it was. Nobody owned up to having the idea though.

The place was crowded, high school kids with rainbow-tinted hairdos making up most of the audience. The rest were uncomfortable parents watching their babies perform in bands with names like Mazeltov Cocktail and No Fat Chicks. As far as crowds go, they were a nice break from the normal regiment of scumbags, skinheads, punks, frat boys, musicians, and wannabes that we had to deal with. Odds were pretty good we wouldn't be involved in any brawls or dragging overdoses out of the bathroom. All things considered, it should have been a cakewalk day.

Shoulda, woulda, coulda.

Me and Junior handled the shift ourselves: me watching the door while Junior patrolled the three floors of the club. Between the two of us, we could easily police a few dozen skinny tweens. We were less bouncers than babysitters with a combined weight of 470 pounds (mostly mine) and about ten grand in tattoos (mostly Junior's). Every parent's dream.

We'd only been open an hour and we'd already confiscated seventeen bottles of beer, two bottles of vodka, one of rum, three joints, and seven airplane bottles of tequila. The way it was going, Junior and I would be able to stock our own bars by nightfall.

A collective groan floated out from inside the bar as the ninth inning closed at Fenway. I poked my head in to check the score. 9–3 Yankees.

And it just had to be the fucking Yankees, didn't it?

As I poked my head back out, the first fat droplets of rain spattered on my shoes, as if the angels themselves wept for the poor Sox. I backed under The Cellar's fluorescent sign, but the wind zigzagged the drizzle all over me.

At least I was in a better place than Junior. The basement didn't have any ventilation and crowds produced furnace-level temperatures. A hot wind would gust up the stairs when the club got crowded, feeling (and smelling) like Satan farting on your back. If I was hot outside, Junior must have been miserable.

The first wave of baseball fans wandered into Kenmore Square. I could hear chants of "Yankees suck" approaching from the Fenway area.

Two guys broke off from the herd, stumbling in the bar's direction. The bigger guy wore an old Yaztremski jersey and a mullet that would have embarrassed Billy Ray Cyrus in 1994. His buddy wore a backwards old school Patriots hat and a Muffdiving Instructor T-shirt.

Really . . . ? Really?

Asshats.

I recognized their tribe immediately, the type of townies who will go to their graves believing they could do a better job than the pros did—if only they hadn't knocked up Mary Lou Dropdrawers senior year.

Those guys.

Mullet looked over, his eyes wide as he saw the crew of punk kids in front of The Cellar. His smile was filled with a bully's joy. He grabbed Buddy's collar and pointed his attention toward the kids.

"Nice hairdo," the townie called out to the kids milling outside. "What are you, some kinda faggot?"

I closed my eyes and sighed.

Away we go . . .

Buddy laughed with a mocking hilarity, pointing a finger and looking to the rest of the crowd for an approval he wasn't getting.

A skinny kid, head shaved close and dyed in a leopard skin pattern, turned. "Why? You looking for some ass, sailor?" the kid yelled back, smacking his bony behind for emphasis. He got some approving chuckles from the passersby and hoots of laughter from the other kids.

Buddy looked pissed off that the kid got the laughs from the crowd that he hadn't.

"What did you say to me, bitch?" said Mullet, quickstepping toward the bar.

The kid flipped the guy off with both hands and ran back into the club.

When Mullet got a couple of feet from the entrance, I stepped halfway across the doorway. He stopped short and we stood there, shoulder to shoulder.

"What's your problem?" Mullet asked, puffing out his chest.

"No problem," I said, blowing cigarette smoke out my nose, moving my face closer to his. "It's just not happening for you here. Not today."

"I wanna get a beer." His breath reeked of soft pretzels and a few too many overpriced Fenway Miller Lites.

"Not here you're not. Get one down the street if you're thirsty."

Buddy suddenly found his shoes real fascinating. Mullet and I kept giving each other the hairy eyeball. "It's a free country, asshole."

"And a wonderful free country it is. This bar isn't, though. Not for you. Not today." I took another long pull from my cigarette and fought the urge to blow the smoke into his face.

"Who's gonna stop me, you?"

"Yup." There it was. The frog was dropped. Let's see if it jumped. I balled my fist around the medium-point Sharpie in my pocket. Bouncer's best friend. Won't kill anybody, but hurts like a bitch when jammed between a couple of ribs.

I stood at the long end of his best intimidating stare, which frankly, wasn't. Mullet decided to give it one last shot.

"What are you? Some kind of tough guy?"

"Well, gee golly Hoss, I haven't started any fights with twelve-year-olds lately, so I'm not sure." I moved my face right into his. One more inch and my cigarette was going up his nose. I removed my hand from my pocket and held it low at my side.

Buddy grabbed Mullet's arm, and Mullet twitched like he'd been shocked.

"C'mon, man. Let's go." Buddy's voice cracked like he'd just been kicked in the nuts. Now I know why he'd minded his own. Hard to talk a tough line when you sound like Minnie Mouse.

"Yeah. Fine. This bar's full of faggots anyway," Mullet muttered as he walked off.

"Fuck you very much, gentlemen. Have a good one." I clipped a sharp one-fingered salute at them as they retreated.

The kids applauded and cheered as the two walked off. I shut them up quick with a glower. I made a hundred bucks a shift, plus a tip-out from the bar. Not enough money to be anybody's pal.

More noise pollution began thumping from the basement. The group quickly ground out their smokes on the wet cement as they filtered back inside.

A girl with brightly dyed red hair lingered outside longer than the rest. I could feel her stare on the side of my neck like a sun lamp. I glanced over and she gave me a little smile. She couldn't have been more than fifteen, but behind the smile was something older. Something that made me uncomfortable.

As she passed me going into the club, she brushed her tiny body against me, tiptoed up, and kissed me on the cheek. "My hero," she whispered softly into my ear and went inside.

I shuddered with Nabokovian creeps and shifted my attention back to the crowd. (And yes, fuck you, I know who Nabokov is. I'm a bouncer, not a retard.)

I kept my thousand-yard stare front and center on the passing crowd, keeping my peripheral sharp for any run-up sucker punches. It happens. I was alert to every degree of my environment except what was directly behind me; which is why I nearly had a heart attack when a booming crash sounded from the back of the bar. Instinctively, I ducked, made sure my head was still intact. Inside the bar, every patron jerked his head toward the hallway leading to the parking lot out back. I bull-rushed through the thick crowd, almost knocking down a couple customers. Somebody's beer spilled down the seat of my pants as I hit the hallway.

Junior was halfway up the back stairs when I hit the huge steel exit door at full clip. The door opened only a couple inches before slamming into something solid, my shoulder making a wet popping sound. The door clanged like a giant cymbal and I ricocheted back, landing on top of Junior. We both toppled hard onto the concrete stairwell. Pretty pink birdies chirped in my head as I lay sprawled on top of him.

"Christ! Get offa me!" Junior yelped.

I rolled onto my wounded arm, and that same something popped back into place inside my shoulder. I roared like a gut-shot bull.

Junior pulled himself up and pressed against the door with all his weight. The door barely budged. Whatever was jammed against the door squealed metallically against the concrete.

I pinwheeled my arm a couple times to make sure there was no permanent damage. Apart from a dull throb and some numbness in my fingers, I'd survive.

"You okay?" Junior asked.

"Seems like it."

"Then do you wanna help me move this fucking thing or should I kiss your boo-boo first?"

"Would you?"

I pressed my good shoulder against the door beside Junior and pushed. Whatever was on the other side, it was heavy as hell. With a painful scraping of metal, the door slowly slid open. We had about an eighth of a second to wish it hadn't.

A flood of garbage and scumwater came pouring through the crack. Plastic cups, beer cans, crusty napkins, and a few good gallons of dumpster juice slopped over our shoes. Somebody had toppled the entire Dumpster across the entryway. The stink was epic.

"Motherfucker!" Junior dry-heaved mightily, but didn't puke. "I just bought these goddamn shoes!"

A horn honked in the parking lot. Mullet and Buddy sat in the cab of a black Ford Tundra. They were laughing their asses off and wagging middle fingers as they peeled out and shot the pickup toward the lot gate.

The truck got halfway across the lot before jamming up in the long line of exiting Sox Faithful. Other cars moved in from both sides and the rear, neatly boxing them in. They had nowhere to go.

Junior stomped across the parking lot, his temper giving him an Irish sunburn. "I'm going to kill you, then fuck you, you cocksucker!"

I'm not sure that was what Junior meant to convey, but I went with the sentiment. "That's right," I called out. "He's not gay; he just likes to fuck dead things."

In the large rearview mirrors, I could see the fear on Mullet's face. Suddenly, I saw him lean over and grab for something. I was pretty sure it wasn't going to be a kitten.

"He's reaching!" I yelled to Junior. We took the last twenty feet at a sprint, and I swung a haymaker into the open driver's side window. My fist cracked Mullet right in the back of his hairdo as he turned back.

"Gahh!" he replied. His hands were empty.

"Hey!" was all Buddy had time for before Junior reached into the passenger side, grabbed his head, and whacked his face hard onto the dashboard.

A pair of high voices cried out from the cab as two small faces in Red Sox caps smushed against the tinted glass. "Daddy!" one of the little boys cried in terror.

Bang.

The world exploded red and I had Mullet's windpipe in the middle of my squeezing fingers.

"*Are you fucking nuts?* Were you going to drive drunk with your fucking kids in the back?" Spittle flew from my lips onto Mullet's reddening face. "Are you out of your *fucking mind*?"

"Please don't hurt my daddy!" Tiny fingers clasped at mine, trying to pry them open. Something deep inside was telling me to let go, but the rest of me wasn't hearing it.

"Let him go, Boo." Junior's voice sounded miles away. I saw his hands on my arms, pulling me, but I couldn't feel him there.

Mullet's lips went blue, and his eyes started to roll up white.

Buddy was also trying frantically to loosen my grip. "Jesus Christ, you're killing him! Let him go." Buddy's blood-slicked fingers kept slipping off mine.

Suddenly, an explosion shocked my hands off Mullet's throat. I stepped back, my hands reflexively going to the place I thought I'd been shot. The truck listed down and to the left. Another explosion and the truck sank further. I wheeled my head to see Junior standing by the limp oversized tire, box-cutter in his hand. "Let's go, Boo. They're not going anywhere."

I blinked a few times, regaining myself. One of the boys was halfway though the partition into the front seat. He was crying, snot running over his upper lip, screaming at me, the monster who was hurting his daddy. "Go *away*!" he shrieked. "Go *away*!" He threw an empty Red Sox souvenir cup at me. It bounced off my chest, clattered to the ground.

Junior took me by the arm and pulled me the long way around to the entrance of The Cellar so no one could tell the cops where to find us.

Junior walked at my side as we passed around the lot. I could feel his eyes on me. Without looking over, I said, "You got something to say?"

“Nothing specific. You okay?”

“Finer than Carolina. We just performed a public service, if you ask me.”

He didn’t ask me. “Fair enough,” he said. “You want a soda big guy?”

“Fuck off.”

Toward the front of the jam, an old lady in a beat up Dodge Omni and Red Sox cap gave me a big thumbs-up.

For some reason, that bothered me.

I could still hear the kids crying when we got back to the bar. I shouldn’t have been able to, but I did.

Chapter Two

Soaked from the rain, we did our best to dry off with bar napkins. The flimsy napkins kept shredding, leaving little white pills on our clothes. Junior kept smirking, looking like he had something to say.

"What?"

"He's not gay; he just likes fucking dead things?"

I held it in as long as I could, but one loose snort later and we both exploded into laughter. Junior doubled over, howling. My ribs ached from the force of my own guffaws. The guilt still gnawed, but I needed the laugh right then.

It was easy to cut the giggles, though, when we realized one of us had to clean up the pile of shit outside.

"Rock, paper, scissors?" Junior asked, wiping away a tear.

"Of course." If it was good enough to settle negotiations when we were eleven, it was good enough today.

"On shoot. One, two, three, SHOOT!"

Rock.

Junior made paper.

Shit.

"I'll get you the shovel, garbage man," Junior said. He hooted evilly as he trotted to the utility closet. I really hate it when Junior hoots.

An hour later, the show closed and I was only about two-thirds done. The crowd exiting the building my way covered their faces and made disgusted sounds as they passed. They were all smart enough not to make any comments. I had a shovel.

The cleanup left me glazed in vinegary old beer, ashes, and some viscous crap I didn't even want to attempt identifying. It also left me deeply, deeply pissy. By the time I was down to the last shovelful, the storm had transitioned from drizzle to summer downpour.

Carefully, I pulled a cigarette from my pocket, mindful not to contaminate any part that was going into my mouth. The wet paper split and tobacco crumbled under my fingertips. I was just about to let loose with one of the longest, loudest, and most profane curses in the history of language when I heard a woman's voice from the doorway behind me.

"Excuse me, Mr. Malone?"

I turned, wanting to see who was speaking before I answered.

"Are you William Malone?" she asked.

I gave her the once-over. Too small to be a cop. Definitely too young to be a cop in a suit. Usually only cops call me Mr. Malone. "That's me," I said, staying right where I was.

"Kelly Reese," she said, extending her hand in a sharp, businesslike gesture.

I didn't take her hand. "No offense, but I wouldn't do that right now. Not unless you plan on getting some serious vaccinations later," I said, trying to wring rain and muck out of my shirtfront.

She didn't get it at first. Then the wind shifted and she caught a quick whiff of what I had been dealing with. To her credit, she managed to cover her reflexive gag with a demure cough. "Oh," she said through watering eyes.

"What can I do for you, Ms. Reese?"

"I'd like to talk to you about possibly hiring your firm."

My firm? "I don't know what you've been told, Ms. Reese, but we're not lawyers."

"Maybe it would be better if we spoke inside. You're getting wet." The wind blew her way again, and fresh tears sprang into her eyes. She subtly made with the scratchy-scratchy motion instead of pinching her nostrils shut. Classy chick.

"I am wet. Can't really get much wetter."

She nodded sickly in agreement. "I'm sorry," she said, and she finally covered her nose and mouth, unable to take the stink anymore. I guess class can only hold out for so long.

"After you," I said. I could feel my ears burn with embarrassment as I turned and followed her up the stairs.

Everything about her screamed "out of place." Her dark, curly hair was cut in a perfect bob. Most of our regulars looked like their hair was styled by a lunatic with a Weed Whacker. She was also in a dark blue suit that looked like it cost more than the combined wardrobe of everyone else in the bar.

Whether your collar is blue or white, in Boston, you stick with the crowd that shares your fashion sense. The city's got a class line as sharp as a glass scalpel and wider than a sorority pledge's legs. The old money, reaching back generations, live up on Beacon Hill and the North End. They summer in places like Newport and the Berkshires.

They see me and mine as a pack of low-class mooks. We see them as a bunch of rich bitch pansies. Kelly Reese's collar was so white it glowed. Still, it didn't keep me from checking out her ass as she walked up the stairs ahead of me. Ogling knows no economic boundaries.

"Want to sit down here?" I indicated a table at the end of the bar.

"Is there anyplace quieter? More private?" She asked, wincing at the volume of the Dropkick Murphys track bellowing from the jukebox.

"Don't worry about it. Nobody else can hear us over the music." As it was, I could barely hear her.

"This—This is fine, then." She looked around the room like she'd found herself on the wrong side of the fence at the zoo.

I sat in the gunslinger seat, back to the wall. She rested her hands on the tabletop but quickly pulled them back onto her lap with a sick expression. The table was sticky and dirty, but there probably wasn't a cleaner one in the place. Princess would just have to make do.

"Would you like a beer?"

She smiled nervously. "Uh, sure."

I waved at Ginevra, the heavily tattooed Nova Scotian waitress who was built like she should have been painted on the side of a WWII bomber. Ginny gave me the one-minute finger as she downed a shot with a table full of middle-aged punk rockers, then walked over to us. "Whatcha need, hon?"

"Two Buds and a shot of Beam."

Ginny wrinkled her nose and looked around. "Christ, what the hell is that stench?" She leaned closer, following her nose down to me. "Damn, Boo. You been washing your clothes in a toilet again? Whoo!" She dramatically waved the air away from her face with her checkbook.

"Yeah, Ginny. Thanks. Thanks for the input," I said, my ears burning again as she walked off to get the drinks.

Ms. Reese raised an eyebrow. "Boo?" Was it a tiny smile or a smirk that touched on her face?

"Long story," I said and quickly got up from the table. "I'll be right back."

I took the stairs two at a time up to the 4DC Security office. And by office, I mean the space next to liquor storage, complete with desk, separate phone line, and one dangling light bulb. All the comforts of home, if home is a Guatemalan prison.

Tommy Sheralt, the alcoholic lunatic who owned the joint, cut us a deal on the space. We got a desk, Tommy got a discount on our rate and the guarantee that we won't tell the customers that he cuts the top-shelf liquor with rotgut.

In the desk, we kept spare sets of clothes for such emergencies, though our usual emergencies involved bloodstains.

I stripped out of my foul clothes and into a clean pair of jeans and a black T-shirt. I still reeked. Junior kept a pint of cheap cologne in his drawer, and I tried to cover up the rest with an Irish shower. I was trading in smelling like a bum for stinking like a Greek man-whore, but it was a step up. Finally, I cracked a bottle of Crème de Menthe and gargled, spitting into the wastebasket while quietly resenting Ms. Kelly Reese for making me give a shit.

When I walked back downstairs, Junior was doing his best seductive lean-in on Kelly. I hurried over and caught the tail end of one of Junior's knee-slappers. "And the farmer says, 'That's the fourth faggot rooster I bought this month!'" Junior cracked up while Ms. Reese tried her best not to look completely horrified.

"Good one, Junior," I said and clapped him on the back. "I'll take it from here."

"Huh? My bad. Didn't know I was stepping on toes here." Junior winked at Kelly with as much subtlety as a bear on a unicycle. Kelly gagged on her beer. "By the way, Boo, we need another bottle of Johnny Blue at the bar. Came in with the Bud," he said, nodding to the bottle in Kelly's hand.

Well, well . . . Ms. Reese just got a whole helluva lot more interesting.

Johnny Walker Blue wasn't sold at The Cellar. Would have been like offering Kobe beef at Taco Bell. Junior just informed me that our little Ms. Reese had come with a police presence.

I didn't have to look at the bar itself. From where I sat, I could see the entire room reflected in the long mirror running across the far wall. He blended in better than the prom queen across the table from me, but I knew immediately who Junior was talking about. He sat nursing a beer and stared straight ahead, all the while watching our table out of the corner of his eye. Big guy with a white beezer haircut and an old black nylon jacket on despite the heat, which told me he was packing. His air was "don't fuck with." Old-school tough.

"You got this covered?" Junior asked, tipping his head back toward the bar and the cop.

"Yeah." I nodded. "You can head back downstairs. I got it up here."

"You sure?" I knew he was only about a third concerned. The other two-thirds were curiosity and just plain nosiness.

"I got it," I said, a little firmer.

Junior nodded and walked toward the front, giving the cop's back a long lingering glare.

I checked the cop in the mirror one more time before I turned my full attention back to Ms. Reese. "So, do you own a bar?"

Her eyes widened. "Excuse me?"

"You said you wanted to hire us. We do bar and club security. That's what people hire 4DC Security to do."

"No, I don't own a bar."

"Club, then?"

"No."

The game of twenty questions was wearing thin. "So assuming you haven't mistaken us for a ballet troupe, what is your business with us, Ms. Reese?"

"Kelly," she said.

"What?"

"Please, you can call me Kelly."

Even that small offering sounded patronizing. She seemed to have been torn between disgust, condescension, and sheer horror since she walked in the place. It was all probably unintentional, but it was crawling under my skin like a fat tick.

"Okay, Kelly, what's your business?"

"My employer would like to hire your services."

"And just who might your employer be?" I said, popping down my bourbon.

"I'm not at liberty to divulge that at this time."

"You're not . . ." I laughed a little too loudly and glanced in the mirror. My outburst made a white beezered head turn at the bar.

Gotcha.

"Let me explain something to you, Kel. I don't know whether you've seen too many spy movies or just have a hard-on for old noir, but I don't work for phantoms, and this cloak and dagger bullshit you're feeding me is going right up my ass. So you can cut the shit and talk to me straight or you can go piss up a rope." I stood from the table, ready to walk. It was one part my shitballs of an afternoon and another part poorly repressed class rage. Either way, it felt good to let her have it.

Her voice shook a bit when she said, "I'm sorry, Mr. Malone. I'm just following my employer's wishes at this time. I didn't mean to get you angry."

She looked much younger than my original assessment right then. On the table in front of her was a small pile of napkin bits. She'd been nervously ripping off pieces and rolling them into little balls. She wasn't just being snobby. She was legitimately scared to be there. And of me.

Hot shame filled my chest. Kelly Reese made me feel like a bully. "Listen, I . . . I'm sorry," I said. "You didn't deserve that."

"No need to apologize," she said, but her eyes didn't leave the table.

"I'm not having the best day, as I'm sure you can smell."

She forced a tight smile. "You do smell awful."

"Thanks. Ask anybody. Any other day and you'd be overpowered by my smoothly masculine musk."

"No doubt." The smile came a little less forced.

"Can we start from the top again? And this time straight?"

"I'm just here to find out whether or not you're available for hire."

"For what?"

"My employer's daughter has been missing for a week and a half. He would like you to try to find her."

I drained the last of my beer. "I don't know who you or your employer has been talking to, but that's not what we do. Like I said, we do club security and every now and then we'll pick up a bail jumper for shits and giggles, but that's it. Hell, more often than not, we know the guy we're picking up. Missing persons usually go to cops like your friend at the bar." I tipped my empty shot glass at the cop. The cop saw my gesture and closed his eyes, disgusted. I gave him a hearty wave.

Kelly Reese raised an eyebrow. "Well, with observational skills like that, you might be the right person for the job."

"The flattery is certainly helping, but again—"

"However, my employer knows that going to the police could mean the situation leaking to the media. Unless it becomes absolutely necessary, he would like to avoid that."

"And your police escort is here . . ." I trailed off, allowing her to fill in the blank.

"My friend at the bar is just here to keep an eye out."

"For what? For me?"

"For anything."

"I see," I lied. I didn't see shit yet. Although my ego deflated slightly that I didn't warrant the singular attentions of her bodyguard. "But as I said, we really don't do that sort of thing."

"He's just asking you to try." She reached into her briefcase and pulled out a cream-colored envelope and slid it across the table. "Here's a picture and a small retainer, should you choose to take our offer."

I opened up the envelope and pulled a smaller envelope out. It was unsealed, and clearly held more than a month's wages in bouncer gigs. I hoped my eyes didn't do a cartoon bug-out. "Okay, then, we'll give it a shot," I said a bit too quickly. Money talks, brother. And in this case it sang a rock opera.

I pulled out the picture.

It was the girl with the dyed red hair.

I leapt up from the table, knocking over my chair, and ran to the door where she had just kissed me on the cheek less than two hours before. Junior saw my frenzy and ran over. "Yo! Where's the fuego?"

I stuck the picture in his hand. "This girl was just here. Find her!"

No questions asked, he ran back down to the basement. I looked around the street in front of the club. Nothing. I ran back through the bar and out the back. A few kids were hanging out there in a cloud of acrid pot smoke and quickly hid their hands. No girl.

I let out that long and profane curse I was holding in.

I stormed back into the bar and over to Kelly. "All right! What the hell is going on? That kid was just here. Who is she?"

The cop decided he'd had enough of the silent partner routine. He quickly came over to the table. "What do you mean she was just here?"

"What the hell do you think it means, Chief Wiggum?" I smacked the back of my fingers across the envelope. "She was just here."

Junior came in through the back. "Nothing. There's a few band members and a couple of groupies downstairs, but not this one. Who is this?"

The cop said, "Where? Who was she with?"

"Who is this?" Junior asked again.

"I don't know," I said to them both.

"Then why the fuck am I looking for her?" Junior asked.

"Where was she?" The cop again.

"Hey!" I yelled at the cop. "Step off! Until you introduce yourself, you can blow me with the interrogation." His face darkened, but he shut up for the moment. "Junior, go back downstairs. Show that picture to everyone down there and ask them if they know her, and if anybody does, where she went and who she was with."

Junior threw his hands up and sighed. "Fine."

I turned on the cop. "You. Who are you?"

He pointed a sausage finger at Kelly. "I'm with her." Kelly just stood at the table, tense and unsure.

"I didn't ask you who you were with, pal. I asked you who you were."

Veins bulged on his forehead. "Danny Barnes." He said his name like it should mean something. It didn't. "And you'd better watch your mouth, boy." He meant it. I suddenly remembered the man was a cop. And according to his bulgy jacket, an armed one.

"Good. Thank you. Now that we're all introduced, why don't one of you fill me in on what the fuck this is all about." Relative calm restored itself, and the three of us sat back down at the table. "Question number one," I said. "Who is this girl?"

Barnes answered. "Her name's Cassandra."

"Cassandra what? Just Cassandra? Does Cassandra have a last name or is she like Cher?"

I thought I could hear Barnes's teeth grinding. "As I'm sure Ms. Reese has explained to you, last names are out of the question at the moment. We need to respect her father's request for privacy."

"Lemme tell you something, I don't need to respect a goddamn thing. Ms. Reese hasn't told me a whole hell of a lot as of yet, so why don't you, Danny?"

Kelly shifted uncomfortably in her seat but stayed silent. Barnes had taken control of their end of the meeting. She seemed more than content to let him have it.

"Look, Malone, you'll know everything you need to know when you need to know it. Until then, you'll just have to make do."

I laughed. "With what? A first name and a picture? Are you shitting me?"

Junior returned from the basement towing a protesting kid with dreadlocks and bad acne by the back of his Mudvayne shirt. "This little jackass was smoking a joint in the downstairs bathroom. He knows the girl." Junior pulled another chair over and dropped him in it hard. The kid tried to shake it off with a defiant shoulder roll. "What's your problem, man?" he said to Junior, feeling safer in the company of witnesses.

"Look at me," I said to him. "Listen carefully. You're going to answer my questions and that's it. Now take a look at this guy." I thumbed at Barnes. Barnes straightened up, confused at where this was going.

The kid looked him up and down. "Who, the cop?"

Barnes frowned and went red. I did my best not to chuckle. "Yeah, the cop. If you don't answer me, he's going to drop your ass in juvie." I turned to Barnes. "What will possession get a kid his age? Three years?"

Barnes finally caught on. "Uh . . . five. Minimum."

The kid's fearless facade shattered. "It was just one joint, man! Please! I don't know anything about Cassie."

Hell, just knowing her name, he had as much info as I'd been given. "Relax. What's your name?"

"Paul."

"All right, Paul. How do you know Cassie?"

"I see her around the Square and stuff. She was just here for the show. What did she do?" He meant Harvard Square, a traditional hangout for the young punk kids and skate rats.

"No questions, Paul. Answers." I thumbed at Barnes again. Paul nodded quickly. "Who was she here with?"

"I dunno. I think she was alone. She wasn't with that creepy dude she's always going off with." If Barnes was a German shepherd, his ears would have shot straight up.

"Who's that?" I asked.

"I don't know the dude. He just gives me the creeps." Paul shuddered to emphasize those creeps. "Y'know. Slimy fucker. Got that big snake tattoo around his arm."

"What else?"

Paul thought about it. "Real skinny. Got greasy black hair, goes halfway down to his butt. Looks like a rocker. Nobody knows why Cassie hangs with that guy."

"Is he her boyfriend?"

"Jeez, I hope not. He's like in his twenties." Paul leaned back in his chair, teenage cockiness back to full. He'd realized he had something we wanted and that information gave him an edge. "Cassie's a cool chick and all, but she's a little flaky. That guy's just . . . I dunno. Like I said, he creeps everybody out."

"Junior, take him up to the office."

"Move your ass, Weedy McTokesalot," Junior snarled.

"Get his number and address."

Paul panicked. "But you said—"

I put my hand on his shoulder. "Relax. It's just in case we need to ask you some more questions. Junior's going to give you my beeper number."

"A beeper?" Paul looked at me, aghast. "Who are you, Fred Flintstone?"

"We can still toss you in juvie, smartass."

He mimed a key between his lips and turned it.

"If you see Cassie anywhere, and I mean at any time, you beep me. Got it?"

Paul snapped me a brisk salute. "Got it."

"C'mon." Junior walked off with Paul.

I looked over at Barnes. "How much?"

"How much what?"

"How much are we going to be paid if we find the girl?"

"There's twenty-five hundred in the envelope to get you started." My heart did a somersault. Twenty-five might not impress Bill Gates, but in my world, we were starting out on the right foot. And that right foot was in a Gucci loafer. "I'll need to talk with my employer on a final amount."

"One more thing," I said. "I meet your employer."

"That's not happening. You deal with me," Barnes said.

"Ooh! I've got an idea! How about no? I meet him before I do another goddamned thing." Barnes started to protest. I cut him off. "You tell him what you just saw. You tell him we meet or he can go fuck a duck. You know where I am." I got up from the table. "I'm done."

Barnes and Kelly stood up. Barnes didn't offer me a goodbye handshake as he walked out. I wasn't hurt.

Kelly said softly, "Thanks for the beer."

She followed Barnes out without a second glance back at me. I did the opposite and didn't take my eyes off her butt as she exited. Then the low-watt bulb flickered over my dome.

Sonofabitch.

As I stared at her exiting skirt muffins, I realized I'd just been had.

Kinda.

Chapter Three

Junior sat at the desk writing down Paul's info on an index card. We planned on getting a computer one day. On the other hand, we also planned on winning a million bucks on scratch tickets and retiring to Hawaii to build custom thongs for Natalie Portman. We were about as close to execution on either plan.

Paul stood, leaning against the doorjamb, arms crossed, looking like he was aching to get the hell out. The kid looked at me. "Am I done?"

"Couple more questions," I said. "What's Cassie's last name?"

He hummed the "I dunno" notes.

Swing and a miss.

"What about the Dutch House?" I asked. Junior looked at me.

"What about it?" It was no secret why kids went to the Dutch House. A big squat in Cambridge, just off the Square, it was a safe place for kids to get high, drink beer, and do anything else they didn't want their parents catching them doing.

"Has Cassie been there?"

"Once or twice. I don't think she dug it. She's not into the scene that much."

"What scene is that?" Junior said, sneering. "Future Junkies of America?

Paul smirked but his eyes reflected hurt. I shot Junior a "leave him alone" look. Junior scratched his chin at me. He forgot to use all his fingers.

"I don't think she's been staying there or nothing." Paul looked at our business card. "What does 4DC stand for?"

"Dirty Deeds Done Dirt Cheap."

He smiled. "Hunh, cool."

"We're done," Junior said, dismissing him with a wave.

Paul started to go, but I grabbed his arm and slid a hundred from the envelope into his hand. He gaped at it. "Holy shit!"

"If you get me to her, there's more. Cassandra's not in any trouble, despite the cop. You're working for 4DC now. You know what that means?"

"Uh . . . no?" His eyebrows met in confusion.

"What it means is you're representing me. You're representing Junior, here."

Junior waved his hands in protest. "Oh, no, no, no. This little shit ain't representing me."

I rolled my eyes. "You're representing us. Nobody else needs to know. Anybody asks, you're just wondering where Cassie's gone off to. Got it?"

"Got it, boss," he said with a crisp salute. He smiled so wide I thought the corners of his mouth would meet in the back of his head.

As he ran down the stairs, I yelled after him. "And if you use that money to buy weed, I'm gonna break your shins."

I looked back at Junior, whose face was a mask of amazement. "Was that a hundie you just gave that little prick?"

"Yep. We've got a gig."

I ran Junior through the basics, since basics were all I had. He sat on the corner of the desk and chewed his lower lip as he mulled the information. My fingers massaged the ache that roosts inside the lumpy cartilage of my nose when I think too much in one day. I've had my nose busted six times—one on Junior. Believe it or not, that bothers him competitively.

After a long silence, Junior said, "That's it?"

"That's it."

"Man, that's not a lot to start with. A picture and a pothead."

"True that."

"This isn't what we do."

"I know, Junior. I told them that. They still want us to try. If they want to hand out money, why not to us?"

Junior thought that over. "That is a shitload of money, though." He drummed his fingers, tapping out a cadence with the letters H-A-R-D tattooed across the knuckles of his scarred right hand. He rubbed his other hand, the one with C-O-R-E across it, over the pocket where he had deposited the twelve-hundred I'd just handed him.

The picture of Cassandra sat on the desk. Junior stared deeply at it, jaws tight. "Boo?"

"Yeah?"

"Who the fuck is this girl?"

We closed the bar at two, and Junior and I hung out shooting pool while the bartender counted out the receipts.

I nursed a beer and bourbon, since all us tough guys drink bourbon.

Well, almost all of us. Junior placed his plastic cup of wine on the lip of the table while he lined up his shot. The only vintages served at The Cellar could probably strip the barnacles off Old Ironsides. Plus most of the iron. I never understood his taste for it, but it was all he drank.

Junior viciously smacked the cue ball off the nine ball. With a hard clack, the nine and the cue bounced off the rails and both dropped. "Shit." Not only did he scratch, but he was playing solids.

I took the stick and smoothly banked the cue off both bumpers without hitting any balls. "Shit." Fewer people got as much as we did for our four quarters. If one of our matches ended in less than a half-hour, we were unusually hot.

Luke, the night porter, rattled the front locks. Somewhere between his sixties and his early hundreds, Luke had been the clean-up man at The Cellar ever since its doors opened twenty years earlier.

He looked over at me and beamed his five-hundred-watt smile. Luke had the darkest skin I've ever seen on a man, which only served to make his smile all the brighter. His face bunched up in a way that made it look like his wrinkles were smiling at me too. "Mr. Boo. How goes it?" he said with a tip of his faded Red Sox hat that looked like he bought it when Ted Williams was in Little League.

"It goes, Luke. It goes."

He looked over at Junior. The smile dimmed a bit. "Junior." A smaller tip of the hat.

Luke stopped calling Junior "Mr." after Junior accidentally let loose with one too many curses while Luke was in earshot. That was Luke's one serious and unforgivable pet peeve. All I needed was one good tongue lashing from him. From then on, I turned on my filter when he walked in.

"Luke," Junior said, lifting his glass.

"Good night?" Luke asked me, while seeming deliberately to not ask Junior.

"A little slow. Day was busy after the game."

"Those Sox. God bless 'em," he said with a warm chuckle. "I'm just glad I got to see 'em win a big one. Never thought I'd see the day."

"Heck Luke, I never thought I'd see the day."

He laughed like it was the best joke he'd heard in a while and clapped me on the back. "Aw, you gots a long ways to go, youngblood. You might see a couple more."

"You're gonna outlive all of us Luke, you know that," I said.

"Lord willing, Mr. Boo. Lord willing." Luke slowly shuffled back into the kitchen to get his mop and broom. The sound of his little radio came through the swinging doors. Same station every night—a preacher giving his late-night sermon to the airwaves, presumably in the hopes of converting the sinners who were still up and listening at that hour. I gave him no mind, of course.

I swallowed my bourbon and poured another. I made two hash marks on our monthly tab under the register. "What are you drinking?"

"White," said Junior. There were only three kinds of wine in the bar anyway. White, red, and pink. I grabbed him another bottle from the ice bin, made another hash mark.

Luke came out from the kitchen, mop in hand.

"Hey, Luke?"

"Yeah?"

"If you were looking for a girl, where would you start?"

"C'mon, Mr. Boo. You trying to tell me that you having a hard time finding girls?" He laughed at the very idea. Junior laughed too, but not in the same way. I was strangely flattered that an elderly black man would think me irresistible to the opposite sex.

"Never mind."

"Don't worry, Mr. Boo. They always come along." The whole left side of Luke's face winked at me as he worked his way down the back stairs.

Junior was still laughing. "He don't know you too well, do he?" Junior handed me the stick. It was the last intact stick in the house, so we had to share.

"What if it isn't her father who's looking?" I said. I dropped the cue ball again, but actually managed to knock in one of my own.

"Who else would be?"

"C'mon, Junior, don't be a dumbass. What if . . ." I thought for a second. "What if she's a runaway from New Bedford or something and some assho—someone took her in and was using her to turn tricks? She leaves him, he loses revenue. He wants her back."

"Where does the cop fit in?" Junior knocked in another one of mine. "*Shoot*." He was getting better at not cursing around Luke, whose presence forced us to edit out 90 percent of our pool banter.

I gave him a look as I handed him his wine.

"Okay, okay, so not every Boston cop is on the up and up." He poured the wine in his cup, then straightened, excited with a new idea. "The girl. The skinny chick." He snapped his fingers. "Kelly! Where does she fit into your little runaway hooker theory? She a coworker?"

Good point. She didn't fit in. We both knew some girls who worked that biz. She wasn't . . . well, she just wasn't. "Fine, I'm just saying, before we hand a kid to anybody, I want to make sure that we're handing her to the right people."

Junior took a sip of his wine and smacked his lips. "So riddle me this, Batman. There's gotta be two hundred PIs in Boston. Why us? This whole Little Girl Lost in the Big City shit? Been there, done that in at least a dozen books that *I* read."

"And you've only read seventeen books."

"Hey, three didn't have no pictures. Two of those didn't even have pictures of titties."

"What was your point?"

Junior stopped. "I forgot. Started thinking about titties. Oh yeah. PIs. Seems like their standard gig, if books have taught me anything."

"And they haven't."

Junior bowed. "Ahthangyooverramuch."

"Most of those guys are retired cops. We've already established that they don't want the cops in this."

"But why us?"

"A different perspective?"

Junior snorted. "That's for fucking sure. But seriously. Why us?"

"Because we're so pretty?"

"I am, but you could scare flies off a shit wagon." Junior winced at his own word choice, hoping Luke didn't hear. "Maybe 'cause we're underappreciated geniuses?"

I lined up my shot. "I am, but you're so dumb, you can't spell PI."

"But I might be able to sound it out."

Junior had a lot of points. All valid. Why us?

Why the fuck us?

I scratched the eight.

Chapter Four

Whenever anyone asks, I say Junior and me go way back. If anyone asks how long is way back, I say none of your goddamned business. Nobody asks a third time.

Truth is, we go back to The Home. As ironic a name for a place as any.

It was always The Home.

Never home.

The real name was Saint Gabriel's Home for Boys. Or Saint Gabe's. Or Saint Gabe's Home. It sure as shit wasn't ours. What it was was half juvenile detention, half state-funded residence.

Most of the kids there were orphans from birth. Me and Junior lived in the minority. We'd had families, once. I got shipped in when I was eight. That's how old I was when I lost everything.

Think about it. Try to remember back to when you were eight. Try to remember everything that was important to that kid. Now imagine losing it all.

Your home?

Poof.

Your family?

Gone.

Everyone who loves you?

Bye-bye.

Even the kids whose bodies were pockmarked by little round burns the same size as a cigarette cherry. Even those whose backs and legs were crosshatched by vicious belt buckle scars. More than those whose wounds rested deeper than any place on their bodies, we were all united by that little piece we'd lost.

Blood from blood.

No matter how shitty our lives may have been, we'd had something. Anything is better than nothing when you're that young.

More so than the never-hads, we instinctively arranged ourselves into groups. The neo-progressives who ran the program called us makeshift families. The counselors still linked to reality called us gangs. Whatever kept our backs safe and our asses covered.

Fact was, until you or your crew could inflict enough physical damage on an attacker, you were a potential victim. You never wanted to get caught alone. Ever.

Me and Junior ran our own crew, The Avengers—named after the comic book. Since there was no comic book called the Make Sure You Don't Get Ass-Raped League, we took what was available. We wanted X-Men, but it was taken already by some older boys. Bigger boys, who would defend their little piece of the world—something so simple as an adopted name—with a violence polite society would find shocking.

So we were The Avengers. It was all just an earlier incarnation of 4DC. Protection and services. At least now we make a little money for it, instead of a couple extra pieces of commissary cake and an unsullied rectum.

We both turned eighteen around the same time and left tracks running out of St. Gabe's. We worked your typical bullshit eighteen-year-old jobs. Never for very long.

Junior worked at Dunkin Donuts until he slapped a customer after three straight mornings of busting Junior's balls regarding cruller freshness. He got forty hours of community service and an anger management class.

I bussed tables at Hoolihan's. That stint ended when the manager grabbed my vest and flapped his jaws at me a little too aggressively. I broke my hand on that same jaw. It flapped a little differently after that. I got a hundred hours of community service and an anger management class.

Clearly the anger management classes didn't take.

The community service did.

Junior and I both had spent the larger portion of our lives under the State's rule. We didn't want to go back to that. Ever.

And the only reason that I wasn't already in a cage was that I had three witnesses that saw the Hoolihan's manager grab me first.

That scared the shit out of me.

It was obvious that we needed jobs with as little answering to higher authorities as possible.

We were drinking our sorrows blind at The Cellar when opportunity knocked. Back then, the door staff was too busy scoring, selling, or snorting to care much about carding. One night, the bouncer got the shit kicked out of him by a couple of townie bikers after he screwed them on a coke deal. Junior and I entered the fray and tossed all of them, bouncer included, into Kenmore Square.

4DC was born.

When we left the bar, the streets were empty and silent but for the sounds of traffic coming off of Storrow Drive on one side and the Mass Pike on the other. Junior hopped on his ten-speed bicycle and rode off. Normally, Junior would have given me a ride, but his car was in the shop for the third time in six months. The car was an old wreck, but Junior loved it, even to the point of suffering the indignity of putting himself on a beat-up bicycle for days at a time. Devotion and indignity. That pretty much sums up our lives.

And beat-up.

Beat-up cars, beat-up bicycles. Beat-up lives.

Nice thing about our business though? Sometimes we got to beat back.

While waiting for a cab, I leaned against the front of the bar and looked at Cassandra's picture.

The picture was taken at a mall somewhere in the suburbs. I could make out a Sunglass Hut and Spencer Gifts in the background. She was a cute kid with a sweet smile: a kid's smile, without the self-consciousness that develops with adulthood. Her hair was slightly shorter in the shot so it couldn't have been more than a few months old. I noticed the unusual maturity I'd seen in her eyes earlier that day wasn't present in the picture.

Whatever put it there happened recently.

I handed the cabbie ten bucks after the short drive up Commonwealth from Kenmore Square to my apartment in Allston. The young neo-hippie who lived upstairs wasn't at his usual post on the front steps. He's usually perched there all odd hours during the summer, never on any type of schedule that might coincide with having a job. Might be a student. Never cared enough to ask.

I have the entire first floor of a two-family house on Gordon Street. It's got three big rooms—more space than I need, but the price is right. The landlord cut me a deal when 4DC shoo-flyed some meth-head squatters from another one of his properties. I converted the front room into a home gym and use the second for a living area. The smallest room, no bigger than a large closet, is my bedroom. Growing up like I did, I tend to find comfort in smaller spaces. Less to defend.

The red light on my answering machine blinked three times. I hit play and walked into the kitchen to open a can of dinner. I dumped the canned pasta into my lucky bowl and tossed it into the microwave. It's my lucky bowl because it's my only one. I also own a lucky plate and a lucky glass. It says Welch's Grape Jelly on it and features Tom & Jerry.

The first message was from Curtis, the manager at The Drop Bar in Cambridge. He needed some extra security on weekends. He said the bar had been attracting a rowdier crowd in the last month and more fights had been flaring.

The machine beeped. Message two. Some woman was overly concerned with my cable TV package. She left a number in case I was as excited about the movie lover's package as she was.

The machine beeped again. "Mr. Malone? This is Kelly Reese. My employer has agreed to meet with you. A car will pick you up at The Cellar tomorrow night at ten o'clock Goodbye." She ended the message without giving me a return number by which to accept or decline the offer. Regardless, I *69ed the number.

Unlisted.

My number's unlisted, too. How they got it was just one more question I would have to add to the stack.

I woke up around noon the next morning—early for one living the night-owl lifestyle. I opened up another can for breakfast and turned on the news.

An elderly woman was killed during a botched home invasion. No suspects were in custody at the time.

A Harvard freshman's suit against the city started the day before. He fell onto the Red Line tracks, losing both his legs.

The mayor was railing against his opponent's stance on "the issues of the citizens." Apparently, the incumbent couldn't dig up any damning personal info to fling yet. Unfortunately for him, his opponent, a long-term DA, had a whole lot on him. Ah, politics . . .

I shut off the TV before the news anchor got to the report that my children's lives just might depend on.

I did a quick workout, punching on a heavy bag until I broke a light sweat. I wanted to keep working the bag, which was always good for clearing my head, but my shoulder was still stiff from the Wile E. Coyote routine I'd re-enacted off The Cellar's back door.

I had a lot of time to kill until my evening pickup, so I decided to do some recon work. I could at least try to fill in some blanks so I didn't walk into the meeting with nothing more than my dick in hand.

My upstairs neighbor had resumed his post on the front steps, soaking in the sun like an otter on a rock. A strong mixture of patchouli and pot wafted off him. He even had an old VW van parked in the short driveway beside the house. I'd never seen anyone drive it since the day he moved in. At some point in its existence, somebody decided to paint a mural of peace signs, rainbows, and daisies on the front but lost interest about a quarter of the way back.

He'd been living above me for three years and I still didn't know his name. Couple years back, I'd tossed him out of The Cellar after I busted him lighting a hash pipe. From that point on, I think he regarded me as a tool of the Man's oppression.

He gave me a nod of acknowledgment as I passed him on the steps. I returned the nod and stopped. I pulled the picture from my back pocket and held it out to him. "You don't happen to know this kid, do you?"

He lowered his sunglasses and stared blankly at the picture. He narrowed his eyes when he looked back at me. "Nope."

Great. Now he had me pegged for a chickenhawk as well as a Fascist.

I hopped the Green Line train back into Kenmore. The Cellar didn't open until three, but by the time the train got there, the bar would be ready for business. I knew Underdog would be inside as soon as the doors opened.

A few years back, Underdog was just another drinker at the bar. He was usually the first to show up and sometimes the last out at the end of the night. Pipe-cleaner thin, he would keep to himself in whatever part of the bar had the least light and steadily drink plastic pints of Busch. After a few weeks, he became a fixture and the staff began to feel sorry for him. The girls who work at the bar have a soft spot for strays like Underdog, and The Cellar was the type of bar that attracted them.

A year back, I'd made a rare daytime appearance at the bar. As I headed up the stairs to the offices, I heard a clattering from the well underneath the steps. I went to see what was going on, since the area was supposed to be off limits.

I got an eyeful of Underdog's ass as I turned the corner.

And the long needle tracks along the pasty flesh of his inner thigh. The clatter I'd heard was a dropped hypo.

I felt duped, personally betrayed by a man we'd brought into our family.

A bloody haze fell over my eyes like a red-filtered Klieg light blazing at a thousand watts.

"Boo, I—" was all Underdog got out before my right hand clamped over his throat and squeezed off his protests. Feeble squeaks of alarm were all he could produce.

I crushed the syringe in my left hand, glass slicing into my palm.

I flung the shattered needle to the floor. With my bleeding hand, I went into his pockets while still choking him with the other. From his shirt pocket, I plucked a small bag of heroin. I dumped the beige powder on the floor, turning the baggie over right in front of his face. Underdog's mouth started foaming at the corners, his oxygen-starved brain ordering his thin legs to kick at my shins. Unfortunately for him, a panicked hundred and twenty pounds doesn't even register when I hit that wall.

And I'd hit that wall.

Hard.

Then his eyelids fluttered and he was beyond caring.

I felt through the front pockets of his jeans. A few loose bills. Keys. Stick of gum. Lint.

In the back pocket of his jeans, I found his badge.

My hand opened on Underdog's throat, and he dropped to the floor, conscious by a hair. "You're a cop," I said, dumbfounded.

Dog lay at my feet, clutching his neck and wheezing asthmatically. He slid himself into the crevice under the stairs like a wounded animal.

"You're a cop," I said again. The answer—the gold shield in a leather case—was already in my hand. I was just trying to push the information into my brain. It didn't want to go.

"Vice," he squeaked from his corner, almost too softly to hear. Then he started weeping deep, heaving sobs like a child.

"Vice," I repeated. I stared stupidly at the ID tucked into the flap of the wallet. Sure enough, it read: Brendan Miller, BPD, Detective—Vice Division—Narcotics. Then I looked long and hard at the photo. Any bouncer will tell you, the best way to spot a fake picture on an ID is by focusing on two things that don't change on a person between license photos: the distance between the eyes and, barring breakage or surgery, the nose. Brendan Miller had an academy crew cut.

Underdog had a shoulder-length mousy tangle.

Brendan Miller was clean shaven, skin gleaming.

I'd never seen Underdog with a decent shave.

Brendan Miller was a healthy looking, young guy.

Underdog . . . wasn't.

The picture on the ID was definitely the same person cowering on the dirty floor before me. But it sure as hell wasn't the same man.

"I didn't want to be this way," he cried quietly.

I towed him up the stairs by the scruff of his shirt before anyone else came looking to see what the hubbub was about. I dropped him in the office and cleaned the bits of glass out of my hand in the upstairs bathroom. When I came back, he was still slumped in the bright yellow chair next to the desk, his sobbing tapering off. His shirt was streaked with stripes of my blood, and when he coughed, a little spray of his own came out.

I glared down at him, then looked at the cuts in my palm. "Any chance you gave me something? You got Hep?"

Softly, "No."

"HIV?"

A shake of the head. "I get tested. I'm an idiot. I'm an asshole. I'm a fucking junkie. But I'm not suicidal."

I handed him some paper towels. "Here. Clean yourself."

I sat in the desk chair and watched him smear my blood deeper into his shirt. He started sobbing again. "I don't wanna die, Boo. I really, really don't."

"So, what's the story here, Dog?" I said quietly, not able to look directly at him. I've seen more than my share of junkies in my day and felt not a lick of pity for their weaknesses.

But dammit, this was Underdog.

He gave me his story in a monotone.

He'd been Vice for six years and on deep cover for the last three. Too deep and not enough cover, apparently. In his dealings, as a show of good faith, he'd shot up a few times with the people he was supposed to be keeping an eye on. Nobody shoots up and believes they'll get addicted. Brendan Miller was no exception.

He was wrong. After a few months of regular use, he became the Underdog before me, snuffling through tears and holding himself tight.

His real troubles started a year before, when in a drugged stupor he told a pusher who was dicking him around that he was a cop. Word spread fast, and soon the whole network of dealers knew. They cut him a deal. Fudge your reports and your junk is free. Brendan Miller was too far gone to refuse. The dealers were thrilled. They had a cop under their thumbs. A Vice detective, no less.

The entire time Underdog was telling me this, he stared at an empty space on the floor. I still didn't want to look at his face, so it was a good arrangement. His feet scuffed a two-step on the tile, and he wrung his hands obsessively.

When he finished the story, he looked up from the floor and held me with heartbroken, bloodshot eyes. "Boo?"

"What?" When I spoke, my voice was as flat as his.

"Please don't kick me out. Please." He was begging. His voice cracked at the end, like he might burst into tears all over again.

That's what he was afraid of. He'd seen what I'd done to other people. People I'd caught messing around with shit a hell of a lot less severe than heroin.

"You can fuck me up if you want to. Shit, I deserve a beating. I probably need it, but please don't . . ."

I realized the people in The Cellar were probably the only ones who had been kind to him in a really long time. They were people who cared about him, who liked to see him when he walked in the door. He was terrified to lose that.

I wasn't going to beat him up. Life had already taken care of that. I took my reserve bottle of Beam from the drawer and poured him a thick shot into a rocks glass and took a pull from the bottle. "I'm not going to ban you from the bar."

His bony face lit up with hope, but his hands still shook hard enough to make the bourbon slosh around the glass. "Boo, I—"

"But if you ever, fucking ever, buy, sell, or do that shit in this building again . . . if you do and I catch you . . ."

I didn't finish with my threat. I didn't have to. He was still thanking me when I told him to get the fuck out of my office.

Underdog had made himself scarce the last couple months. I think he was avoiding me. I'd hear about him being in the bar, but he'd be gone by the time I showed up for my shifts.

He hadn't been caught again.

That's not to say he wasn't still using.

He just wasn't caught.

Iggy and the Stooges blaring out of The Cellar's open door could only mean Audrey was working. She'd been bartending at the place almost as long as Luke had been cleaning it. Big, loud, and with more brass than your average marching band, Audrey was something of a local legend. Legendary for her heavy hand when pouring the Jack Daniels for customers—and herself. Legendary for laying out said customers who dared to give her an ounce of shit. I'd lay good money that she could punch harder than me. That long a tenure at The Cellar, and she'd have had plenty of practice.

It was still early enough for the scent of Luke's pine cleanser to have the advantage over the stink that would soon fill the air. Audrey's ample behind wagged a greeting at me when I entered. She leaned over the bar, smothering somebody with her maternal bartending. She had two grown daughters of her own, but never had an empty nest. She stuck all of us in there instead, whether we liked it or not.

"Hey, baby, can I get some fries with that shake?"

She wheeled around, a wide grin breaking across her cherubic face. "Willie!" she said in her sandpaper voice, thirty years of Winstons and whiskey sitting on her larynx. Audrey was the only one who could call me Willie without making my skin crawl.

Coming around the bar, she bear-hugged me, nearly lifting me off the floor. My ribs shifted under the power of her hug.

"Look, Brendan!" she said. "Willie came out to play today."

"Dog," I said.

"Boo." He nervously bobbed his chin in greeting.

Audrey smiled like she'd just reintroduced two old playground buddies. "Me and Brendan were just gonna play some gin rummy. You want the winner, Willie?"

"Maybe later, Audrey. I need to talk to Underdog."

Dog's head shot up, and I waved him toward a table in the back. He picked up his pint and shambled over. He looked even skinnier than I remembered from the last time I'd seen him. His clothes hung off him like socks on a chicken.

Audrey freshened up her Jack and water. She would freshen it at least a dozen times a shift and never show it. Thirty years ago she could have been my dream girl.

"I just remembered why I drink," Audrey called out to us. It was the closest thing she had to a toast, and the reply was mandatory.

"Why is that, Audrey?"

She swallowed half the glass. "Because I fucking like it."

Before I could say word one to him, Underdog was already scrambling.

"I didn't do anything, Boo. I swear." He kept his voice hushed so Audrey wouldn't hear. A loud *ka-chunk* sounded through the old speaker system as Audrey changed the tape. Jimmy, the legendary skinflint who owned the club, was still too cheap to spend the thirty bucks it would have cost to buy a CD player, much less an iPod. The Muffs started screaming about a lucky guy, and Audrey bobbed her head vigorously to the beat, oblivious to our conversation.

Underdog stared at me with an earnestness intense enough to pop greasy beads of sweat on his brow. "You've got to believe me. I'm not going to lie to you. I'm not going to say I'm totally clean, but I swear, I never do anything here. Not anymore."

"Dog—"

"Boo, I swear . . ." He held a sweaty palm up to show his honesty.

"Dog—"

"To God!"

"Shut up," I snapped. "Jesus!"

"Huh?"

"Shut up. I just want to ask you about some people." Underdog still possessed enough unscrambled brain cells to hide his addiction and keep his job. He wouldn't be joining Mensa anytime soon, but if he were stupid, he'd already be dead or behind bars himself.

Relief splashed across his face like a bucket of ice water. "Oh. Oh . . . okay. Shoot."

I handed him Cassandra's picture. "You ever seen this kid around?"

He stared at the picture. "What mall is this?" For a second, I thought I heard Brendan Miller and not Underdog's voice in the question.

"I dunno, why?"

"I need to find a Sunglass Hut. My shades are busted."

I snatched the photo from his hands. "Dammit, Dog, do you know the girl or not?"

"Nope. Why?"

Strike one. "Somebody's lost her, and they want me to find her."

"Hey, Boo, I can help you with this!" He'd perked up at the thought of being useful.

"Fantastic." I tried to keep the sarcasm out of my tone, but it crept in at the edges. "Does the name Kelly Reese mean anything to you?"

He rolled his eyes back in thought. "Kelly Reese. Kelly Reese . . ." He stared at the floor in concentration. "Kelly Reese, Kelly Reese . . ."

It looked like he had something on the tip of his tongue.

"Kelly Reese," he said. "Kelly, Kelly . . . Oh, wait!"

The batter swings. "What?"

"Kelly Reese. Big Irish guy. Bartends at The Dublin Pearl. IRA refugee, right?"

And misses.

"That's Kelly Reed. And he's not IRA, he's a douchebag. It's a bullshit line he gives the sorority girls to make them think he's hardcore. He grew up in Quincy. He's about as IRA as Jackie Chan. Kelly Reese is a girl."

"What? No. Wait. Yeah. That's right, Reed. Nope. Don't know any Kelly Reese."

I sighed. The ache paid a return visit to the bridge of my nose. "What about a Danny Barnes?" I remembered the way he introduced himself. Like the name meant something. Maybe it would to Dog.

His face blanched instantly. "Aw no."

"Aw no, what?"

"Not Danny the Bull."

"Is Danny the Bull a cop? Maybe ex-cop?"

"Unless you know another one, yeah. And I hope to God there aren't two of them running around."

"What's his deal?"

"Bad news, Boo. Stay away from that crazy bastard." Dog glanced around the room as though he feared Barnes might jump up from behind a table. Just speaking Barnes's name made Dog nervous. Which was making me nervous.

"What's his deal?" I asked again.

"He used to run the Organized Crime Division for years. Stuck his badge in the business of a lot of scary people."

"You keep using the past tense. So he's not a cop anymore?"

"No. Retired a few years back. But once in blue—"

"Blue for life," I finished for him.

"You got it. Barnes built a rep for having an ass harder than a diamond. The guy was flat-out notorious."

"For what?"

"For everything a cop can be. Probably still the title holder for brutality reports filed against the department."

Considering most of the cops I'd dealt with, that was one hell of a title to hold. "What's he up to now?"

"Damned if I know. Don't want to know." He shuddered.

"You afraid of this guy, Dog?"

"I was . . . would be today if he came walking in the door."

"Well, he walked in the door yesterday."

"Jesus! Why? What does he have to do with any of this?"

"That's what I'm trying to figure out. Whoever wants this girl found has Barnes on his payroll. You ever work with the guy?"

Dog shook his head. Dandruff or dust floated onto the table. "Different divisions. He worked Organized Crime. Led the task force that put the screws on everybody connected with The Mick. I mean, he nailed all of them. From the right-hand guys down to the runners who picked up the football cards on Saturday afternoons."

"But not The Mick."

"Nobody ever got to The Mick. That's not to say that Barnes didn't try. Or that The Mick didn't try to get back at him. They just never got each other."

If you yelled out "Mick" in a Boston bar, 90 percent of the room would turn around. And if you yelled it loud enough, another two dozen would come in the door. But I knew exactly who Underdog was talking about.

Francis "Frankie The Mick" Cade. Boston's answer to John Gotti, if John Gotti had been federally investigated on a couple of occasions for filtering money to the Irish Republican Army. The charges bounced right off him every time. The guy was rubber in a sweat suit.

And Boston being Boston, Cade was treated like something of a local hero, a Southie Robin Hood who provided Irish grandmothers with free hams every Christmas eve.

When The Mick's daughter passed away a year back, the funeral procession down Dorchester Ave would have made a Kennedy jealous.

A few years back, a rumor circulated that one of Frankie's old buddies was set to testify that he'd seen Frankie stomp a degenerate gambler to death, back when he was doing collections in the late '70s. Full federal protection. Ten days before trial, UPS delivered somebody's right pinkie finger to the witness safe house. The next day, a ring finger. Complete with a custom-made Claddagh ring. The same Claddagh ring that said informer gave his niece on her sweet sixteenth. The guy's story made a U-turn before the sun set.

It said something about Barnes that he'd gone toe to toe with Cade and was still sleeping on the right side of the grass.

"I dunno what he's got to do with you or that girl or anything, Boo. But I changed my mind. I don't think I want to help with this anymore." Underdog stood up from the table. He picked his pint up with hands that shook so badly beer sloshed over the lip. "I may be a colossal fuckup, but I'm still smart enough to stay out of any business that has Danny the Bull attached. Whatever it is, Boo . . . it's bad. Barnes doesn't do good."

Fingers of unease were crawling through my stomach. "Basically, all you can tell me is to watch my ass with this guy."

"No, I'm telling you to walk away. You don't want to be on any side of any situation that has Barnes involved. If I were you, I'd keep one eye on Barnes, one eye on yourself, and grow a third on the back of your head to make sure no stray bullets are heading your way."

Chapter Five

We got a better-than-usual crowd for a Monday. One of our sister bars, The Smash Up, had a bug-bombing scheduled. All their regulars were forced to drink with us for the night. They knew we'd be open. The Cellar never closed for the exterminators. The place hadn't been fumigated once in my twelve years there, and I wasn't sure it ever had been. We'd even named some of the larger bugs.

Junior leaned against the doorjamb. I could tell he was pissed off by his crossed arms and bulldog face. When Junior's got a problem on his mind, he furrows up his forehead. The scar tissue between his eyebrows piles up, and his mouth arches down right under his nose. It really does make him look like a bulldog.

"You gots a sexy mouth, boy," I said.

"Don't know why I gotta sit here," he muttered, glaring at the passing foot traffic.

"One of us has to stay here, Junior. Don't bust my balls on this."

"Then why don't you stay here with your thumb up your ass and let me go meet with these jerkoffs."

"Because they called me and told me they were going to pick me up." I might have emphasized the "me"s in the sentence a bit too much. "Why are you turning this into something it's not?"

Junior didn't answer. He knew I represented the de facto brains of our little organization; he just didn't like feeling left out.

A college kid with boy-band hair rambled toward the door. Already drunk enough to be tagged unwelcome a block and a half away, he fumbled with his wallet and unsteadily held out his ID toward Junior.

"Get the fuck out of here!" Junior said, pointing away.

The kid's alcohol-dimmed brain didn't register anything for a second. Then, surprised indignation. "I—"

Junior stomped his foot at him and actually growled. The kid took off at a quick stagger. As he made his hasty exit, he checked over his shoulder to make sure Junior wasn't giving chase. Possibly to bite him.

"Did you call any of the boys to cover?" I asked.

"Yeah. Nobody could come in."

"Not even Twitch?" I was kidding. I knew he didn't call Twitch.

Junior barked a laugh at the very idea. "Shit, and leave him here without either me or you?"

"If that's the last option we've got . . ."

"Shit." Junior spat on the sidewalk. "No thanks."

Twitch wasn't trouble per se, but trouble sure as fuck found its way to him. He was just that guy. The guy somebody would inevitably have to fuck with.

And by the time Twitch was done with that somebody, The Cellar would be a pile of smoking rubble. I'd feel better leaving the bar in the loving care of al Qaida. At least they might not piss on the rubble.

Twitch was another St. Gabe's veteran, and as such, was as close to family as we had. But Twitch wasn't so much a potential solution as our last resort.

At about twenty past ten, a black sedan rolled up in front of the bar.

"Here we go," I said to Junior. "The fat man walks at midnight."

Junior reached into his back pocket and held out his brass knuckles, keeping it low so whoever was driving the sedan wouldn't see. "You want my face crackers?"

I was touched Junior would offer me one of his weapons. If I took it, he might be left with as few as three on him. "Nah," I said, opening my arms as I backed toward the sedan. "These is respectable peoples."

"That's why I'm fucking worried. At least with us scumbags, you can see us coming."

He had a point.

Kelly Reese got out of the front passenger side and opened the rear door for me.

"Ooh, full service?" I said, smiling with the old charm turned up to eleven. She didn't acknowledge that I'd spoken. I stopped and leaned over the top of the door. "See, normally when I give the ladies my young Connery-esque grin, they smother me with thrown panties. You could at least say hello."

"Hello." All business and colder than a welldigger's arse.

Ah Boo, you old hound dog, you.

Fuck it. One small step for man, one giant leap into the shit pile. I climbed into the car. Kelly shut the door and put herself back in front.

The car was upholstered in black leather softer than milk. Smelled nice too, like a new jacket. It wasn't a limo, but a smoked Plexiglas partition divided the front and rear like in a gypsy cab, sans the money chute. If there was any conversation up front, I couldn't hear it. I tapped "shave and a haircut." The divider rolled down a couple inches. I could only see the tops of Kelly's and Barnes's haircuts.

"What?" Barnes grumbled. Nice to know we were still buddies.

"You've been working this," I said to the crack, "am I right?"

"What?"

"Trying to find her yourself."

Silence.

"Ms. Reese there told me the kid's been gone a week. I'm gonna assume her family noticed before yesterday."

"You're a fucking genius."

"So am I also correct in assuming you've fallen flat on your ass?"

He rolled the Plexiglas back up. I looked out the window. The car was turning off Commonwealth and getting on Storrow Drive heading east. After a couple miles, Barnes pulled off at South Boston, driving toward the harbor.

I won't go into details on the rest of the drive, but in case you didn't already know, Boston's streets are a wheelman's wet dream. Unlike in cities that were actually designed, Boston's planners simply paved over the old horse trails. There's never a simple route from point A to B. To get to B, you have to turn toward point N, bear left, head north past point square root of 173, back to N, then ask directions.

The car came to a final stop on Atlantic Avenue. Rows of converted industrial warehouse lofts faced the skyscrapers by the harbor. The street was empty, most of the offices closed up and lights off for the night.

We sat for a couple minutes, engine idling. I rapped on the Plexi again. The partition came down less this time. No friendly "what" either.

"Gotta suck to be that close. I mean, she was in The Cellar. Literally just minutes—"

Just before the crack disappeared again, I could have sworn I saw veins bulging in Barnes's ears. I was driving him batshit, but he still wasn't going to give anything away.

Barnes shut the ignition and unlocked the doors. Until then, I hadn't realized I was locked in. The lock pulls fell completely into the hole when they were engaged. That bugged me. I don't like knowing flight isn't an option, even if I find out after the fact.

Fuck, who am I kidding? I wouldn't know flight if I fell off a cliff and grew wings.

I opened the door and got out. Another black sedan sat idling in front of us.

Showtime.

Barnes opened the door to one of the loft complexes. Kelly was close behind him. I lagged back a bit. Try as I might, I couldn't figure out what would put those two together in a zip code, much less connect them to the girl.

I gave the names on the door buzzer a quick look-see, in case I needed to know later. Loft one was scratched off. Two was Carbon Graphics. Three, David Pfeiffer Photography. Four through six were for Infonet Streaming. None of the names meant anything to me. Barnes walked to door number one.

The loft with no listing.

Perfect.

The loft was cavernous, dimly lit, and very empty. A painter had used it at one point, but not in a while. Dried paint in varying hues was smeared along the floor. Bolts of canvas stood by the door, and paint cans covered in thick dust sat next to a mural that read *Andrew Lipp—Murals and Painting Gallery*. This detective shit wasn't going to be all that hard. Not with my steel trap of a mind.

Kelly and Barnes headed toward a lone man silhouetted in the yellow streetlamp light coming through large windows facing the street. He wore a dark suit that looked tailored for his broad shoulders. I didn't recognize him from the suit, the salt and pepper crewcut, or his ass, which were all I could see. Then he turned and the gears clicked into place, even if the machinery wasn't running yet.

I suddenly knew the reason for the secrecy and hush-hush.

And it was a fucking doozy.

"Mr. Donnelly," I said, extending a hand that had gone clammy.

"You must be William Malone," Donnelly said in a rich bass, taking my hand in his own. His grip was firm and strong. I suddenly worried about the moistness and limp weight of my own. Jack Donnelly does a lot of hand shaking. I'm more of a smack on the back or punch in the arm kind of guy.

"You know who I am." It was a statement.

"I pick up a newspaper now and then." And on the occasions that I did, Jack Donnelly would inevitably be in there, often on the front. Big Jack Donnelly they called him.

District Attorney Jack Donnelly.

Mayoral candidate, district attorney, Big Jack Donnelly.

"Then you understand the sensitivity of the . . . issue with my daughter. The reason behind all of this 'cloak and dagger bullshit.'"

"Yeah," I said. "I understand the papers would go ballistic if they knew the frontrunner for the mayor's seat misplaced his young daughter."

He bit the inside of his cheek, but didn't bite at my snark. "She didn't come home from her theater camp a week ago."

"You send her to theater camp?"

Donnelly shook his head, confused. "Yes. Why?"

"And you're wondering why she ran away?"

Donnelly's eyes narrowed to dangerous slits, but he took my jab right in stride. "May I continue?"

"Please."

"I've neither seen nor heard from her since. Mr. Barnes and Ms. Reese informed me that you actually saw my daughter yesterday afternoon."

"She was at the club where I work."

"You know that she's underage."

"It was an all-ages show. No alcohol."

What the fadge? Just like that, he'd put me on the defensive.

I lit a smoke, trying to head off my simmering temper. "Look, I'm not an asshole, Mr. Donnelly. You're the DA. You've got as much mojo in this town as anybody if you need somebody found."

He nodded.

"Your daughter's been gone a week. That means I'm not your number-one candidate to head the search party. Now, I'm sure Barnes here dusted off the old badge and came up zero. Maybe a few of your other buddies around the force gave it a shot, too. Thing is? They all stink of cop. Cop walks into a location where cops aren't in the highest regard—which, frankly, seems to be every place your girl is hanging—nobody would tell them shit if they stepped in it. I'm guessing you figured that much out and that's why you sent the piece of ass to talk to me first instead of Barnes." I waggled my finger at Kelly, but kept my attention on Donnelly. "You knew I wouldn't have a thing to say to him either."

Silence.

I waited, wondering if I'd pushed too hard.

Donnelly rolled his neck like a prizefighter, as if his necktie was suddenly too tight. "I'd like to speak with Mr. Malone in private for a moment."

"Jack . . ." Barnes was definitely in favor of Plan B, dumping my carcass off the Tobin Bridge.

"Please, Danny." There wasn't as much a request as a command in the tone.

Barnes wasn't happy and Kelly was redder than a baboon's ass, but both of them turned and walked. Barnes yanked the door open with enough force to send a canvas bolt toppling to the floor. Kelly stormed out right behind him, her heels clicking an angry cadence on the concrete floor.

"What do you want to know, Mr. Malone?"

"I know why you need us. What I don't know is *why* you need us."

"I'm not sure I understand your question."

"If you just wanted a bruiser, you could throw a stick in Kenmore Square and it'd bounce off a dozen thick necks. Why us?"

Donnelly gave me another once over before he spoke.

"Certain people in my circle have been impressed with your company's work. They are all of the impression that you are a capable, smart, and professional young man."

I was getting the dick-around. So far, I hadn't given him any evidence of being capable, smart, or professional. "Why us?"

"Because those men tell me that you understand when to use your discretion."

"In other words, I can put my foot up the right asses and keep my mouth shut about on whose behalf I'm inserting it."

The corner of Donnelly's mouth curled, and he sucked his canine tooth. "Can I have one of your cigarettes, Mr. Malone?"

"I didn't know you guys smoked anything but hundred-dollar cigars."

"And we light them with checks stolen from welfare mothers. Are you going to give me one, or am I going to have to have Danny shoot you in the back of the head?"

I wasn't sure whether he was kidding, so I reached into my pocket and popped a Parliament up in the pack with my index finger.

He took the cigarette. I lit it with my Zippo and he inhaled deeply, his eyes closed. "I haven't smoked since my wife was pregnant. Congratulations. You've driven me back to it."

"I drive most people to drink. Nice to know I can diversify." I said it like I didn't care, but I thought it was odd my attitude had a stronger effect than the stress over his missing daughter.

"Let's cut to the chase, shall we? My daughter is a little bit spoiled and a lot of teenager. A hell-on-wheels combination no matter what the circumstances, and hers have been particularly rough. My wife, her mother, passed away three years ago and that hit us both hard." He paused, his eyes going elsewhere for a moment, the loss of his wife still very much a surface wound. "I'm not going to win Father of the Year anytime soon, but I love my daughter very much. You commented before that I 'misplaced' Cassandra. I didn't correct you. I did misplace her, as far as my priorities were concerned. When Cassandra's mother died, I buried myself in my work, effectively losing my daughter in the process. I've made mistakes with her, and I realize this." He coughed into his hand. "I need you to find her."

"And do so before the papers catch on."

"That would be optimal, yes."

I shook my head, still trying to grasp it all. I'm paranoid by nature, but something still smelled like ass about the whole deal. "I hate to pick up the dead horse and carry it around the room, but I still can't figure out the why and the us."

Donnelly blew a short stream of smoke from his nostrils. "You have access that neither I nor my associates have. True?"

"True." This was ground we'd already covered. I had the sudden impression that I'd walked into something pointy, face-first.

"I have access that you don't."

"What are you talking about?" A sick feeling began slithering around my gut. All of a sudden, the hand I'd been playing didn't seem so hot.

"I may not be able to find my own daughter, but my office has access to information and people you don't. State records and such. Records you might find valuable."

The sick feeling started to spread. "Make your point."

"Plain and simple. I can find somebody you can't."

Bang.

The fucker pulled an ace.

An emotion I'd thought long forgotten ricocheted painfully off my ribcage. He clearly saw me react, despite my best efforts to keep my expression neutral. Not only did I fail at neutrality, I just about puked on his very expensive-looking shoes.

His stare bore down into me. He had me by the short and curlies and damn well knew it.

"Can I count on your help, Mr. Malone?"

"Sure," I mumbled through numb lips.

"Excellent. I'll make sure Ms. Reese gives you all the information you'll need." He turned to go, then stopped, his back to me. He said, "When you saw her, how did she seem?"

I thought about that curious light in her eyes. "She seemed fine." It felt like a lie.

He nodded slowly, then walked out. I started breathing again when headlight beams swirled in the windows as one of the sedans made a U-turn and then was gone.

My knees went out from under me, and I slid against a concrete pillar to the floor. I closed my eyes and concentrated on breathing slowly.

In the nose.

Out the mouth.

I didn't puke, even though I still felt like I might.

I guess we were on the job.

I guess I didn't have much of a choice.

If I could find Cassandra, he could find Emily.

This wasn't about money. This wasn't about my particular style of brawn. It was about information. He knew he could use that information to make me do the job.

He knew he could use me.

He could find Emily.

The possibility terrified me.

I was pissed at him for pulling that card. I was pissed at myself for not being able to tell him to shove that card up his ass. I should have. Why wasn't I able to?

I lifted myself off the floor and walked out. The sedan that delivered me was still idling. Kelly stood by the open car door. She stormed over when she saw me, fury still burning in her eyes. "How dare you!" she yelled.

"Back off," I croaked, my self-control thinner than a piece of floss.

She stepped up, right in my face. "I am not some piece of . . . of . . . ass!" She was so enraged, I wasn't sure whether she was finishing her sentence or calling me an ass.

The floss snapped.

"Are you fucking kidding me?" I yelled right back in her face. "You were used, babe. Face it. You're a tool, just like I am, to be exploited by these fuckers as they see fit."

"What are you talking about?"

"Of all the people who work for Donnelly, you think you were sent into the lion's den because of your people skills?"

"No . . . What? What do you mean, you're about to be used?"

I though of the carrot Donnelly had dangled in front of my nose. "Until your boss decides to share that tidbit with you, sweetheart, file it under 'none of your fucking business.'"

She took a step back from me, stunned at the venom I was spitting. "Whatever you think about this . . . you have no right to . . . I have to—"

"No. The only thing you have to do is wiggle your tight ass back into that car. I'll call you when I'm good and goddamn ready. You got that?"

She pursed her lips, retreating back into Ice Queen mode. "That will be just fine." She turned briskly and walked back to her waiting car. The car pulled away, leaving me without a target for my fury. When the taillights disappeared around the corner, I swung wild punches into the air, wanting something, someone to beat on.

Then I realized I'd just fucked-off my ride back.

✵

I caught a little luck and was able to hop on one of the last inbound trains of the night. I got back to the bar close to midnight. Junior stood at the door, arms still crossed and attitude intact.

"Everything go okay?" I asked.

"Peachy. You?" He lifted his chin toward Commonwealth Avenue. "I see you didn't get chauffeured back."

"How did you know?"

"Bout a half-hour ago, Barnes rolled up and handed me an envelope. Said, 'Give it to Malone when he gets here.'" Junior gruffed his voice and did a shuffling waddle. Not a bad impersonation. "I don't think he's too taken by your charms."

"I'm an acquired taste. You look in the envelope?"

He shook his head. "Not yet. I was going to, but a little brouhaha broke out in the bar and I had to regulate." Junior absently sucked on a scraped and red knuckle. "I left it on the desk." Junior checked the IDs of two girls and let them pass. "So what happened?"

I reached in my pocket and found some gum and smokes. I went with the cigarette, of course. "For starters, I called that Reese chick a piece of ass. She didn't like it too much."

Junior barked a laugh. "Most girls would take that as a compliment."

"Most girls we know, anyway."

"So what's up? Who's the boss-man on this cluster fuck?"

I could see Junior was champing the bit, waiting for me to get back with some answers. I took another long drag, toying with his patience for my own enjoyment. "You're not going to believe this."

"In a good way, or a bad way?"

"Both. Jack Donnelly."

He waited for more. "What about him?"

"That's who's doing the hiring."

He stared at me blankly, waiting to see if I was fucking with him. "Great googly moogly! Big Jack Donnelly?"

"Shhh!" I waved at him to keep his voice down. "DL, stupid. DL. The whole reason we're being asked is because we're supposed to be able to keep a lid on things."

"This is big, man. *He's* a big man."

"That's why they don't call him Little Jack Donnelly."

Junior frowned. "Don't be a dick. You know what I mean." If Junior was a cartoon, little cash register tabs would have cha-chinged behind his eyes.

"Cassandra's his runaway daughter. We're going to find the poor lost lass amongst the social dreck of our peers."

"I do so love it when you talk like a PBS fruit." Junior grinned and bounced foot to foot like a kid on Christmas morning. "How much?"

I sat on the sidewalk and leaned against the brick. The sick feeling had doubled up on my train ride, when I really had time to think about what was being offered. "How much what?"

Junior squinted at me. "You okay?"

I took a long drag and exhaled the smoke out my nose. "He said he could find Emily."

"He said that?"

"Not in so many words."

"What words did he use?"

"He said he could find people, too. Who else could he mean?"

"But he didn't say Emily, exactly—"

"No, but—"

"No, but my hairy ass. Before you get your panties all twisted, maybe he was talking bout the broad who gave you the clap in Oh-6. You always wondered who that was."

I didn't reply, just stared at the cigarette in my hand, brain slipping away toward memories of Emily.

"You want her found?" Junior asked.

"I don't know," I said, as much to myself as to him.

"Ain't that a dick in the ass."

"Yeah."

Junior nudged me in the shin with the tip of his boot. "Enough about your sorry bullshit. Let's talk about what really counts."

"And what is that?"

"Me, jackass. Money. My moolah. How much money we getting to find the kid?"

"Shit."

"What?"

"I forgot to ask."

After Junior had himself a hissy fit and called me a couple of colorful names, I went up to the office to check out the envelope on the desk. Plain yellow manila with nothing written on it. I tore open the end and dumped the contents onto the desk.

A business card for Kelly Reese. Business line read: Donnelly for Mayor Committee. Chairperson under her name. It listed an office number, extension, and e-mail. If I'd owned a computer, I might have dropped her a note and apologized. Again.

Three pictures of Cassandra. The first one a school picture complete with forced smile. She was in a private school uniform with a coat of arms patch on her blazer. Surprisingly, her hair was a natural chestnut in the picture.

The second looked like a blow-up of a family photo, carefully cropped not to show anyone else in the picture. The third showed her on a beach, grinning. She was running into a wave and hugging herself from the cold. They were all solo shots of her. I pulled out the picture from my back pocket and looked at it again. Then the beach shot again, seeing the subtle but present signs of damage done.

What the hell happened to you, kid?

Chapter Six

In the dream, I was eating a huge Italian grinder. Really big. The size of a coffee table. Then the red peppers started to beep and I woke up. Even my subconscious was busting my balls.

Hardy-har. Biting off more than I could chew. Very subtle.

Goddamn brain.

I swept my hand across the nightstand, looking for my beeper, grumbling curses to the air. I knocked over a glass of water, my *Harry Crews Reader*, and an ashtray before my fingers found the beeper and turned it off. I squinted at the number. Didn't recognize it. I shuffled over to my phone and dialed.

The line picked up after one ring. "Call back later, dude. I'm waiting for a call." It was Paul.

"It's me, jackass. What's up?" I was already dripping sweat. Another boiler of a day.

"Oh. Hey, Boo. I didn't think you'd call back so fast."

I yawned so hard my jaw cracked. "Yeah, well, I did. What do you want?"

"Did I wake you up?"

"Paul . . ."

"It's eleven, dude. You're missing the day."

"Paul!"

"Okay, okay. You know The Pour House?"

"On Boylston?" Where the hell were my smokes?

"Yeah. I'm here now. I got some stuff to tell you."

"What?" I picked my pants off the floor and rifled the pockets. Success! Lighter?

"I'll tell you when you get here. Bring money. You're buying me lunch. Ha-*hah!*" With that, he hung up on me. Little prick.

I lit my smoke and stumbled to the shower.

And yes, I can smoke in the shower. I have a technique.

I got to the restaurant a little after noon. When I walked in, the mingling smells of beer, hot sauce, and frying hamburger made my stomach croak frog-noises. The stupid dream had made me hungry, so I wasn't all that upset at meeting at The Pour House. They made the best burger in town. Cheap too, thank God. When I found Paul in a table toward the back, he was finishing a plate of buffalo wings and a basket of mozzarella sticks.

"About time, man. My burger's almost here."

Before I could say anything, the young waitress came over for my order. For breakfast, I went with a double bacon cheeseburger and a Sam Adams. Paul watched her exit as she walked off with my order.

"I think she wants me. What do you think?" His lips were red with wing sauce. He popped another in his mouth. The kid ate like he hadn't been within three feet of a meal in days. For all I knew, he hadn't. I remembered that kind of hunger. The ghost of it echoed in my gut as I watched him tear into his food like he was worried somebody would take it from him.

I stifled a yawn. Probably should have ordered coffee instead of a beer. "What have you got?"

He held up his finger and pulled the bone from his mouth, meat sucked clean off. Jesus. Maybe the answer to Cassandra's disappearance was because Paul ate her.

"Nothing," he said through a mouth full of half-chewed chicken.

I stared at him. "You beeped me, called me here, to tell me you found nothing?"

He gave me look filled with indignant hurt that nobody over the age of sixteen can quite pull off. "Nothing is something."

I continued to stare. "What the . . ." The waitress brought over my beer. I practiced Zen breathing. Slow and even. It wasn't working. I tried rubbing the remaining sleep from my eyes. "What are you talking about, Paul?"

"It's weird. I been asking everybody, real casual like, you know? Just like, 'Hey, seen Cassie around?' Nobody has."

"It's only been two days since you saw her at The Cellar."

He looked at me like I was missing an obvious point. "Dude. It's summer. We're off from school. Only got a couple weeks left before school starts again. Somebody should have seen her somewhere. It's not like she's some computer nerd or one of those inside-kid weirdos reading *Twilight* and shit. She's normally out and about. Hanging, you know?"

"I know." He was starting to make sense.

"I mean, she's not at home, right?"

"I can't tell you that."

"Shit, man, I'm not eating a retard sandwich, here. If she was home, nobody would be looking for her, right?"

Super. Outwitted by a kid with less hair on his lip than Jennifer Lopez.

"Am I right?" He asked again, pleased by his rightness.

"Right."

"So, if she's not home, she's got to be somewhere, right?"

"Right again, Watson."

"Who's Watson?"

"Never mind. Go on." Goddamn public education system costing me a punch line.

"Anyway, if she was anywhere, somebody would have seen her there."

Despite his roundabout reasoning, the logic was solid.

"I mean, there's only a few places where we hang out. You know, where we can hang out. She hasn't been at any of them. She's not anywhere. She's gone, man."

After lunch, I went back to the office and gave Ms. Reese a call rather than head home and take the nap my body craved.

"Kelly Reese," she answered.

"Hey. It's me."

"What can I do for you, Mr. Malone?" Frost began forming on the earpiece.

"First of all, I'd like to apologize for last night. I was out of line." Two apologies in a week. A personal best.

I knew it wasn't her fault she was being used. I also had the impression she legitimately didn't know the depth of what was going on. Either way, I needed an ally. Barnes sure as hell wasn't going to be sending me a cookie basket anytime soon.

Silence.

"I laid some shit on you that I had no right to."

More silence.

"Listen, this is going to be a lot easier if we can at least be civil to each other. I may be a fucking goon, but I'm owning up. At least give me that much credit."

A sigh. "You're right."

"So you accept my apology?"

"No, I agree you're a fucking goon, but I accept the apology. Now what can I do for you?"

"You my buddy?"

"Please."

"Say it."

"I'm your buddy." Score one for my minimal charm. I thought I could hear a smile behind the words. "Now, if you're through interrupting my work, what can I do for you?" Maybe it was clenched teeth.

"I need you to call Mr. Donnelly and tell him I'd like to take a peek around his daughter's room." Crap, that sounded creepy in my ears. "See if there's anything there. Sooner is better than later."

"I'll call you back as soon as I speak to him."

"Great. Smell you later."

"In your dreams." Click.

Great. Now they knew my dreams, too.

Kelly called me back and gave me an address and time. Me and Junior headed over to 3 Harrold Towers, Suite 1605. It was the nicest building I've ever been in, glowering doorman and all.

Junior farted in the elevator.

I knocked on 1605. The door pulled in, but wasn't opened. Barnes was stepping away when I pushed the door wide enough to enter.

The massive apartment was furnished in deep browns and burgundies. A lot of expensive wood and glass. Very tasteful. Ethan Allen or Mary Potterybarn would have approved. I hoped I didn't smell of Junior's fart.

There was even a fireplace. I never knew apartments could have fireplaces. On the mantle sat the family picture that had been cropped. Cassandra had her mother's hair and eyes, her father's strong facial structure. My mind briefly flicked back to all the guys at The Home who never got to see who they inherited their features from.

"Cassandra's room is upstairs. Hers is the door on the left."

Donnelly walked in from another room, adjusting his cuffs. "Gentlemen." The district attorney was dressed in full black and whites. In a large mirror, he made the final adjustments on his tuxedo.

"Mr. Donnelly." I almost called him sir. Junior would have righteously kicked my ass later, so I was glad I caught myself. I didn't like the unease that crept over my skin while I was around these guys. It felt like I was on permanent detention in the principal's office.

"I have a benefit dinner in a few minutes," Donnelly said. "Danny will help you with anything you need. If you must take something, let Mr. Barnes know."

Junior frowned. Under his breath, he said, "Is he going to count the silverware after we go, too?"

I shot him a look. He shrugged. Then he elbowed me a reminder in the ribs. "That's fine," I said. "We'll be careful with your daughter's possessions."

Donnelly turned to go.

"Mr. Donnelly?"

He stopped and turned, glancing at his shiny, shiny watch. "What is it?"

"Before you go . . . We haven't discussed money yet."

"Oh, of course. Any expenses you incur, itemize them and give them to Ms. Reese. Five hundred a day, plus said expenses, for two weeks. If you don't have any luck in those two weeks or if Cassandra seems to be in any danger, I'm afraid that, election or no election, I'll have to go the police."

"I understand." I just hoped Junior hadn't lost control of his salivary glands and drooled all over the pretty Oriental rug.

Donnelly glanced at his watch again. "I'm sorry, gentlemen, but I really must be going." He stopped short of closing the door and turned back. "Oh, and one more thing. Should you find her and return her to me quietly and safely, there is an additional twenty-five thousand."

I managed not to piss myself, so I guess it wasn't all bad.

"Twenty-five fucking grand!" Junior was fit to bust as he rifled through Cassandra's bureaus looking for anything other than clothes.

I was in the desk, pulling out drawers and looking along the bottoms. No luck. I made a mental leap and looked inside the drawers as well. Zip. "Anything?"

"Just the creeps," Junior said. I knew what he meant. Cassandra's room was a masterpiece of pink. Pink walls. Pink bedspread. A generous number of stuffed animals. Even the desk was a light shade of pink. I think it's called Conch Shell or something ridiculous by people who give a shit. The air was scented subtly with flowers and vanilla.

We were spies in the House of Girl and uncomfortable with it.

"Feels like if we hang out in this room long enough, we might go gay or something," he muttered.

Same planet, different worlds. "You might."

"And you'd love me." Junior licked his thumb and ran it between his man-cleavage.

I almost threw up in my mouth.

4DC Security. Professional investigating at its best.

We divided up the room lengthwise. I took the left side, Junior took the right. Fifteen minutes later, my head was stuck under the bed when I heard something hit the carpet, followed by the sound of something delicate breaking.

"Shit," said Junior.

"What? What did you do?" Knowing Junior, he'd managed to find a Faberge egg and tried to eat it.

"Goddamn unicorn," he said, pointing at the floor. "Bounced right off the carpet." A small glass unicorn lay on the hardwood seam between the carpet and the wall, its dainty head off from the delicate neck.

"It shouldn't have hit the carpet at all, ass."

"Maybe . . ." Junior attempted to fix the unicorn by clinking the two pieces together. Lo and behold, the glass didn't fuse itself back together with force. Instead, a leg broke off with a snap. "Dammit."

"Just leave it alone."

Junior looked out the door and slipped the pieces into his pocket.

"All right," I said, sitting on the soft, light pink bedspread. "Think back. When you wanted to hide something at The Home, where would you hide it?"

He wrinkled his brow in thought. "Shoes."

"Checked them when I did the closet. Books?"

"Did 'em. Checked for pages glued together, too."

I'd forgotten about that one. "Where else? Think."

"My ass."

"What?"

"Sometimes I hid a couple of things in my ass when I had to." He caught my horrified expression. "Small things."

I cradled my face in my hands. "Well, why don't you check and see if Cassandra hid her diary or an address book in your ass?"

"I'm just going train of thought here."

"Is that train up your ass, or is the room already getting to you?"

"Up your ass. There's nothing here."

"I know." I lay my head back on the bed and felt something crinkle in a stuffed animal. It had been a while since I'd owned one, but I didn't remember stuffed animals crinkling.

"So, you geniuses find anything I didn't?" Barnes leaned in the doorway with a smug expression smeared across his face. I didn't want to manhandle the stuffed animals with him watching. He looked to me. "If you're going to take a nap, take it at home."

Junior sneezed hard into his hand. It sounded quite a lot like "dickmuncher," but I could have been wrong.

"Excuse me?" Barnes said. His tone indicated he didn't really want us to excuse him.

Junior sniffled and smiled wide. "Allergies."

"We'll be done in about ten minutes," I interjected. "Say, you didn't happen to find anything worthwhile when you gave the room a once-over, did you? Diary? Address book of any kind?"

"Nope. Not a damned thing."

"Because it would really make you a jerkoff if you knew something that might help us and you were just being a bitch about us sniffing around."

Junior sneezed again. This time, it sounded like "asswipe." That Junior and his allergies.

That big vein bulged out on Barnes's head. "You two swinging dicks just have no idea what's going on here, do you? I've got just as much as you do—more—riding on finding her. I'm in charge of Donnelly's security, and my own stock goes up when he gets elected mayor. I want the kid found before she blows the whole thing to hell for her father *and* me." He turned to walk back out.

"Your concern for Cassandra is really touching. Truly, it is." I didn't bother masking my sarcasm.

"You know what?" He came back halfway into the room. "She's a spoiled little rich bitch who has no idea how much she's fucking things up for a lot of people here."

I had to admit, the kid's room did smack of more than a little privilege.

"Be out in five minutes." He slammed the door behind him.

"He's just a big old shmoogie-bear, isn't he?" I said.

"I'm gonna look under the carpets."

I turned my attention back to the stuffed animals. One of them had that mystery crinkle going on. Pink elephant. I squeezed it. Nope. I checked the seams. Nope. Raggedy-Ann. No sound, but a shoulder seam was split a half-inch. I stuck my pinkie finger in and rooted around. Nothing. Then I saw the kangaroo. Built-in pouch. Nature's hidey-hole. I poked the belly.

Crinkle.

The pouch was held together by Velcro. I opened it and felt inside the stuffed velveteen. My fingers closed around something, and I pulled out a single Polaroid. The photo was of a man's torso. Long and stringy black hair covered his face. He was looking down in the picture. What he was looking at made me freeze—and made me blink a couple times to make sure I was seeing it right.

"Yo, Boo! You done with your tea party over there?" Junior tossed the edge of the carpet back onto the floor with a thump. "Shit. There's not even dust under here."

"Junior? I need you to see this."

"Whatcha got there?"

He walked over to the bed, and I handed him the photograph. He did the same double blink. "*Whoathefucka*?"

"Yeah."

"I mean, good God, man . . . *Whoa*!"

"I know."

Junior looked again and pointed at the suspect region. "Is that fake?"

"I don't think so."

"It's gotta be fake." He shook his head.

"I don't know."

"Jesus H. Christ, that guy must have a helluva slouch."

A snake tattoo coiled around the man's forearm. The diamond-shaped head lay across the top of his hand. We had our man. Or at the very least, we had a picture of Paul's "creepy dude."

Kinda.

"Let's get out of here. Now," I said, my creeps turned up to eleven. I stuck the picture in my back pocket and speed-walked out the door, Junior right behind.

"See ya," I said to Barnes, who seemed a bit startled by our hasty exit.

"Hey!" We were gone before he got out of his chair.

The elevator still smelled like Junior's fart.

Chapter Seven

"Lord. That is one big dick," said Underdog. He bent over the desk, squinting at the Polaroid. He didn't touch the picture, and I understood why. Shit, I washed my hands after taking the photo out of my jeans. Might burn the jeans, too.

"The tattoo look familiar?"

Yeah, I could have shown Barnes the picture before we bolted. Fuck Barnes. Instead, I got Dog on the horn and told him to meet us at The Cellar. When he got there, I dragged him up to the office, since the issue was definitely not for any of the regulars' eavesdropping ears to listen in on.

Besides, we were going to be discussing a massive schvonce.

You get my fucking point.

Dog continued to squint. The tip of his tongue stuck out of his mouth while he wracked his drug-abscessed memory banks. "I've seen some like this before, but not this one."

"Is it some kind of gang symbol?" asked Junior. "Looks like it could be a biker tat. Not any gangbanger shit I've ever seen."

Underdog shook his head. "Nah. Doesn't look like any biker gang stuff I've come across. I mean the style at least. Might mean something anyway."

"Beyond the obvious reference to the snake hanging between his knees?" I asked. I lit a pair of smokes and handed one to Junior. My stress was making me smoke like a foundry. My pack of gum was in the trash.

"Maybe it's a secret society tag," Junior chuckled. "The Big Dick Association of America."

"All right, Junior. Enough with the dick jokes," I said.

"You weren't invited to join, were ya?"

"For a man who likes his cars bigger than most Pacific whales, you think you might be compensating?"

"That's enough!" Underdog's tone was razor sharp. "Doesn't it bother you two that you found this in the room of a fourteen-year-old girl? Doesn't it bother you at all?" Brendan Miller was in the room. The grungy little junkie had turned back into the cop.

We were both silent, shamed. "It does bother us, Dog" I said. "We're being jackasses because this whole deal has got us on edge."

Underdog sighed. "I'm sorry too. This just . . . I don't like it when shit like this, you know, involves kids. Look, I can have a buddy run a crosscheck on the station computers. See if we get a match on the tattoo."

"Any suggestions on what we can do next?" I asked.

"You could show this picture around. I know you can't show the pictures of the girl too much, but who gives a shit about this guy? Sounds like if you find him, the girl will be there, too."

"Maybe we could start at some tattoo shops. See if anybody local did the work."

"Whoa, whoa, whoa." Junior stood up. "I'm not going to canvas Boston's tattoo shops with a picture of John Holmes Junior there and ask if anybody knows where I can find the guy."

"Junior . . ."

"Just cover the dick up with your thumb," Underdog said.

"No good," I said. "You'd be hiding too much of the tattoo." I showed him.

"Oh, man. Just seeing you do that is freaking me out. I'm not putting my thumb over any man's dick."

"Come on, Junior. It's just a little picture." I waggled the photo in his face.

He swatted my hand away. "Get that thing outta my face. No man, seriously. My rep."

"Is your rep worth more or less than twenty-five grand?"

He stopped dead, rolling his cigarette between his teeth. "Hmm. Good point. Twelve thousand, five-hundred on the nose, actually."

I paused. "You've thought about this before, haven't you?"

"Damn straight."

Three days passed. Nothing. Not a word or a trace.

Junior and me hit the ink shops with the picture of Snake and came up with zilch. A couple smartasses claimed the picture was of them. One guy got himself throttled by Junior when he made the mistake of cracking wise about our sexual predilections. The guy sobered up real fast when Junior grabbed his collar and shook the dude's head like a maraca.

One place had two girls working the needles. They just snickered. I hoped I didn't turn as red as Junior did.

The price tag on our reps was starting to feel pretty damn cheap.

"This is such bullshit!" Junior protested, slugging down another wine. We celebrated our humiliation the only way we knew how. We sat in The Cellar's darkest corner and got loaded.

"It was worth a shot." I was on my sixth round of beer and bourbon. My buzz took hold around the fourth round. The last two were insurance.

"Well, it was a bullshit shot. I can never get another tattoo in this town again. Christ! Probably not even in the whole goddamn state!"

"What's left to tattoo, your taint?"

"What do you know about my taint?"

"As it is, you're a walking Louvre." Across the room, I could see Underdog stumbling through. Scanning the bar. I held my hand up and he saw me, returning the salute. He plopped himself in the chair across from me. "Drink?" I offered.

He waved his hand. "Nah. Prob'ly shouldn't have any more." Drunk as I was, I could tell he was on a whole other level of intoxication. I hoped it was just booze. "So!" He smacked his hands on the table, making the glasses rattle. "My buddy ran the picture for you. Got eleven matches on the snake tattoo. Factored in the probable age and hair type. Boiled it down to two."

Junior and I looked at each other and sat up straight. "And?"

"Okay. First one. Marshall Conigliario-io-io." Either Dog was having a hard time wrapping his tongue around the name or he was breaking out into a verse of Old MacDonald. "From Brockton."

"So, what's the deal? Is he our guy or what?" Junior asked.

"Nope," said Underdog.

"Why not?" I asked.

"He's up in Bridgewater doing eight to ten on armed robbery. Been there for two already." He burped loudly. I smelled grapefruit juice. He held up his finger. "Second guy: Richie Dean in Allston."

"You're kidding me." Wouldn't that be a kick in the ass if the girl had been in my own neighborhood the whole time?

"You got an address on the guy?" Junior asked. "Let's go over there right now and tear him a new one."

That would have been just dandy. A rescue at one in the morning by two drunks and a junkie.

"S'not him either. He's dead. Motorcycle accident back in April."

I was going to need another round to continue the conversation. I waved at Ginny and circled my finger over the table. She nodded.

"So what th' fuck you telling us, Dog? You got nothin' either?" My own words were starting to slip and slur.

"Not exactly. I was getting my copy of the picture back in the Vice office when one of the guys . . ." Dog blew out another acidic burp. "Yama. Japanese guy. You know him?"

"No."

"Nice guy. Anyway, Yama sees the picture and recognizes it. Yama!" Underdog banged the table, like we would know him better the second time around. "Japanese guy?"

"Well, who the fuck is it, then?" Junior had had just about enough.

"No name. Just recognized the picture. Dick, too."

"Yama's a dick?"

"Noooooo. He recognized the dick."

"Is it his own?"

"Nope."

Junior grimaced. "Man, the day I recognize another man's dick . . ."

"See," Underdog continued, unfazed by Junior's homophobia, "this is where it starts to get really messed up. Apparently, our boy Snake is a filmmaker."

I didn't like where this was heading. Ginny brought our drinks over just in time.

"Please tell me he videos Bar Mitzvahs," I said.

Underdog shook his lead slowly. "Porn." Underdog held up his glass. "Our boy is Boston's answer to Roman Polanski, both as a filmmaker and baby fucker." He lowered his glass and twisted his face. "Shit, that was a terrible toast."

I didn't lift my glass.

I wanted to puke.

Some of it was the alcohol.

Most of it wasn't.

Chapter Eight

After Dog's revelation, the three of us ripped into a bender that would have made Keith Moon blush. The rest of the night is piecemeal. I don't remember getting a cab, but I remember the driver pulling over so I could puke. I don't remember getting out of the cab, but I recall vomiting hugely into the bushes in front of my apartment. The hippie was on the steps smoking a joint the size of a burrito. I started vomiting off the porch and he was gone. Then his hand was on my shoulder, his other offering me a bottle of water. The unexpected kindness brought drunken tears to my eyes. I remember hugging him.

My last memory is of opening the book under my bed and unfolding the piece of paper. Tracing the outline of my one and only valuable. A flake of dry crayon fell off the picture onto the floor, crumbling into dust. The color remained on the old manila, the ghost of the crayon's touch seeped deep into the rough paper.

The Boy sat on the bed next to me, shirtless, a monstrous scar curled down his sternum to his navel. I didn't look at him, but I knew he was there, knew what the scar looked like.

The Boy sniffled, his breaths becoming hitched. I knew he was crying, tears streaming down his wide face.

He wanted me to hold his hand and cry with him, but I didn't.

I can't.

I won't.

I lay down and closed my eyes tight, waiting for his crying to stop.

Next thing, it was afternoon.

Junior and I didn't do much detective work that day. It was hard enough to keep my apartment from dancing a tango around me. A whole day slipped away. Later that night, I remembered to check my answering machine. No beeps. No business. No messages from Kelly or Barnes. No lunch date offers from Paul. Not even a telemarketer. I ripped the machine off my table and threw it into the wall. It detonated in an explosion of black plastic and circuits like I'd stuffed a cherry bomb into it. A whole fucking day wasted.

Dog said nobody in Vice knew Snake's real name since he was careful not to show his face in any of the videos. Only the faces of the girls.

It now looked like Cassandra was in real danger. And we'd responded to the newfound urgency by incapacitating ourselves for a day and a half. Some rescuers we were turning out to be.

Four days since I'd first met Kelly and Barnes. And there I was.

Without a goddamn thing.

Around midnight my phone rang. I was going to let the machine get it. Then I remembered that my machine was strewn all over the kitchen in pieces.

I snatched up the receiver, angry at having my sulking interrupted. "What?" I barked.

"Uh, Boo?"

"What do you want, G.G.?"

"I think you oughta come in." G.G. was swinging the bouncer shifts for Junior and me while we played private eye. He was a solid guy who could handle himself and the bar. A good part of the reason I gave him the shifts was because he didn't call me when he was working.

"G.G., I'm really in no mood for the bar tonight. Can't you take care of whatever it is?" My brain hurt, particularly behind my eyes. Had it been six hours since I took my last Advils?

"There's a girl here. She's a mess, man. I mean this chick is lit up like Times Square."

"Kick her out, then. What's the problem?" Hell with it. I took two more tablets. Never heard of anybody ODing on Advil.

He paused. "She says she's waiting for you."

"What? Me?"

"Says her name's Kelly."

That got my attention.

"She a friend of yours?"

"She's drunk?"

"Smashed. What do you want me to do here?"

"Just keep her corralled. I'll be right there."

This I simply had to see.

G.G. was the biggest guy on my payroll. Six-foot-eight and three hundred pounds, he played right tackle for the New Orleans Saints for a season before he got his knee pretzled. He also had the misfortune of being a genuinely nice guy who worked at The Cellar. The man played pro ball against guys who were the size of city busses and hit just as hard. But sixty-five inches and a hundred pounds plus change of Kelly Reese had him in a tizzy. He was sweating like a moose in a sauna.

"Man, thank God you're here. That is one messed up little white girl." He pulled a bandanna from his pocket and wiped his forehead.

"Where is she?" I asked, trying to look around his massive frame toward the bar.

"She's at the bar by the waitress station, sitting with Audrey."

"With Audrey?" That couldn't be good.

"Yeah. Fast friends. They were yakking it up when I got here. Audrey's been keeping her under wraps." G.G.'s eyes darted back in the direction of the bar. Kelly really had his panties in a bunch.

"How long has she been here?"

"She was here before me."

"And she's been drinking with Audrey the whole time?" G.G.'s shift started at eight. That would be at least four hours that Kelly had been at the bar. That amount of time drinking with my girl Audrey would have been a good stretch for hardcore boozers, much less Polly Pureheart.

They sat together in the corner of the bar. In their own way, they could be mistaken for mother and daughter out for a drink.

Or twenty.

Audrey clutched her ever-present Jack and water. Kelly was laughing, a pink martini on the bar in front of her. She was still in her business attire, but she'd lost the jacket amid the rounds. Her white blouse was open a few more buttons than what I believed to be her custom.

Suddenly I understood G.G.'s sweating. What the hell was wrong with the air conditioner? I wondered why no one else was sweating.

Audrey saw me first. She beamed and waved at me to come over. Kelly saw her waving and looked, lifting her chin and giving me a half smile.

Goddamn.

The bartender put a Beam and beer in front of me without asking. Audrey held up her drink. "Willie's here!" As always, Audrey's genuine happiness at seeing me made me blush. But still, her calling me Willie in front of Kelly made me wince.

"About time, *Willie*." Kelly held up her martini, joining Audrey in the toast. I caught a flash of light pink bra when she lifted her arm. "You taking the night off?"

G.G. wasn't exaggerating. The girl was plastered. Her eyes looked like a street map of St. Louis. "Boo will do just fine, Ms. Reese."

"You don't like it when I call you Willie?" Audrey said in a hurt tone, putting her drink back on the bar.

Dammit, I knew that was going to happen. Everybody's so goddamn sensitive. "I only like it when you do it, sweetness," I said, pinching her chubby cheek.

She grinned again and picked her drink back up, motioning for me to do the same. "Don't be so touchy, ya big Mary."

"Who? Me? Wait . . . Mary? What?" My lame attempts to play it off were backfiring. I could feel my ears burning at Audrey's teasing. Kelly was making another area heat up. Between the two of them, I was getting my ass whipped. Not fun.

"Drink!" Audrey commanded. "You know? I just remembered why I drink."

I took my cue. "Why's that?"

Kelly answered in unison with Audrey, both hollering, "Because I fucking like it!"

Audrey squealed with delight as they clinked their glasses and drank. I froze in astonishment. I guess Audrey had been tutoring Kelly. I downed my shot and chased it with my beer. The hair of the dog made me feel a bit better. Kelly was staring at me when I put my glass down.

"What?" I said.

"Surprised?" she asked with that same sly smile.

I looked over at Audrey, who beamed, wiggling her eyebrows suggestively.

Jesus.

"Actually, I am. What brings you to the low-rent part of town?"

"I wanted to see you," she said, then added hastily, "to find out if you had anything . . . found out. If you'd found out anything."

Was that a Freudian or a drunken slip? Either way: Advantage, me.

"Nothing yet," I lied. No need yet to panic anybody about Snake. Besides, none of this conversation should have been public.

Kelly slurped down to the bottom of her glass. The girl behind the bar heard the telltale sound of an empty glass and looked, but she didn't come over. She was smart enough to know Kelly was done. I was about done with the evening myself, and I'd just arrived.

"You need a cab?" I offered.

"For what?" she asked. She stared into the empty glass.

"To go home. You've had enough."

"You know? Nobody's ever said that to me before. You always hear people say that to drunk people in the movies."

"Do you want me to call you a car or what?"

"I'm not ready to go."

"I think you are, so come on. I'll—"

"Call me a cab, you said it twice already. Yadda, yadda, yadda." She opened and closed her hand in my face with each "yadda."

Audrey howled like it was the best joke she'd heard all day. "This one's a pistol, Willie."

I felt my ears go red again. "Yeah. She's something." A pain in my ass.

Kelly leaned in and whispered into my crimson ear, "See? I can be bad, too."

That was it. I grabbed her roughly by the upper arm and pulled her toward the back. "Hey!" she protested.

"Willie, she was just playing with you," Audrey yelled. I ignored her. I pulled Kelly into the hallway leading to the back.

Some guy was standing by the metal door yelling into his cell phone. He yelped when I shoved him through the door into the parking lot, then slammed the door behind him. I wheeled on Kelly. Through clenched teeth, I said, "Please. Do me a favor. Take your judgments, roll them up, and jam them up your skirt."

Shock and adrenaline sobered her up enough to process that I was truly pissed. "What? I—"

"Bad? You're being bad? What the fuck is that? You see the people out there? They're not bad. They're just different from you, and a lot of them are friends of mine. That doesn't make them bad people. But I'll tell you what. They're not a bunch of snobs like you and your fucking yacht-club scene."

"I didn't mean—"

"Shut up. I'm talking now. You think that if you come in here, lose a couple buttons on your starched shirt, belittle me where I work, and get drunk that you belong here? Well, you don't, sweetheart. So go back to whatever frat-boy-fuck-bar you picked up your last corporate lawyer boyfriend in." I started to storm off.

"What about you?" she yelled at my back.

"What?"

"What about you? Do you know me at all? No! You don't know me at all, but you call me a snob. I've never been in a yacht, much less a yacht club, in my life. I work hard to get what little I have, and you've judged me worse than I've ever judged you. I have never dated a lawyer, and I still came here despite you being nothing but an intimidating jerk to me."

"I—I have not been intimidating to you." I realized I didn't have much of a defense, considering I'd just physically dragged her away from the bar.

"Yes, you have." She wiggled her finger in my face. "Your whole personality is wrapped around your ability to intimidate people. Well, tough guy, I'm not letting you intimidate me any more." She whacked me in the chest to drive her point home.

Shit. Suddenly, I was on the defense. Again. "I wasn't trying to . . . Besides, who's hitting who?"

Good one, Boo. I call violence on you!

"Whatsa matter? Am I hurting you?" She whacked me again. "You don't have to try to intimidate people. It's who you are. Damn it, you might even be a little attractive if you could just drop the thug act for a couple minutes."

I closed my eyes and breathed deeply. "Look, Kelly—"

She cut off yet another apology by vomiting spectacularly all over my pant leg.

Then . . . a *long* moment of horror and silence.

"Oh . . . my . . . oh . . ." she said softly. Then she burped.

I stared numbly at the frothy pink mess all over the front of my pants.

Her barely focused eyes filled with embarrassment. "I-am-so-sorry."

"You ready to leave now?"

I needed to change my pants in the office for the second time in a week, but I'd forgotten to bring a fresh pair in after the garbage incident. My choices boiled down to dried-up Dumpster juice or fresh puke. I decided to go with the vomit. At least I could wipe most of it off with paper towels. I called a car service to pick up Kelly.

By the time I got back downstairs, Kelly was back at the bar with Audrey. The adrenaline had worn off and she was stone drunk all over again, swaying in a nonexistent breeze.

"You ready?" I asked.

"Mmnyeah. Night, Audrey." She gave Audrey a big hug.

"Nice to meet you, sweetie. Hope to see you again." Audrey looked at me around the hug. "Willie, you gonna make sure she gets home safe?"

"I called her a car."

Audrey's face turned to a mask of horror. "You are not just going to stick this girl in a car. You are going to take her back to her apartment and make sure she gets in safely." She punctuated her points by poking a thick finger into my arm. I knew better than to argue with Audrey. God help me if Kelly actually came back to the bar and Audrey found out I'd disobeyed a direct order. "Jesus, whatever happened to chivalry?"

"Fine, fine. I'll get her home," I said, defeated in more ways than one.

Kelly turned back to me and smiled. "You are so sweet." Then she hugged me firmly. I told myself it was just another drunken mood swing. One minute I'm an intimidating jerk, the next I'm the bee's knees. She held the hug. It felt good. Very good. I tried reciting Red Sox ERAs in my head, but I hadn't been following the last week or so and my mind froze. I hoped she couldn't feel my ignorance of current statistics pressing against her leg.

The car was waiting outside by the time I peeled her away from both the bar and Audrey. The driver nervously eyed Kelly as I poured her into the back seat. "Yo! She ain't gonna puke back there, is she?"

"No," I said with a certain amount of confidence. "I think she's empty."

I managed to haul Kelly up the stairs of her third-floor walk-up without slipping a disk, falling down a flight, or getting puked on again. Considering the way the evening was playing out so far, I marked that on the win column.

As soon as we walked in the door, Kelly ran to the bathroom. I expected to hear more retching, but only heard water running in the sink. Then I heard the brushing of teeth.

A few framed pictures sat on a small unfinished bookcase. Before I realized what I was doing, I checked each photo for a telltale shot of a boyfriend. One picture showed Kelly with an older woman. Another with an older man. Parents, I figured. None of the three together. Probably divorced. A couple group pictures had guys in them, but she didn't appear intimate with any one guy in particular. The water stopped running.

Kelly walked out of the bathroom, face still damp and shiny. "Well, this is it. My humble home."

"Okay, then. You gonna be all right?"

"In a minute," she said, and she planted a kiss on my mouth. Her kiss was firm, her lips slightly cold from the brushing. Our tongues met softly. She tasted nicely minty.

She pulled away and swooned in my arms. I'd like to think it was a result of my animal magnetism, but it was probably still the booze.

"What was that for?"

"That was for me." She kissed me again and pulled me toward the bedroom. We held the kiss as she fumbled with the doorknob. She managed to get the door open and spun me around. The room was tiny, the edge of her bed only a foot from the door. She pushed me back, and I fell on top of her thick comforter. She dropped on top of me, and we kissed again. Taking my hands, she placed them over her breasts. I could feel her nipples standing at attention against the fabric of her shirt. Then she started kissing my neck.

Dammit. My erogenous Achilles heel and she zoned right in on it.

Despite the devil on my left shoulder howling to tear her clothes off, I pulled her hands back. "Uh, Kelly?" She didn't answer me but stopped working on my neck, thank God. I waited for the angel on my other shoulder to provide me with righteous words, but he must have been on a coffee break. I went on without him. "Listen, don't think that I don't want this."

Still no answer. Her breath was hot on my neck.

I fumbled on. "But I've got a hardcore rule that I have to live by. It's a bar thing. You're really drunk. Even if you really do want to . . . You know? Another time, maybe?"

She answered me with a rattling snore.

As gently as I could, I pulled myself out from under her and sat at the foot of the soft bed. I inhaled deeply and slowly blew out the air as I regained control and psyched out my erection. Suddenly, exhaustion hit me like an ocean wave. I looked at my watch. Almost two in the morning and I felt like I'd been worked over with a Louisville Slugger. I walked into Kelly's living room and flopped onto the couch. Before I knew it, I was out, drifting in a blessedly dreamless sleep.

A sharp scream woke me up suddenly. I sprang to my feet and promptly dropped onto the floor. In my awkward sleeping position, my left leg had fallen asleep and couldn't support my sudden leap into action. Heaping injury on top of injury, I came down square on my balls, which had turned six shades of blue, thanks to the previous evening's coitus interruptus.

Kelly stood in the doorway of her bedroom in a purple towel, mouth agape. I didn't know how much she remembered. Enough, I hoped. Her mouth hung open for a couple seconds. It wasn't quite an expression of total horror, but enough to sting my fragile male ego.

"Morning, Puddin' Pie," I said. "What's for breakfast?"

With a shake of her head, she mumbled, "Late." Then she scurried to the bathroom. Within minutes, she was ready to roll. "Dammit, I'm going to be so late," she kept muttering. She hadn't directly acknowledged me yet, the time crunch giving her something else to focus on. But she had no choice but to deal with me when she was ready to leave. She squeezed her eyes shut tight and sighed before she spoke. "Boo, I'm sorry, but I've got to go."

"Don't worry about it."

"Don't worry about what?" She was playing it casual, but a little too much.

"Nothing happened. We kissed. That was it." I didn't lay the blame on her for the kissing, even though she started it. It wasn't like I was an unwilling participant.

"We did, huh?" Bright red stormed into her cheeks and she looked away, probably disappointed that the frog hadn't turned into a prince.

"Listen, it's no biggie." I felt my own face flushing, suddenly embarrassed to be the ugly fuck I am.

"We really have to leave, though." She looked at her watch again, furrowing her eyebrows. "I am so late."

We made our way down the stairs and into the harsh morning light. I walked her to her car, and she unlocked her door and stopped. "I didn't . . . offend you or anything last night, did I?" She made another pained face in anticipation of my response.

"At the bar? Yeah. With the smooch? Not at all."

She winced. "Sorry about that. Thanks for not . . . You know."

"I know." I didn't want to ask what kind of guy she thought I was. I already knew. "Forget it."

With a tight smile, she got into the car and pulled away. I stood there, angry with myself for reasons I couldn't put my finger on.

Chapter Nine

"Where the fuck you been?" It was nice to know Junior cared.

"Sorry, Ma. Did I break curfew?" I had called the office to check for messages and was surprised when he answered the phone. I was at a pay phone in the little coffee shop where I'd stopped to get breakfast. Once again, it was way early for me and the three cups of weak coffee couldn't cut through the wad of cotton where my brain used to be. My muscles were still stiff from the awkward position I'd slept in, my stomach full of greasy eggs.

"Nobody likes a smartass, Boo. That little prick Paul called the office six times before I checked the machine this morning. I tried you at home and couldn't leave a message. Why didn't you pick up?"

"I wasn't at home."

He paused, waiting for me to continue. I didn't.

"You can tell me later. I came in here to catch the kid the next time he called, and get this . . . he only wants to talk to you." Junior said the last line in a nasal singsong.

"I think you scare him, buddy."

"Good. He's gonna be more scared if I get my hands on him. Where are you?"

"Cosmo's Diner on Mt. Vernon. Did he say when he'd be calling back?"

"He said he'd call back every hour."

I checked my watch. It was a quarter to eleven. "Listen, when he calls back, tell him to meet me here. Have him take a cab and I'll pay for it. Where will you be?"

"I'm going back home and sleeping. Way past my bedtime."

Almost forty-five minutes later, Paul arrived, towing a squat Goth girl who was dressed in what looked like a black wedding dress. Their expressions gave me pause, the two of them wearing faces like a pair of slapped asses.

Black eyeliner had dried in streaks down the girl's face, and I wondered if they were from her crying or had been drawn on intentionally. Enough goop was caked under her eyes to give her a vaguely raccoonish look.

They looked fucked up. "You two on anything?"

"What?" Paul asked.

"I'm not supplying you two with a munchie feast if you're stoned, Paul." Bad enough I was feeding Paul. I didn't need to feed his chubby girlfriend, too.

"Yo, man. That's messed up. Besides, Tammy's straight edge." Paul clucked his tongue. "I bring you news, and you act like my old man. That's so messed up."

"What have you got, Paul?" I sipped another mouthful of the dirty water in my cup.

The girl answered me with huge whooping sobs. "He hurt her so bad."

I shook my head, her non sequitur throwing me for a loop. "What? Who? Who hurt who? Who's he?"

The girl just wept harder. The waitress shot us a look, and I felt my face burn with embarrassment at the spectacle.

"Cassie," Paul whispered.

My skin rose like an ice cube had been placed on the back of my neck. "Who did?"

The girl kept crying.

"Who hurt Cassie?" I said, a bit too sharply. I didn't have the patience to play the crying game with an overwrought mascara case.

"I don't know!" Her words were spaced by sobs. Fresh trails of makeup ran down her round cheeks. Black tears splashed on the table, pooling into an inky puddle.

"Where? Where is she?"

"Tammy saw her at a party last night," Paul said.

"She saw Cassie at a party last night?"

"She saw a DVD. A movie at the party."

Holy Shit at the Pearly Gates.

"What party?" My goosebumps decided to call some friends over.

Tammy couldn't answer me. She was lost in her fear and pubescent anguish.

I jumped up from the table and ran back to the pay phone. With trembling fingers, I called the office again. The phone rang four times before the machine picked up. I hung up and called Junior's apartment. His machine picked up immediately. "Junior! Pick up! Emergency! Yo, Junior!"

The phone beeped again. "What is wrong with you, man? Can't a brother get some beauty sleep?"

"Is Miss Kitty back yet?" My foot was tapping impatiently. Screw the coffee, I was wide-awake now.

"Yeah. Just got her back yesterday. Why?" Junior yawned.

"I'm still at the diner on Mt. Vernon. Get here, ASAP."

"What's going on?"

"Now, Junior."

"Don't start barking at me, dickwad. I'm there." Click.

You cost her, my mind kept repeating. You cost the kid while you were drinking like a fool and crashing on couches. I didn't know what the price was, but I had the feeling the interest was going to be a bitch.

I forced some of the shitty coffee into both kids while we waited for Junior. Neither one of them seemed to enjoy it any more than I did, but they drank it. Tammy managed to calm herself down a bit, and the caffeine gave Paul some color back.

A screech of tires announced Junior's arrival. I paid the tab, and the three of us hopped into the brown '79 Buick that Junior called Miss Kitty.

Yeah, I don't know why either.

"So, what's the deal?" he asked, scratching at his morning stubble.

I turned to the back seat. "Where was the party last night, Tammy?"

She looked at Junior and me with the eyes of a caged animal. "I'm not going back there. That guy is a freak." Her lower lip started to tremble. "He laughed. When he saw me watching, he laughed at how scared I was."

I reached back and took her hand. "We need to go there, Tammy, and we need you to help us. Cassie might be in trouble, and the faster we get to her, the better her chances are. Please, sweetheart. Help us." I squeezed her pudgy hand and tried to look concerned through the impatience I was feeling.

She didn't say anything for a few seconds, just gazed into the air. "It was in Brookline. Just off of Boylston. I don't know what street, but I'll recognize it when we get there."

Junior gunned the car, and the powerful engine shot us off like a cannon. I filled him in as delicately as I could without upsetting either of the kids again. The more I talked, the tighter he gripped the steering wheel. He clenched his jaw so tight his temples throbbed.

We drove down Huntington slowly, letting Tammy get her bearings. She jumped up in her seat when she spotted it. "That's the street, right there. I remember the Kinko's on the corner." We'd already passed the street by the time she noticed it. Junior stopped at the light and U-turned back at the intersection. We pulled to a stop on the corner.

"Which one is it?" I asked.

"That one. Right there." It was a large prewar building. No doorman. That made life easier. "Can I go home now?" She stared at the building, tears welling in her eyes again.

"Not yet. We need you to buzz the apartment and get us in," I said as gently as I could. "Do you think he'll remember you?"

"I'm so scared. Seven was laughing at the video. He was getting off on it."

Seven.

I'd forgotten to ask who threw the party. Junior and I were both well acquainted with the victim-to-be.

Junior and I looked at each other. Seven was the lead singer of The Genitalonious Monks. Goth band. Or, as Junior liked to call that particular scene, "men with eyeliner." The last time they played The Cellar, I had to put the kibosh on their show just as Seven was about to give a strangely willing audience member an enema right on stage. He called me a Philistine. I made sure Seven and his three-ring circus of a band never got booked at The Cellar again.

Junior bared his teeth in a wolf's smile. "Honey, you scared of that guy? With me and Boo here?"

"I dunno. He's weird. Like, crazy weird." She chewed her lower lip.

"Would it make you feel better if we smacked the shit out of him if he gets out of line?"

She actually giggled into her hand. "Would you?"

"For you, sweetness? Anything." Junior had turned on the charm, and by God, it seemed to work.

Tammy was blushing all the way down to her collar when we stepped out of the car. She led the way. I whispered in Junior's ear. "Sweetness?"

He whispered back. "Death wish?"

The four of us stepped into the large tiled foyer. I knew which intercom buzzer was Seven's without being told. *Antichrist* was written in fancy calligraphy next to the button for 3B.

I turned to Tammy. "Tell him you were at the party last night and left your purse."

"I . . . I can't," she said. I could see tremors squirming through her body. "I can't go up there again."

Junior stepped in. "He's not going to fuck with you, sweetie. I promise you." His face was set hard as he lifted her chin and looked straight into her watery raccoon eyes.

"Me, too," Paul said, protectively wrapping his arm around Tammy's shoulder. Junior turned so Paul couldn't see him smirk. I think he was actually starting to like the kid. Or maybe he was just smiling at the notion of smacking the shit out of Seven if necessary. I really hoped it would be necessary.

With a trembling hand, Tammy pressed the button for 3B. A shrill screech blared from the box, making me wince. A few seconds later, a tinny voice came back through.

"What do you want?" I'd forgotten about the horrible, fey English accent Seven affected.

"Um, hi. This is Tammy? I left my purse up there at the party last night." She looked at Junior for approval. He nodded at her.

A pause. "I found no purse." The guy was a real charmer.

"It's really small, and I was sitting on the couch. It might have fallen between the cushions." Nice touch. Junior gave her a thumb's up.

Another pause. The door clicked and buzzed as Seven let us in. It was on.

I pushed the door and held it. "Tammy, we just need you at the door so he'll open it." I considered telling Paul to wait, but I didn't want to emasculate the kid in front of the girl.

Tammy knocked on the door. There was a peephole, so Junior and I flanked opposite sides before she knocked. Seven undid what sounded like two dozen locks before he opened the door. He stood in the doorway in a long red silk robe that slung low around his waist, barely held together with a sash.

"Come in," said the spider to the fly.

Then the pit bulls charged the web.

Junior firmly pushed Seven back into the apartment. The walls were painted blood red, and Nag Champa incense clouded the space so thickly my nose hairs gagged.

"Wait," Seven said in an offended tone. "Who are you two?" I noticed his fake accent seemed to be tinged with German right then. His body was completely hairless, which made him tough to read. If he was surprised, he didn't have the eyebrows to show it. If anything, he almost seemed pleased to see us. He pointed a long finger at Tammy. "I remember you. You cry."

I grabbed him by the silk lapels and flung him into the wall. His head bounced off it with a pleasant whack.

"Hey! Hey!" he protested. I let him go. "I remember you, too." Then he looked at me with calm appraisal. "Philistine." He said it like a nickname for an old friend.

"I'm real flattered you remember me, dickhead."

"You stopped my art. You have no vision."

Junior stuck a thick finger into his face. "And you're gonna have no teeth unless you give us what we want."

"What do you want?" he asked, sounding bored. I had to admit, the guy was cucumber cool.

"The DVD," I said.

"I don't have DVDs. Or CDs or tapes for that matter. I am a performance artist." He trailed his fingers slowly down his body. His long, manicured fingernails made a soft zipping sound on the silk. "All of my shows are individual works."

"We don't give a good shit about your whiny, pansy-ass music or 'performances,'" Junior said. "We want to see the video you played last night."

I gnawed my lower lip, itching to pound the pose right off him.

His smile was lascivious. "Ah, yes. The red-haired girl. Her fear was delicious." The room started to tinge redder than the walls, redder than his robe.

"So was yours," he said to Tammy. He stared at her, unblinking. I followed his gaze to her. She was frozen, terrified. He held her eyes like a snake paralyzing a mouse. The poor kid was so scared, she couldn't even cry anymore. She just took short, sharp breaths while fresh black tears rolled down her cheeks.

Junior broke the spell with a clean right hook to the mouth. Hard. Seven's head snapped back with what sounded like a whip crack. He dropped to his knees and grabbed his mouth.

"Ahh! You fuck!" Seven yelped. It sounded like "fuh-muck" through his mashed lips.

"Yo, Seven," Junior said, leaning down, his face right in Seven's. "You really should have been paying attention to us, not the kid. You might have been able to dodge that if you were."

"Take her down to the car," I said to Paul. Paul nodded and took Tammy out the door by her upper arm. In her state of shock, she was easily led.

"I'm gonna sue your asses off!" Seven cried, stumbling back up to his feet. "I have a performance tonight!" Blood poured from his ruined mouth. Remarkably, Junior's punch had only unleashed more attitude.

I grabbed his left ear and twisted it like a piece of taffy. He screamed, and I socked him in the gut with my other hand to shut him up. Worked like a charm. Felt *real* good, too.

He dropped back to the floor, gasping. He didn't try to stand again.

"This is the last time I ask. Where's the DVD?"

"Do you have any idea how much that cost me?" His voice was a wheeze. I noticed he forgot the accent entirely. A natural Quincy twang replaced it.

"You need to listen when I say I'm not asking again," I said, drawing back my hand. "Now you get the pimp hand."

He squealed. "No! It's in the coffee table!"

I let the pimp hand go just for the pleasure of it. I cupped my hand and caught him right on the ear I'd just squeezed. He howled and covered up the side of his head. Must have hurt like hell. I walked over to the coffee table. It was a glass-topped box shaped like a coffin, complete with plastic skeleton inside. Under the bones of the left arm sat a short stack of unmarked black DVD cases.

"Which one is it?" I asked.

"It's one with the red sticker on top," he said as he pointed at the table. The long finger wasn't so steady anymore.

I flipped through the DVDs. There were five of them. Three with red stickers. I dropped each case without a sticker to the floor and crushed it with the heel of my boot. "Which one?" I asked.

"I don't know. It's one of those." He put a finger in his mouth, probing his teeth.

"Where did you get these?" I asked.

He shook his head. "I can't tell you."

"Junior, go to the car and grab my needle-nose pliers. I'm gonna pull those pretty fingernails off backward. Then we'll see what he can and can't tell us." It was only a half-threat. I wouldn't have pulled them off backward. That would have been mean.

"No!" Seven screamed when Junior walked toward the door. "I can't tell you! Please! These people, they're crazy. They'll kill me!" Flecks of bloody foam formed at the corner of his mouth. For what it was worth, the guy was scared off his cracker.

"Blah, blah, blah. Stop being such a cliché," Junior said, whapping the top of Seven's bald head like Benny Hill.

"And what a loss you would be, but that's not our problem," I said. "First of all, they never have to know it came from you."

Junior said, "Second, what do you think we'll do to you if you don't tell us? We're gonna fuck ya, then kill ya. We're not gay."

Seven looked at us both, confused.

I glared at Junior. "Point is, we're going to hurt you. A lot."

Junior closed his eyes and shuddered violently in his imaginings. "*Grande mucho*."

Seven's eyes bulged white as he looked back and forth at the two of us. His head dropped. "Sid's Vids on Comm Ave. By BU," he said in a whisper.

"Who do we talk to?" I asked.

"Sid," he said snidely. He felt around the inside his mouth again. "I think you cracked my tooth, asshole."

Junior kicked him right in the face with a size-twelve Doc Marten. Seven's head bounced off the wall like a tennis ball. "There. Now you can be sure."

With great effort, Seven simultaneously tried to crawl into a corner and stay conscious. I stalked him slowly across the floor. "Those kids out there? You ever—and I mean ever—come across them again?" I booted him a shot to the ribs. Seven wheezed and flopped over. "You say one fucking word to either one of them . . ." I kicked him again.

"Or look at them . . ." Junior punched him solidly on the thigh, sending a vicious charleyhorse through the muscle. Seven looked like he wanted to scream, but there was no air left in his lungs from my kick.

"Or breathe on them . . ." I kicked him again, and he went fetal.

"Don't even think too hard about them," Junior said, adding the heel of his boot to the fray. "That would also be bad for you."

"Have we made ourselves clear here?" I asked. Kick.

Seven wheezed dryly before he managed to mouth a "yes."

"Got that, you G.G. Allin wannabe motherfucker?" Kick.

Kick.

Kick.

Kick.

Kick.

Kick.

He was still wailing hoarse yesses at us as we walked out the door. Probably be a while before he'd be singing again.

I'd be a liar if I said it didn't feel good.

Real fucking good.

Paul sat on the wide hood of the Buick, hugging himself. His skin tone still wasn't a color I would consider healthy. He looked like he could puke at any second. Credit to the kid, though, he was hanging in like a trooper.

"Tammy took off," he said. I felt bad about how we had put her in that situation. I consoled myself with the thought that she'd be fine after she listened to a few Dead Can Dance albums. Maybe sacrificed a goat. Who knows what cheers up a Goth kid, anyway?

"Now what?" Junior asked.

"Yeah. What are we going to do now?" Paul rubbed his hands together, the excitement perking him back up. This was all one big adventure for him.

The gig was shaping up to be a long evening of indiscriminate violence. "First, we drive you home," I said to Paul.

"Aw, man! C'mon," he whined. "I hook you guys up with Baldy and the videos and you're gonna do me like that?"

I handed him another hundred. He shut up. "We appreciate your help, Paul, but we need to take it solo from here."

His eyes were full of Benjamin Franklin, but there was disappointment in his voice. "No, no. That's cool, I guess."

"Where can we drop you off?" Junior asked.

"Forget it. I'm gonna go to the Square," he said. "Besides, the mom's boyfriend has been drinking his unemployment check away all week. Best to stay mobile, you know? Later." He flashed us a peace sign and was off.

Junior and I silently watched him off for a moment. Junior said, "Boo?"

"What's up?"

"Every goddamn time I hear something like that . . ." Junior shook his head.

"Yeah." I felt for Paul, though he seemed pretty well adjusted to his situation. The two of us knew all too well the art of adaptation. Either you made your way within your shitty life or they found you dangling from an extension cord in the janitor's closet.

As I went to light a smoke, I noticed a tiny smear of Seven's blood on my finger. I wiped it off on my pants leg.

Junior started Miss Kitty's engine and gunned it, making her roar. "Now what?"

"Let's go rent some movies."

"*Ugh*. That was terrible, Boo. That was like, Steven Segal script terrible."

"Just drive."

Chapter Ten

Sid's Vids sat sandwiched between a Vietnamese restaurant and a Store 24 on Commonwealth, right down the block from where the BU campus began. The window facing the street looked like it last met Windex sometime during the Cold War. Sun-faded videotape boxes sat limply on display. I did a double-take.

Videotapes? Even I, the man with the beeper, owned a DVD player. The titles popped up more red flags than a Chinese Army parade.

Caddyshack 2.

Joe vs. the Volcano.

The place didn't even hawk good videotapes.

Obviously we'd found the right place. The piece of real estate the store occupied didn't come cheap. And Sid's Vids wasn't working too hard to interest customers off the street. The money wasn't coming off rentals. The only thing missing was a neon sign flashing *FRONT*. But I must have passed the place a thousand times before and never noticed the quirk of it.

A little bell tinkled over the door as we walked in. The place smelled of stale dirt and something ripe and sickly sweet like old meat. The air conditioner over the window had to be broken; otherwise it should have been turned on by law. Putrid humidity hung the stench at eye-level in the small room. I could hear the sounds of a television and labored breathing coming from the rear. My heart pounded as we walked down the aisle. I wasn't sure what I was going to do if I saw a snake tattoo.

Bad things.

Bad, bad things.

What I did see was one of the fattest beasts outside a zoo that I'd ever laid eyes on. The person sitting behind the counter was at least four hundred pounds. Limp, stringy hair lay across its forehead like overcooked spaghetti.

I was looking right at it, and I had no idea if it was a man or a woman. There were tits, sure, but in the dim light, I couldn't be sure there wasn't stubble or an Adam's apple wedged into the thick folds of its neck.

"Oh, yuck," Junior muttered under his breath.

I cleared my throat. "Excuse me."

"What?" The beast still didn't look up from the TV.

"I want to talk to Sid."

"I'm Sid," the beast said, pointing a thumb the size of a bratwurst back at itself.

"You're Sid?" Junior asked.

"The fucking sign says Sid's Vids, don't it? You expecting a man?"

Well, at least we cleared that much up.

"It's Portuguese," she went on, "short for Sidonia."

"We were told we could get some movies here."

With a tremendous effort, Sid turned her head to look at us better. "Wow. You two managed to figure out that you could get movies at a video store. You two must be the fucking pride of MIT." Sid laughed a wet gurgle at us.

"Movies with girls in them."

Sid turned back to the television. "On your left. Through the curtain, Romeo." To the left was a beaded curtain, a handwritten sign next to it that read, *18 And Over Only*.

"I don't think you'd have these movies on your shelves," I said.

Sid's broad face darkened as she turned back. "I don't know what you're talking about."

"Sure you do," Junior said. "Rough stuff. With girls. And by girls, we mean *girls*." Junior plucked a pair of quotation marks in the air with his fingers.

"I don't know what the fuck you're talking about." Sid's voice didn't have the same conviction the second time. Beads of dull sweat popped out on her face. Might not have been nervous sweat. Could have been exertion sweat from having to turn her head twice in less than an hour.

"C'mon," I said. "Seven told us this is where he gets his."

"Seven what? Little dwarves? I said I don't—"

"Whatever," Junior said. "You don't want our money? Fine. But just so you know, we've got a few people who want those kinds of movies and we've got cash." Junior brought out the flash money—a hundred wrapped around a thick wad of ones. To Sid it must have looked like a Burger King's ransom.

Sid licked her thick lips at the sight of the money. I suppressed my gag reflex.

"You two cops?" she asked.

"We look like cops to you?" I asked.

"Cause you have to tell me if I ask. It's illegal for you to not tell me if I ask. That's entrapment."

"I'm not a cop," I said. I didn't know if Sid's information on the law was true or not, but I figured I'd humor her.

"What about you, Red?"

Junior sighed. "Nope. Not a cop."

"Say it. Say the words. Say, 'I'm not a cop.'"

"I. Am. Not. A. Cop," he said, hammering it out like a kid at a spelling bee.

One more shot, for reaction's sake. "Listen, just call the snake man and tell him we want three copies of every movie he's got."

Sid jiggled and wheezed at his mention.

We have a winner.

I sighed, feigning boredom at the conversation as we walked. "Make some calls. We'll be back tomorrow. Have an answer."

Outside the store, Junior said in a mock-serious tone, "I thought you told Seven you wasn't gonna bring him into this."

"Did I now?" I said with equal amounts of mock-forgetfulness. "Well, gee. It must have plum slipped my mind."

"Shame on you." Junior waggled his finger at me. "And your plums."

"Yes," I said. "Yes. Shame on me. Leave my plums out of this."

Junior sat on Miss Kitty's hood, mulling over the situation. "Well, ain't this a bitch," he said, chewing on his thumbnail.

"What is?" Humid sweat made my clothes stick. As I separated the fabric from my skin, I could still smell the stink of Sid's Vids coming off me, as though the odor had dug itself into my pores.

"This throws a monkey wrench right into our investigatory style, now don't it?" he said, throwing his hands into the air. "I mean, hell . . . we can't just kick the shit out of her to find out what we need, can we? She's a girl." He said the last with an aggravated sweep of his hand toward the storefront.

Girl might not have been the term I would have used to describe our little Sidonia, but I knew what he meant. As a blanket policy, we try not to hit women. Even ones with as questionable a womanhood as Sid. Once I had to deck a townie biker chick when she went for my eyes with a corkscrew. Another time, a drunken skinhead girl chased Junior halfway to Roxbury when she decided she wanted a fight and picked Junior. That's how far he'd go to avoid physical conflict with a woman. Literally.

As extreme as the circumstances were, we couldn't come up with a good enough reason to pound on Sid. Besides, I wasn't convinced we could dish out anything that would register on her thick hide. Be like punching a waterbed.

This was going to call for creativity. Not our deepest well to draw from.

"Wait a sec," I said. I walked back over toward Sid's Vids. I was reasonably sure Sid wasn't going to come waddling out the door unless it was time to close or the building was on fire. Over the windows, about seven feet up, was the broken air conditioner. I felt in my pockets for something to hitch up the vent flaps with.

Pack of Parliaments, keys, and Sharpie pen.

Bingo.

My lucky self-defense Sharpie.

I tiptoed up and arched my body to stay out of Sid's line of vision. I heard her voice over the television before I lifted up the slats. I couldn't make out what she was saying but I knew she was on the phone. Nobody was in the store when we went in, and nobody had gone in since we'd left.

Detective of the Year Award, here I come.

With the slats opened, I caught snippets of her side of the conversation.

". . . know who the fuck they are . . . [wheezing] yeah . . . I think that . . . [more wheezing] . . . pay fucking Seven a visit . . . [wheeze] . . . stupid fucking pussy ass faggot . . ."

Too easy. Either we were better than we thought we were or these people were wicked retarded.

Then my beeper sounded, nearly making me shit myself. I jumped down and tried to muffle the buzzing by cupping it in my palms as I ran down the street. I wasn't worried about Sid giving chase.

Kelly's number popped onto the screen. As I walked past Miss Kitty, Junior rolled down the window. "The fuck was that?"

"Got a beep. Gonna use the phone in the store."

I dropped a quarter in the pay phone in the Store 24. Much as I hated to admit it, I was going to have to get a cell phone. Pay phones were becoming scarcer in Boston than Yankees fans.

"Kelly Reese."

"You beeped?"

"Yeah. About that. You have a beeper?"

"Yup. I'm kinda old school." I waved at the cashier. When he looked over, I showed him the Twinkie package I'd picked up. He waved it off, so I opened it and took a big bite of chemical deliciousness.

"That's one way of looking at it."

"Hey, you beep me to bust my balls, or you need something?"

"Touchy."

"Only when people make fun of my beeper."

"Can you meet up with me for a coffee in the next couple hours?"

"I'm available right now. Sure you don't want anything stronger?"

"Want me to vomit on you again?"

"Coffee it is."

She was sitting outside the Starbucks across from Back Bay Station when I got there. She handed me a large iced coffee. (You can fuck yourself if you think I'm calling it a *venti.*) I knew a hangover when I saw one, and she looked like she was coping with a doozy. Lot of that going around, apparently.

"How you feeling, kiddo?"

"Oh, ready to die." She nodded toward the paper bag on the table. "Didn't know how you took it, so there's some sugar in the bag and milk in that little cup."

"Thanks. So . . ."

"Again, I just want to apologize for last night. I don't want you to get the wrong idea."

Her behavior had given me all the right ideas, but none I could repeat in public. "Like I said, no problem. You call me up to apologize again?"

"Beeped you, actually," she said, smirking.

"What did I say about making fun of my beeper?"

"Sorry. Forgot you were old school for a second."

"Thank you." I lit a cigarette and saw her expression shift. "So, which is it?"

"Which what?"

"Are you a pain-in-the-ass cigarette hater, or did you want one?"

"I quit a year ago." She took a long pull off her straw.

"Great. You're the worst of both worlds."

"Give me a drag." She plucked the cigarette from my hand and took a longer pull, closed her eyes, and groaned in a fashion not far from sexual. I wondered if she'd quit to impress her boss, the other ex-smoker I'd handed a cigarette to recently. "You're a very, very bad influence, Mr. Malone."

She had no idea. "So other than using me to enable your vices, why are we here?"

"Mr. Donnelly was wondering how you were doing."

I took the cigarette back and puffed. I got a strange pleasure from the taste of her lipstick on the filter. "Oh. Um, we're making progress."

"What does that mean, exactly?"

I decided to edit severely, and dodge the exactly. "Have you ever heard her talk about boys at all? About a guy with a snake tattoo, specifically?"

"Honestly? I've never really talked to her all that much. I've picked her up from school, driven her to the mall and stuff, but she's at an age where anyone over twenty is the enemy."

"That may be the case, but the guy we think she's with is well over puberty."

"That sounds bad." She pulled a chunk off an apple fritter and popped it into her mouth, chewing it slowly.

"It probably is." I didn't say just how bad.

"Oh God, I think I'm going to be ill."

"Not on me this time."

"You're never letting that go, are you?"

"Probably not. She do any of that computer stuff? Friendster?"

"Friendster? You're not old school, you're retirement home. All the cool kids are on Facebook. Besides, her dad keeps all her passwords saved. He regularly checks her online activity."

"He spies on her?"

"Monitors her. But kids are crafty. They're so much better than adults with the technology, with adapting to it. Most kids, they want to hide online activity from their parents? A moderately savvy kid could do it easily."

I didn't do any of that shit. I didn't "friend" people on a fucking computer. I didn't Twoot on Twatter or whatever the hell that crap was called, either. Maybe she was right. Maybe I wasn't old school anymore so much as just out of touch. "So there is a possibility that she met some kind of pervo online, and her dad would have no idea, even with the monitoring."

"That is a possibility." She shuddered at the thought. "Anything else? Anything less on the potentially skeevy side?"

"Sorry. Skeevy is all we got right now."

"All right, then." She stood and wiped the creases off her skirt. "One more drag." She opened her fingers to grab the cigarette.

I pulled it back. "Tell me I'm cute again."

She immediately blushed. "Did I do that?"

"Yup."

"Crap. Well, you are, for old school." Defty, she plucked my cigarette out of my hand and walked off with it.

"Hey."

She winked at me. "I might not be old school, but I'm not as good as you think I am, Mr. Malone."

"No doubt, Ms. Reese."

No doubt.

I met back up with Junior at a small Chinese restaurant about a half mile down Commonwealth. We didn't talk much while we ate. We were both trying to think in between chews.

Junior spoke first. "How do you think you'd fuck something that big?"

"I wouldn't," I said through a mouthful of pork fried rice. Great partner he was. I was trying to figure out how we could get information out of Sid while he was trying to figure out the mechanics of sex with her.

"I mean, you'd have to have a dick like a Pringles can to get under that belly."

My gorge did a little hurdle at the thought. "Junior, please. I'm trying to eat."

"You think Snake fucks her?"

"Junior . . ."

"He'd be capable, just—"

"Junior! Fucking stop!"

"Sor-ry," he said, dripping sarcasm. "Didn't mean to offend your delicate sensibilities."

"Did you see what time the store closed?" I asked, desperate to change the conversation.

"Nope," Junior said, mopping up the last swirls of oyster sauce with a piece of bread. "Why?"

"Figured we could tail Sid. See where she goes after work."

"Well, she ain't going to no gym," he said with a snort. "Not too far a stretch to guess she goes for food. You don't get that big unless you eat a good ten meals a day. And I'm not kidding. Take my aunt, Gretchen—"

"No, thank you."

"Wakka-wakka, Shecky."

"That was Henny Youngman."

"Huh?"

"Henny Youngman, not Shecky Green."

"Fucking hell, you wanna let me talk or you gonna display your knowledge of the Borscht Belt all over my story?"

"The mike is yours, bubelah."

Junior paused a second, debating whether or not I'd called him something potentially offensive, and whether or not to eat the bread in his hand or to stick it up my nose. He chose to pop the bread into his mouth and continued.

"Anyway, Gretchen, same deal. Actually, she was smaller than Sid, but nobody was calling her to do any underwear modeling, you know? She ate two meals between breakfast and brunch."

Just thinking about it made my appetite grind to a screeching halt. I dropped my fork down on the plate with a clatter and tossed my napkin on top of it. I was still hungry, but with Sid and Aunt Gretchen in my head, I might not eat for the rest of the week. "Was there a point to that story?"

"Sorry. Did you need one?" Junior nodded at my rice. "You gonna finish that?" I handed him my plate, and he dumped my food onto his. "Anyway, other than thinking about what to eat next, I don't imagine Sid doing much else."

"So we'll follow her when she leaves the store."

"Should be easy to tail. Not like she's gonna outrun us."

"Can't say that about too many people."

"True that. Problem is, what do we do once she stops?"

I scratched at the stubble on my chin. "Getting physical on her is out of the question."

"Not if we call Twitch." Junior didn't look at me when he said it, as though he were ashamed for thinking it, much less saying it.

I shuddered at exactly what Twitch could be capable of. "That's not the way I want to go about this."

"Me neither," Junior said. "But what other options we got? Clock's ticking."

"We'll do this on the fly. Let's see where she goes first. Who knows? I think we rattled her. Her next stop might be Snake's. Now, he we can fuck up."

"Sounds like a plan. Kinda." Junior shoved the last of the fried rice into his mouth.

Yeah. Kinda. Problem was, I had no idea what to do next if Sid didn't follow my imaginary script.

Our first stakeout. They should make Hummels to mark the occasion. For supplies, we brought six cans of metallic-tasting iced coffee, a carton of smokes, and three pounds of candy from the candy shop right across the street from Sid's. Good thing neither one of us was diabetic. If we were, we'd find out soon enough.

We parked behind a construction trailer on the far side of the street. Just enough of a sight line for us to see the front of Sid's and not be obvious about it. If anyone in the neighborhood was wondering why we were sitting in our car for a couple hours smoking and bitching about the quality of canned coffee, they didn't care enough to ask.

"'Oh, Sheila,'" I said to Junior as I popped another jelly bean in my mouth.

"Prince. You're slipping. That's an easy one." Junior was munching on a big bag of Sno-Caps, the front of his T-shirt covered in tiny white sugar granules.

"So easy you're wrong."

"What? That was so Prince! He wrote it about Sheila E."

"I don't know if he wrote it, but he didn't sing it."

"Morris Day?"

"Nope."

"Shit. Who was it?" Just then, a stunning young thing in ripped jeans and a tank top came strolling by with a ferret wrapped around her neck. Only in Boston. From our angle, we could see a big tattoo of the Pisces sign on her lower back, right above her butt cleavage. "Jeeeeeesus H. Crow," Junior said in awe.

"Yeah," was all I could manage as I squinted in the last few seconds of her before she turned the corner and was gone. "You know, I'm starting to think we're not the best guys for this work."

Junior shrugged as he licked a finger and dipped it into the white sugar orbs accumulated at the bottom of his bag. "I dunno. I think we're doing a pretty damn good job so far."

"Yeah, but look at us. Put together, we don't have the attention span of a squirrel. We're supposed to be watching the store."

"Boo?"

"Yeah?"

"If something like that ever walks by and I can't take my eyes off Sid? Shoot me in the face."

"Got it."

"I mean it. In the face. Close the lid. I don't deserve the dignity of an open casket. Sno-Cap?" He sucked the sugar off his finger as he offered the bag.

"No thanks."

"Suit yourself." He dipped his wet finger back in for another go.

"Ready for the World."

"I'm ready for anything."

"No, they sang 'Oh, Sheila.'"

"Damn. It was them, wasn't it? I thought it was Prince."

"Nope." So far, I had the lead. Sixteen to nine. Hollow victories are still victories.

"Oh, yeah. Fine, then. Gloves are off. 'Pac-Man Fever.'"

I sang the opening riff. "I got a pocket full of quarters, and I'm headed to the arcaaaade . . ."

"No way. No fucking way do you know this one."

"Way. Buckner and Garcia."

"Goddamn it." Junior flicked a Sno-Cap at me. I switched my jelly bean bag for my gummi worm bag.

Time crept along, and we waited. My legs started to stiffen, and my back ached. How the hell did cops do this shit? Maybe they didn't in real life. So far, all we had for references on procedure were John D. MacDonald novels and Junior's *Miami Vice* DVDs.

Then the Sid's Vids sign went black. I checked my watch. Quarter past eight. The sun was just starting to lower itself into the horizon, turning the sky into mango.

Timing was perfect. We would have the cover of dusk to follow Sid. Unfortunately, it was too hot to wear trench coats. That would have been cool.

We waited. Another fifteen minutes passed. The lights in the store went off.

Another half-hour. Fully dark now. No Sid.

"Uh . . . You don't think she went out the back, do you?" Junior asked.

"Shit. I don't know if there is a back way."

"Shouldn't we have thought of that?"

"Probably."

"Wait here. I'll go check."

Junior scrambled out of the car, hunched low and moving in a serpentine path from car to car like he was on recon in Baghdad. Nice and inconspicuous.

Jesus.

I kept my eyes on the front of the store. Nothing. It was half past nine. Something was fucked up in Denmark.

Junior came back behind the car, still hunched like a gorilla with Scoliosis. "Found her," he said, grinning.

"Where?"

"Upstairs. We were watching the stupid store so tight we didn't notice the lights in the apartment above go on. I guess it's hers. There's a little lot and a rear door into the apartments back there."

"How do you know she's up there? All the shades are drawn on this side."

"Shadows, my man. Either Sid is up there or they're renting the apartment out to a wheezing buffalo. Got a dog up there, too."

"Damn. How big?"

"Sounded like one of those little dogs with fuzzy ears that just piss and shake."

"Good. I don't want to head up there and rassle with a Rottweiler." Along with women, I don't dance with dogs. I know guys who have; guys like Lefty and Petey One-Nut.

"If what I heard was any longer than my dick, I'll buy you a steak."

"Wow. That's a little dog. Or a barking ladybug."

"Hardy-har. You're a fucking riot. You want the front or the back?"

"I'll take the back door," I said, climbing out of the car.

"Heard that about you," Junior said with a cackle as I shut the door.
Point to Junior. That was a good one.

Luck came in the form of a pizza and a prayer. I waited in the back, leaning in the empty rear doorway to the shop next to Sid's Vids. I watched shadows play in the windows. The shadows looked big, but I couldn't tell what might be tricks of the light. I could hear the sharp yipping of an aggravated pet. It did sound smaller than a breadbox, which was a relief. Other than that, Sid seemed to be alone up there.

Junior came around the corner of the building, a large flat box in his hands, a huge grin on his puss. "Lookie, lookie," he said, "Junior found a cookie. It appears Sid here ordered herself a big ol' pizza that I seem to have intercepted." He tipped the paper cap that read *College Pizza.*

"Nice hat."

"Any headwear looks good on a man like me." Junior hit the buzzer for Sidonia Sliva.

Sid's voice replied from the console. "What?"

"Itsa pizza," Junior answered in an Italian accent that would have embarrassed Chef Boy-ar-dee.

She buzzed us in. Either Sid never met an actual Italian before, or she was just too hungry to care.

One flight of creaky stairs up, I knocked on the door.

"C'mon in. The door's open," came the reply from inside.

So we went in. The apartment had the same reek as the store. It wasn't as bad as the Dumpster incident, but it was still awful, like old meat and dirty underpants. My sinuses wanted to bust out of my head and run to the nearest aromatherapy clinic. How the hell could someone live in this?

Sid sat in a wide recliner, frozen. From the television she'd been facing, Homer Simpson said "*D'oh!*"

"Yo, Sid," Junior said. "Dangerous habit leaving the door unlocked like that."

Sid tried to leap out of her chair. She really did. All she managed to do was rock spastically from side to side. "What the fuck is going on here? What the fuck are you two doing here?" she croaked at us. She almost made it up into a half squat. I nudged her in the shoulder with the tip of my boot. Sid fell back with a thud into the recliner. The vinyl farted under the impact. I hoped it was the vinyl. She looked like a turtle who'd suddenly found itself wrong side up.

"Do you guys know who you're fucking with? Who my business partners are?" Sid bellowed.

"Let me guess," I said. "Colonel Sanders? He's dangerous. Military background."

"Fuck you."

"Wait, I got it. You're in with the McDonald's Mafia, aren't you?"

Junior was trying to find a place to put on his badass lean but couldn't seem to locate a surface that wouldn't ruin his pants. "Dude. Maybe we oughta think about this. That Grimace is a baaad mutha—"

"Shut yo mouth!"

Junior shrugged. "I'm only talking 'bout Grimace."

"I can dig it."

"Fuck you!" There still didn't seem to be any fear in Sid's voice. That wasn't good. If anything, she was just getting more and more pissed.

"Well, I'll tell you who she doesn't know. Mr. Clean." Junior picked up what looked like a leather handbag with eyes from behind a garbage pail. "Sid, your housecleaning skills suck."

"Worse than yours?" I asked.

"At least I don't have little piles of shit on my floor left by Free Willie of the canine set." Junior held up the pudgiest chihuahua I'd ever seen. His tiny legs poked out from a body the same size and definition as ten pounds of cookie dough. His tail stub wagged happily.

The dog was the plan. Since we couldn't very well threaten Sid physically, we had to threaten her dog. Looking at the cute little fat bastard, I felt guilt seep into my gut. I like dogs better than I do most people.

"Hey, buddy," I said, scratching him behind his ears. His little tongue darted out at my fingers. Then tiny teeth gnashed where my fingers had been a moment before. "Hey!"

The fucker started snarling and snapping for Junior's fingers too, but the dog couldn't turn his neck far enough over his fat shoulders to get him.

"You let him go," Sid said in a low and deadly tone.

"What's the little guy's name, Sid?" I asked.

"Put him *down*!" Sid didn't try to stand again, but the armrests creaked ominously under her grip.

"Now, Sid. You don't want to go yelling and get all the neighbors riled." To my right, small stacks of DVDs sat on a bookshelf. Red stickers and all. "Because if the cops come, I'm gonna have to show them those discs you got over here, now won't I?"

A flicker of fear danced across her eyes, but the fierce glow quickly returned. "Put the dog down," she said.

"We will, Sid, we will. First, you to tell us where we can find the guy who stars in your videos."

"I don't know where he is. When I need the videos—" She cut herself off.

"What? You call him? Don't suppose we could get that number, do you?" I was hoping we wouldn't have to go any further than asking.

Sid didn't say anything, but she looked frantically between the dog in Junior's arms and me.

Damn it.

I nodded at Junior. The dog yipped in pain. Even though I knew Junior only gave him a tiny pinch on the hind leg, it still hurt to hear the little guy cry like that. I knew it hurt Junior even more to have to do it.

Neither one of us expected what happened next.

Sid started sobbing. Big, whooping sobs that sent her frame shaking like Jell-O on a paint mixer.

Junior and I exchanged guilt-ridden glances. This wasn't us. Sid might have been a horrible waste of humanity, profiting from pain on video, but as far as we knew, she'd never hurt anybody.

Then the dog peed a yellow arc onto the floor.

"Whoa." Junior held the dog over the wastebasket.

Sid covered her face with wide hands. "Puh-puh-leease. Let my dog go. I'll tell you wuh-wuh-whatever you want."

I leaned in close, the guilt making me nauseous. "That's all we want, Sid." I turned to Junior. "Put the dog down."

I turned back just in time to see . . . Sid smiling through her fingers, then a fist the size of a canned ham bee-lining for my face.

The impact was tremendous. Like a sack of M-80s exploded in the back of my skull. She caught me square on the jaw with a straight right that would have made Brock Lesnar proud, with all of her weight behind it. I found myself airborne and looking up at my feet and the cracked ceiling. I landed on my neck and upper back, the wind knocked out of my lungs and my senses knocked clean to Tuesday.

If I wasn't so jacked, the following scene might have been enjoyably comic.

Junior ran like a fullback chased by the biggest and scariest defensive tackle in the league. He hurdled an end table, shuck-and-jived around the television stand, and pushed over a large fern to block the charging Sid—the entire time with the chihuahua tucked under his arm like a hairy football.

And he was singing.

"C'mon, Sid! Can't touch this! Duh nuh nuh nuh. Nuh nuh. Nuh nuh. Can't touch this!" he sang as he dodged.

Sid just continued her rush, making low animal noises as she grasped for Junior and her dog.

Still woozy, I wouldn't have been surprised to see little chirping birdies swooping around my head. My lower lip was shredded, warm pennies in my mouth.

Impossible as it would have seemed moments before, Sid was still going full-bore, tearing through her apartment like a maddened mama gorilla. The dog yipped like a frightened squeeze toy. Junior cackled like a madman. He stopped cackling long enough to throw me a warning. "Yo, Roundheels! Coming back your way! *Get the fuck up!*"

Sid had finally given up her pursuit of Junior. Hands on her knees, head down, she gulped huge, spent breaths. She wasn't looking toward me either, though she began lumbering back toward where I lay sprawled.

I followed her gaze. She was headed for the kitchen and . . .

Oh shit . . .

. . . the big block of butcher knives on the Formica countertop.

I had just enough time and sense left to fling myself at the back of her knees as she passed. The clipping move might have drawn a flag in the NFL, but this was strictly amateur hour.

Down Goes Frazier! Down Goes Frazier! Down Goes Frazier! ran through my head in Howard Cosell's voice as she fell.

Sid toppled with both arms reaching forward in a last-ditch effort to get her hands on a knife. Problem was, that didn't leave her any hands to break her fall. She seemed to drop for a considerable amount of time. The first body part to connect with anything solid was her face on the countertop. The Formica cracked like a gunshot. Dishes jumped in the cast iron sink five feet away. Sid's head snapped back, blood already streaming from her split brow, and she crumpled like a sack of beans.

Out.

"Aw *shit*," Junior whispered when the dust settled. Even the dog stopped barking. And I'd swear his little jowls hung open in surprise.

"Aw shit," I reiterated. Sid didn't move. A small pool of blood blossomed under her face.

"We killed the great white whale," Junior said.

Not the plan. Not the plan at all.

This is what me and Junior get when we start thinking this shit out and actually come up with a strategy. Junior came up with the next one on the fly.

"*Run!*" he yelled as he dropped the dog and booked it down the stairs. I grabbed an armful of the red-stickered DVD cases and followed him out in a full sprint.

"Ohfuckohfuckohfuck," Junior kept babbling as we bolted from the scene of our crime to the car. Junior did a perfect Bo Duke slide across the hood and leapt into the driver's seat. I'd have to compliment him on it later.

My lip had stopped bleeding, but the whole side of my face was swollen and throbbing. The inside of my mouth felt like I'd brushed my lower teeth with a steak knife. Junior slammed his foot onto Miss Kitty's accelerator.

Junior said, "Dude, we're boned."

"We're all right. I don't think anybody saw us." I turned and checked to make sure no one was pointing and staring, writing down license plate numbers.

"Your goddamn blood is all over that floor. That DNA shit is gonna point right to us!" He was gulping in huge panicked breaths. "CSI, motherfucker! CSI!"

"Shut up. Let me think."

"I mean, if it was a dude? Like if that was Snake on the floor? I wouldn't give a shit. Courts probably wouldn't either. But we just smoked a female. A female!" He was too freaked to even bust my balls about getting cold-cocked by the aforementioned female.

"I don't think DNA testing gives a name and address. I think it just does blood type and hair color and that shit."

"How the fuck do you know, Professor Malone? You been following the technology in *Scientific Weekly World News*?"

He had a point.

Junior drove into the parking lot behind The Cellar and screeched to a halt behind the Dumpster. For a second, I thought he might knock the damned thing over again. I unlocked the back door to the club with my keys and staggered into the rear of the bar. I was hoping nobody would see us. Junior let the door slam shut behind him.

The huge metal door.

It sounded like two Mack trucks colliding. All conversation stopped in the packed bar, and all eyes turned to us—including the last pair of eyes I wanted to look into at that moment. Barnes sat in exactly the same seat he was in the week before, smirking at us. We had only one option.

Be casual and lie, lie, lie.

We walked through the room like Clint Eastwood in *The Good, The Bad and The Ugly*. Unfortunately, we were felt neither good, nor bad. Just dazed, pale, sweating, and blood-covered. I moseyed up to the bar right next to Barnes. I can mosey real well when I try.

"Ice, please."

Barnes stared straight ahead and sipped his Heineken. He was playing it casual too, and pulling it off better than we were. You try to be casual when your face has been pounded into tuna tartar.

"So," he said in a chipper tone. "Should I even bother?"

"Cut myself shaving," I said.

"Fell down the stairs," Junior said.

"I fell down the stairs while shaving."

"Poor bathroom design," Junior said with a snicker.

"Funny," Barnes said, taking a sip of his beer. "Got anything for us?"

Junior and I just looked at each other. The bartender brought me a bar rag filled with ice. I pressed it against my broken face. Heaven. Barnes waited for a response.

Junior looked at me. "You know? I like it better when they send in the girl."

“Me, too. Seems less obvious for us to be talking to a broad—any broad—than Mr. Trying-not-to-look-like-a-cop, here.

“True. Wasn’t discretion supposed to be a big factor?”

I shrugged. “I thought I heard them say that. And look at you, using a big-boy word like discretion.”

Junior beamed. “I know, huh? Being around all these classy edjamuhcated people must be rubbing off.”

“Osmosis.”

“Like Donny and Marie Osmosis.”

Barnes snorted, shaking his head. “Thought so. You two fuck-wits have five more days.” He tipped the last of the beer into his mouth.

“Five? You guys said two weeks.”

“The two weeks were conditional. We both assumed you might have idea one before today. You got five more days.”

I pulled the ice from my face, the terrycloth a Rorschach in crimson. “Fine. Won’t even need that many. Wanna bet we can name that tune in three?”

Barnes snorted again as he got up and walked out. He didn’t dignify my bravado with a response. He didn’t have to. My bluff sucked. I didn’t believe me either.

Chapter Eleven

"Sid's Vids," came the voice over the phone. The voice was unmistakably Sid's. She sounded a bit fuzzy, but alive. Dead women answer no telephones.

I hung up the pay phone outside the bar and sighed with relief.

"What happened?" Junior asked. Dark saddlebags camped under his eyes, matching my own. We'd spent the night in the office, pacing and smoking like mobile forest fires, wondering on Sid's fate and consequently our own.

"Sid lives," I said.

Junior sagged noticeably without the weight of Sid's possible demise riding him. "Thank Christ. Man, I would not want to go down for having killed a broad. Even if it was an accident."

I agreed with him insomuch as Sid wasn't the person we wanted to damage. She was strictly a cobblestone on our road to Snake. I tried not to let my evil imaginings linger too long on what kind of damage I would inflict once I got my hands on that chickenhawk piece of shit.

Bad things.

"We gotta look at the DVD," Junior said suddenly.

I shook my head. "No. No way am I watching that shit."

Junior chewed off a piece of his thumbnail and spit it to the floor. "If you got a better idea, lay it on the table and we'll go with it."

I didn't have any better ideas. We didn't want to tap Sid again. One look at us, and she would opt for the shoot-first, ask-questions-later scenario.

Junior continued. "Whether or not it's our girl in the movie, there might be something there that could clue us to where the guy holes up."

The idea wasn't bad. I just had no urge to watch kiddie porn even if it gave us an address, business hours, and directions from my front door. "It might have been shot in a studio, Junior. It might be in somebody else's apartment. Shit, after what we did to Sid, the guy's probably halfway to Mexico himself."

"And if ifs and buts were candy and nuts, we'd all have a merry fucking Christmas."

"Give me a sec," I said.

"We've been through this all night, bro. We're at the end of our options here. I don't wanna see what's on that video either, but if it's gonna help put twenty-five thousand rocks in my hand? If it could help us get the kid away from that freak?"

The bottle in my hand was almost half empty, and since prayer was never my strongest anchor, I took one last pull. "Let's go."

A fist-sized lump swelled in my throat as Junior slid the first DVD into my machine. The player closed silently and hummed. A few seconds of blackness, then slow focus from the dark.

A man sitting on a white cushioned chair, completely naked but for a snake tattoo coiling down his arm and a black leather mask covering his head. The S&M kind with the zipper over the mouth.

A soft knock sounds. The camera pans over to the door, the lens passing over the windows. Heavy black curtains cover the glass.

"Come in," the masked man says.

I listened for anything familiar in the speech pattern. Snake's voice was a low baritone with a slight touch of local accent. Quincy, maybe? Beyond that, nothing.

A girl walks in the door.

Not Cassie. This one's around the same age, though. Too young. Way too fucking young.

She's tiny, blonde, and scared. Wide ears poke out from under her hair, making her look like a frightened mouse. A low chewing sound.

For a moment, I was afraid the DVD player was starting to fritz. Then I realized the sound was coming from the teeth grinding inside my head. If we didn't get this over with soon, I was going to need that twenty-five grand to buy myself a nice pair of dental crowns.

"Are you here for your lesson?" Snake says.

"Y-Yes," the girl replies, badly acting her part. "I've been very bad."

Snake stands up and walks over to the girl. He strokes her face with a disturbingly gentle tenderness. Then he balls his fingers tightly in her hair, yanks her head back, and flings her across the room onto the bed. The girl mewls in pain and fear as Snake backhands her. He kneels over the kid, straddling her chest, and tears her shirt open. The camera zooms in on her terrified face, as though her fear is the most important thing caught on the film.

I looked away, unable to watch anymore. The contents of my stomach had churned into rotting cottage cheese.

All I heard was one more heart-wrenching word. "No."

Junior slowly rocked back and forth in his chair. His eyes never left the screen. "Shut it off," he said in a monotone. "There's nothing more to see on this one." I guess Junior forgot he had the remote clutched in his hand.

I stood up to hit the stop button. My finger shook and missed it the first time. I closed my eyes and pressed the button carefully. If I missed a second time, I was going to shut it off with my fist. "I didn't see anything. You?" My voice was as flat as his.

Junior shook his head. "Put another one in."

"Junior, this guy's careful. There were curtains up over the windows. He wore a mask. There's nothing on the goddamn discs."

"Put another one in. We don't know there's nothing on the other ones. We gotta look."

I took a deep breath, and I switched the discs. They felt like they weighed a hundred pounds each. I hit the play button again. The second disc didn't open with a cryptic attempt at a storyline.

The picture kicks right in to Snake, still masked, spanking a girl with a large paddle. She's on all fours, freely offering her backside to Snake's blows. The girl's a bit older—maybe even legal. The action goes a little beyond typical S&M. She's not just receiving a playful tapping on the ass. Thin lines of blood run from huge red welts on the back of her thighs. The girl moans orgasmically with every blow.

We watched until we were sure there was nothing on that DVD either.

We started the third. From the get-go, the feel of the video was different.

Snake stands on one side of the door, shuffling back and forth like a kid who has to pee. He seems excited, eager to begin the scene. Cassandra opens the door.

My throat closed.

She's wearing the same clothes as when I first saw her at The Cellar. Her bright red hair sticks to her scalp, as though she's been caught in the rain.

I'd been stuck in the same rain. "This was shot the same day," I said.

"Same day as what?" Junior asked.

Snake pounces from behind the door. He smacks Cassandra hard enough to send her sprawling onto the curtains. The camera follows her. She screams.

Junior and I both leapt to our feet, reacting to the violence in real time.

"Motherfucker," Junior muttered.

Snake grabs a fistful of hair. He says, "You've been a bad girl, Cassie."

"I'm sorry. I'm sorry," she whimpers.

"You need to learn a lesson." He cracks her another one, still gripping her hair. Cassandra's head snaps around and she swoons, stunned from the blow. Snake easily tosses her onto the bed.

He reaches into the nightstand by the bed and pulls out a large hunting knife. Viciously, he slices the clothes off her. Cassandra doesn't move, either in a state of shock or still stunned from the blows. Snake roughly forces her legs open while she struggles weakly.

"This motherfucker's dead," Junior said, looking at a space far beyond the television.

I tried to respond. My jaw clenched so tightly, the muscles around my mouth started trembling.

The world bloomed red. The room pulsed deep crimson in perfect time with my heartbeat. Heat surged from my eyes.

I stood up and pressed rewind. I ran the video back to the first blow when she walked in the door.

"I can't watch that again, Boo."

I pressed play.

"Goddamn it, Boo!" Junior's voice sounded like he was yelling from the other end of a hallway.

I watched it again frame by frame. Watched Cassie's fear with a sharp eye. Remembering it. Watched her in slow motion stumbling toward the heavy curtains. Her tiny hand brushing the curtains ever so slightly.

Ever so slightly enough.

Outside the window, at an angle toward the street, was a portion of a sign. I couldn't make out any details, but I knew someone who could.

Gotcha, fucker.

Chapter Twelve

It was the spring of 1994, Opening Day at Fenway, when we first officially met Ollie. All the kids at The Home were buzzing with the welcome distraction from our shitty day-to-days. At St. Gabe's, you found hope wherever you could, even as misplaced a hope as the Red Sox might provide.

Having a regular broadcast game was a treat, an event. But our one TV in the rec room was always flipping between light snow and blizzard conditions. Not blessed with cable or a serviceable antenna, we'd pocketed enough tinfoil from the dining common to wrap the television like a cocoon. The only parts visible were the knobs and screen. Problem was, the night before, the TV decided to shit the bed all the way. Most of us had spent a large part of the day figuring out what the fuck we were going to do come game time.

After lunch, a large group of us headed to the rec room, tinfoil in pockets, hoping to wrestle some life, if not reception, into the old Zenith. We would suffer reprimands and punishment for cutting classes, but fuck it. Hope had a price, and we were willing to pay it.

We walked into the rec room, then stopped short enough to get nearly knocked over by the kids behind us. Mouths hung open in shock at what lay before us. The kids in the back swept around us, all trying to see what had stopped us in our tracks.

Somebody said, "The *fuck*?"

A lanky new kid named Ollie had not only unwrapped years' worth of carefully calibrated foil, but also managed to get the TV apart. We all stood there, gobsmacked at the sight of our beloved television, its parts laid out like chess pieces on the checkered linoleum. Ollie only looked up at us briefly, adjusted his Coke-bottle glasses, and furiously went back to his task.

Grumbling began to well up from the stunned mob. Grumbling that ran along the lines of how to make the new kid's head fit up his ass. It may have been a shitty TV, but it was ours. We didn't have many things we could call ours.

The threats grew louder and more ominous. One boy picked up a folding chair, tested its heft, and made his way over to Ollie in order to brain him properly. As the chair was raised overhead, Ollie plugged in the set. The screen lit up on Roger Clemens warming up in the bullpen. The grumblings erupted into cheers and handshakes. Ollie was smiling nervously and sweating through his shirt in a dozen places. He had to know how close he'd come to getting crippled. The kid ready to do the crippling lowered the chair and opened it front and center, a seat of honor for Ollie. Ollie watched the entire game seated in the chair that almost caved in his skull.

The Red Sox won the game, 9–8.

At St. Gabe's there were only two ways to insure your safety: be dangerous or be useful.

Ollie became one of the strays who wandered in with me and Junior's crew. He may not have been a brawler, but he earned his keep. And those smarts had brought him a lot of cash since his days at The Home. He wasn't a complete flake job like Twitch, but he was koo-koo for Cocoa Puffs in his own fashion. If the Unabomber was pro-technology rather than anti, he might have been Ollie.

Ollie's basement apartment looked like a utility closet on the Death Star. The walls were painted sterile white, all four layered with computers, pieces of electronics, and what looked like miles and miles of wires twisting around themselves in a three-dimensional Jackson Pollack.

"You guys gotta see this," Ollie said, leading us to one of the many screens posted along one wall. "I can't tell you guys which, but one of the major airlines just dropped a chunk of cash in my hands to test their electronic defense systems. Look."

On the screen was a radar layout. Little dots slowly moved around the screen, identifying numbers beneath the dots.

"That's the system?" I asked.

"Nah, it's a simulation program they've linked me into. Basically identical to the real OS they use, same security and whatnot."

"Solid system?" I asked, as though I had any idea what we were talking about.

"This?" Ollie huffed at me like I'd just defended the Ewoks. "This is shit work. Any hack with half a brain, half a system, and a little bit of patience can break into it." Then Ollie smiled and held his hands apart like a magician about to yank a rabbit out of a hat. "Ever see a man crack a Federal Black Ice firewall in under a minute?"

"Uh . . . No?"

"Watch this." Ollie went to work. He leaned forward in his chair as his fingers flew over the keyboard. Numbers that were meaningless to me raced down the bottom of the monitor. Junior gaped at the screen like a chimp forced to translate ancient Egyptian. He stuck a cigarette in his mouth and popped open his Zippo.

Ollie whipped a pointed finger at Junior. "Do *not* light a cigarette in here. These machines are exceptionally sensitive." His eyes never moved off the dancing numbers. The hand remaining on the keyboard picked up speed, as if to compensate for its missing brother. I wouldn't have been surprised to see smoke curling off Ollie's fingertips.

Junior frowned and flipped off the back of Ollie's head. He tucked the cigarette into his T-shirt pocket.

"Now," Ollie said, "watch *this*." With the last few flicks of his fingers, the dots on the screen disappeared. It looked like the computer had shut off.

"Taa-daa!" Ollie sure was excited by the blank screen.

"Uh, I don't see anything."

"Exactly. And neither do they."

"Where'd the planes go?" Junior asked.

"Oh, they're still up there. I haven't hacked into their individual systems, but their ground control is completely blind. About eighteen hundred tons of airplanes are about to go crash kaboom."

"Well," Junior clapped his hands. "I'm not getting on a plane again. Ever."

"Man, the boys monitoring these boards must be shitting their pants right now." Ollie wiggled with pleasure in his seat. It was the way he laughed. He never made a sound, just wiggled happily.

Like most things Ollie, the humor was lost on me. "I thought you said this was a simulation."

"It is. But they still have guys monitoring the boards to see if we can whack 'em." Ollie leaned back in his chair and groaned, as though he'd just finished a hugely satisfying meal. "So, what's this video thingy?"

"We need to get a closer look at one part of a frame. Can you do something like that?"

"Can Captain Kirk bang a green chick?"

"I'll take that as a yes."

"I'll just drop the DVD into the 'puter and rip the file. I'm pretty sure I can jury rig some sort of video capture/enhancement program. It might take me a couple hours to convert the hardware and then render the MPEG into a negotiable file. Is MPEG an okay format? I know it's almost archaic at this point, but so is the vid software I have."

I recognized enough English in the sentence to feel retarded. "Whatever works for you, Ollie. The stuff on the DVD . . . it's some messed up shit. It's really important that you forget what's on it, okay?"

"Gotcha. Can you give me a rough idea of where?"

"At three minutes, thirteen seconds, a curtain gets knocked aside. That's what we need. We need to see better what's outside that window."

Ollie sucked in his upper lip and chewed on it, thinking. "Can do. Gonna take me about an hour or so. You wanna pick up some lunch?"

"Anyplace good around here?"

"Grinder shop down the street. Grab me a meatball parm?" Ollie began flipping through disks of software. "Just think. A couple years ago, I probably would have had to run a firewire through an AVID system to get this kind of video editing. Now it's all inside here." Ollie patted his computer like it was an old family pet.

"And you'd have to frammajamma interface with the hibbity-dibbity," Junior said with a chuff.

Ollie found the right software and placed the CD into the computer tray. "Wouldn't need a hibbity-dibbity for this." Junior's smile fell. Ollie shot Junior a wink, then reached behind the table and started reconfiguring wires.

An hour later, our stomachs full of greasy meatballs, we returned to Ollie's. The door to his studio was open when we returned. He was nowhere in sight.

"Ollie?" I called out. No answer. I looked at Junior. He shrugged. I called again. "Oliver? You here?" A horrible sound came muffled from behind one of the wired walls.

Junior and I ran over to the wall. "Ollie? You all right?" The strangled choke came again. It was definitely behind the wall. I looked for a convenient place to put down the grease-soaked bag with Ollie's grinder in it, but was afraid the wrong spot could cause a fire.

I dropped the bag on his desk chair, and Junior and I started moving sophisticated boards of God-knows-what and tangles of wire along the wall. About halfway down, under yet another colorful tangle, was a white doorknob. I pulled it and the thin door covered in shelves and bric-a-brac opened. Behind was a small bathroom. Ollie was sprawled on the tiled floor, face in the toilet. The horrible sound we heard was him emptying his stomach into the bowl.

"Ollie? You all right, man?"

"Jesus Christ, Boo!" was all he managed to say before his body spasmed over the toilet twice more. "You could have warned me a little more about what was on that fucking DVD before you left!"

I found a glass next to the computer and filled it up in the sink beside the toilet. I held it out to Ollie. He took it in a trembling hand.

Ollie was right. I should have given him a more specific warning regarding content. There's tough and there's hard. The Home made Ollie tougher than his exterior indicated. But he wasn't ever going to be hard.

"Ollie, I'm sorry, man. I didn't think. Junior and I have been looking for this girl and I just figured it was hard for us to watch, because, well . . . I dunno." I did know. I couldn't say it was because we knew her, because we didn't. I couldn't say it was because we cared about her, because as objective tough guys, we shouldn't.

But I did. Or I was at least starting to, and that thought bothered me, because I knew why.

Unsteadily, Ollie got to his feet. "Boo, that video would have given Jeffrey Dahmer a nervous breakdown." He walked over to his computer, typed for a second, and the screen shot appeared. The falling Cassandra. The pulled curtain. The sign.

"I still can't make it out," Junior said.

"I haven't done the pixel rendering yet," Ollie said, a little snippily. He looked at the bag on his chair. "What is that?"

"Your sandwich."

Ollie's gullet lurched audibly. "Ugh. Take it away." I picked up the bag and stashed it in the mini fridge to the left.

Ollie sat at the desk. Again, his fingers flew over the keyboard faster than my eyes could follow. The capture focused, then enlarged. Focused and enlarged. A third time. The piece of the sign was clear. Distinctly, I could make out part of two words. They were all in caps, one word atop the other in red and yellow neon. APA above PANA.

Junior cocked his head at the screen. "What the hell does that say?"

"Apa Pana," said Ollie. "Sounds Spanish. Either of you speak Spanish?"

"*Un poquito*," Junior said. Unfortunately, I knew *un poquito* accounted for about a quarter of the Spanish phrases Junior spoke. The other three were filthy.

"I think it's parts from two different words," I said.

Ollie looked at the screen again, head cocked at the same angle as Junior. "Oh. Oh, yeah."

"Panama?" Junior said. "Japanese?"

"Junior," I said. "Does Japanese Panama make any goddamn sense to you?"

"Just train of thought, man. Could be a travel agency."

"Next time you travel, fly Japanese Panama Airlines."

"Okay, cheesedick. You think of something."

I couldn't. "Can you print that out for us, Ollie?"

"Already did." He handed us both blowups of the picture on the screen. "Listen, Boo. Because I saw that, it doesn't make me accessory to anything, does it?"

Oh, yeah. Forgot to mention. Ollie's also one paranoid bastard. He didn't eat fish for two years because he thought the government was spreading AIDS through seafood. I'm not kidding. He had a reason. It also made sense.

I squeezed his shoulder. "How could you be? You never saw the video, remember?"

"Yeah, yeah. My memory is already hazy. What are you going to do with this guy?"

Junior and I looked at each other. "That all depends on him. We'd love nothing more than to punch him so many times he shits sideways for a few weeks. But our job is to find the girl and get her back to her father. How much pain we inflict is directly in correlation to how much resistance he puts up."

"I'm gonna fuck him up, either way," Junior said.

"Aw, who am I kidding? We're fucking him up either way."

I looked back to Ollie. I really didn't like what I saw. The color had run out of his face like rainwater down a drain. I thought he was going to be sick again. Softly, he said, "Oh, shit."

"What?" Junior asked.

"You guys didn't watch the whole thing, did you?"

Ollie couldn't stay. Couldn't watch it again. He left us to go get some beer from the packie. I'd never known Ollie to touch alcohol before.

Junior and I stared at the monitor, sick dread a lump in my stomach. Or maybe it was just the meatballs. Felt like dread. I hit play.

The scene played out like it had before, but silently. Either Ollie didn't have speakers connected to the computer or had the sound turned off. For whatever reason, it made the viewing worse. Cassandra's screaming was still there, but it was inside my head, along with the sound of the blood pounding through my veins. The rage flared red before my eyes.

We reached the point where we'd stopped watching. The video played on. Snake did . . . things. Things I'm not going to recount. After a minute, Cassie stopped struggling, resigned to the abuse, the humiliation. She just lay there, no fight left in her. Easier to let it happen.

That is, until Snake picked up the knife again.

When she saw the knife in his hand, she bucked underneath him, kicked her legs.

He rode it out, letting his weight keep her pinned. I couldn't hear it, but I knew he was laughing. He held the knife aloft, letting it catch the light, taunting her with it and his power over her.

A quick flash.

A spray of red along the headboard and wall.

One tiny arm reached up briefly, then fell to the bed. One last spurt of blood arced across the wall. Then the video faded to black.

Out of the corner of my eye, I saw Junior move to the bathroom. I stared at the black screen.

"You gonna be sick?" I called.

"I dunno." He made a horrible gassy sound, then, "I think I might be. You?"

"No." There was surprise in my answer, since a part of me felt like I should be. I wasn't. Instead, I kept right on looking at the dead monitor. The red haze was gone. Instead, my vision took on a sharp clarity, as though the world had its edges filed to points. I felt no anger. I felt no sadness or pity or revulsion. I felt neither hot nor cold. Even my clenched jaw stopped hurting.

I felt absolutely nothing.

Chapter Thirteen

By the time I tracked down Underdog, the sky had gone purple, Kenmore Square filling up with Sox fans heading to a night game, the Fenway lights giving an eerie glow in the night sky behind The Cellar. Audrey said I had just missed him and he might have gone to Wolf's Grill. I called Wolf's, but nobody picked up. I took a cab over to Wolf's. No Underdog. I realized I hadn't eaten since Ollie's. I ordered some ribs and asked the waitress if she'd seen Dog. She said he was headed to The Cellar or The Model. I called The Model. He wasn't there, but they had a good idea where he might be. This went on for the better part of two hours. Eight calls to various bars and two call backs later, I finally reached him back at The Cellar.

"Hey, Boo. How's it going?"

"I gotta talk to you, Dog. It looks like you might be needed on this thing after all." I'd barely touched the ribs. Maybe the pile of sauce-slathered, meaty bones was hitting my psyche too close to home after what I'd seen.

"Oh. Okay." He didn't sound eager to help. He'd weighed it all against his fear of Danny the Bull and come up short. "Where are you?"

"I'm at Wolf's"

"That's weird. I was just there."

"Listen, Dog. I gotta talk to you ASAP."

"Well, I can just wait for you here."

"No. I don't want to talk about it there. You got a place?"

"You mean away from prying ears?"

"Ears, eyes, tongues, and anything else you can think of."

"Let me think . . ." A soft, grating sound came out of the phone as Underdog scratched his stubble in thought. "Hows about you meet me at the pier right by the aquarium? You know which one I'm talking about?"

"That'll work."

"An hour okay?

"See you in an hour." I hung up.

I chain-smoked during the wait. The hunger still roared in my stomach, and my recent sleeplessness was catching up to me. My eyelids felt like someone had glued a pair of bricks to them. A misty breeze blew off the harbor and moistened every surface around me. When I'd first arrived, I'd sat on the concrete ledge of the pier and gotten rewarded with a soggy ass.

So I paced and I smoked. Once in a while I mixed it up and smoked, then paced. Except for the soft red glow of the cherry, it was nearly pitch dark by the aquarium, the light swallowed by the fog. I hadn't been there since I was a kid. I remembered a dolphin statue somewhere, but I couldn't see it. One of my most vivid memories of my mother was of her waddling around the sculpture, chasing me and quacking penguin noises while I laughed and ran from her.

Part of me was glad I didn't see the statue. The memory was beginning to fill me with shame for who that kid became.

A voice snapped me back from my childhood. "Boo? Where are you?" Dog's voice carried well on the misty air, and I could see his silhouette on the border of the well-lit world.

"At the pier," I called back. "Right where you said to meet you."

"Shit, it's dark." He was hugging himself, shivering against a cold that wasn't there. I kept the observation to myself.

Underdog gave the area a quick look over. "So . . . what's up?"

I took one last drag on the dying cigarette and ground it out under my shoe. The tip sizzled on the damp ground. Bright cinders danced a ballet in the breeze. "We're close to ending this."

"That's great." Then he realized there wasn't an ounce of great in my statement. "Isn't it?"

"She's dead. Snake killed her. Me and Junior saw it on a video."

"Wh—what?"

"It's a snuff video. Snake's moved up from kiddie porn into blood-freak theater."

"That stuff's mostly urban legend, Boo. Most of that shit is faked. Buncha twisted fucks looking for a quick buck in the loony market."

I shook my head at him. "Most is not all. I saw it, Dog. Shit wasn't faked."

Underdog looked away toward the Harbor. "Bastard . . . that fucking bastard," he said softly.

"We're getting close to him." I lit another cigarette. I was still pacing, but I'd slowed it down to a conversational speed.

"When you do, call me. Do you still have the video? I'll have Vice on his ass like—" Then, quietly, "Shit. It's Homicide now, isn't it?"

I shook my head again. "He's gone. We find him, nobody else does. Not Vice. Not Homicide. Nobody."

Before he could respond, a yellow flashlight beam caught me right in the eyes, blinding me. I held up my hand to cut the glare, but flash burn still coated my vision. Peering through my fingers, I could see a pair of silhouettes slowly walking toward us. The saunter spelled cops, even at fifty paces.

"Whatcha doing out here, boys? Aquarium's closed." The arrogance of authority rang in the voice.

My eyes adjusted, and I could make out the pair. Two young cops. Younger than me.

"We're just talking, officers," Underdog said.

"You sure?" the other one said. He was smaller than the first and that much cockier. "Because it looks like you two are up to something, lurking around in the dark here."

As they got closer, I could see the taller one was blond, a wispy cop moustache over a thin mouth. The shorter one had a dark buzz cut and power-lifter muscles under a generous layer of fat. Both wore matching sneers.

"There a law against conversation?" I asked.

"On closed property there is."

"Hey," the shorter one said. "Maybe the crackhead was just about to suck off big boy's dick, here. Maybe we interrupted a date?"

"That right?" the other asked. "You two faggots about to exchange a little kneel and bob?"

"Actually, we were waiting for your dad to show up," I said.

"You fucking—" The little one was reaching for his club when Underdog jammed his own badge halfway up his nose.

"I know you're an idiot, but I assume you can read." Brendan Miller had made a sudden appearance—one that probably saved me a long sentence at Cedar Junction.

The taller one's face blanched as he looked at the ID. "Oh. Oh! We're sorry, Detective. We didn't . . ." He couldn't seem to find a satisfactory way to finish his sentence.

The muscle midget scowled and gave the card a once-over, like he was expecting a fake. Even in the dark, I saw his color turn three shades of green before he swallowed hard. "Yeah. We were just . . . We didn't . . ."

"You didn't what?" There was a real edge in Dog's voice. "You didn't know you were interrupting a ranking officer's conversation?"

"No sir, we didn't." The taller one had completely lost his swagger. The smaller one still looked fit to bust, but was keeping himself under control. I debated patting him on the top of the head, but as far as the totem pole of power went, I was still at the bottom of the present quartet.

Underdog poked the tall one in the chest with his loaded finger. "So, in the event that I was *not* a detective, you two assholes saw fit to verbally abuse and possibly assault a pair of citizens."

"There have been trespasses by graffiti vandals." The short one's voice had started to whine.

"Shut your mouth, Pee-Wee," Underdog said. "Obviously you didn't see us tagging the wharf, so you and your excuses can kiss my hairy ass." Underdog was only a few inches taller, but the dig worked. The midget deflated, punctured by Dog's tone. "What district are you idiots out of? A-1?"

"Yes sir," they said simultaneously.

"Larson's your captain, then?"

The two exchanged a quick, nervous glance. "Yes sir," in unison again.

"All right. Unless you two want a disciplinary phone call made to Captain Larson in the morning, you're going to head back to your car and fuck off."

"Yes sir," in unison one more time, heads hung like a pair of beaten puppies. They turned to go.

"And put on your goddamn hats. You officers are out of uniform."

They flinched at the last comment and walked off. In the distance, I saw them both put their hats on the second they climbed into their cruiser.

"Damn, Dog. That was tight."

"And you—" He spun on me, the same loaded finger trained right in my face this time. "Did you just tell me that you and Junior are going to kill off this Snake character when you find him?"

"You didn't see that DVD, Dog. He cut her fucking throat. You didn't watch that little girl die. I did. So did Junior."

"You know what, Boo? You know I'm a loser." He jammed his finger hard into his own bony chest. "*I* know I'm a fucking loser. But I am still an officer of the goddamn law. And you just confessed to me intent to murder. *Murder*, Boo!"

"You want to see it? I'll fucking show it to you. Watch the video. You decide whether this cocksucker deserves to die or not."

"I don't want to watch it," he said. "And it's not up to you or me to decide. Get this guy. Turn him in. You've got evidence."

"No way. No way am I trusting this guy to the system."

"Bullshit, Boo! Bullshit! More often than not, it does work."

"But sometimes it doesn't."

Dog sighed and turned away from me. "If the law is so ass-backward in your estimation, if we're such fuck-ups on my side of the fence, what do you want from me?"

"If push comes to shove? I want your alibi."

Underdog huffed a short, sharp laugh, but he still didn't look at me. "Why? Because my alibi just might hold a little weight because I'm a cop?"

"Well, yeah."

Dog turned his head slightly to me, but he was still unable or unwilling to look at me. "You are some piece of work, Boo Malone. Really. A piece of work." With that, he walked off.

I'd gambled on Underdog. On his support. I was a fool to do so. But it still didn't change a thing.

As I walked back toward Haymarket and the Green T line, a movement caught my attention out the corner of my eye.

Deep in shadow, stood The Boy.

He looked up, one small hand touching the dolphin sculpture.

Chapter Fourteen

How the hell was I supposed to see Kelly again and not tell her what we'd seen? How could we face Barnes, much less Donnelly? "Hi. Didn't find your daughter, but I have a video of her being raped and stuck like a piglet. Can we have some money now?"

Not to mention Emily, and all that the information on her could have represented—even though I still wasn't positive I wanted it.

So I walked. I walked past Faneuil Hall. The evening fog swirled in the low walk lights as small groups of tourists milled about. A few couples on romantic strolls, holding hands. I was the only solo pedestrian in the area.

Being alone was a set of feelings I'd long come to terms with. But this was a new kind of alone for me. I don't know. It hurt. It hurt me in places I didn't know were still wired into my nervous system.

I didn't know what I thought Underdog would say. Maybe a part of me wanted him to try and talk me out of it.

So I wandered. I didn't feel like hanging at The Cellar. It was too easy there. I would start drinking again, and drunk was a comfortable womb I'd been finding my way into far too often lately.

Another hour and a half of wandering, and I was standing in front of the coffee shop I'd gone to after corralling Kelly home. It was almost 1 A.M. As far as ideas went, it seemed like my least stupid of the week, at least. I retraced my steps to her door and rang the buzzer before reason and common sense could lead me elsewhere. I wound up there for a purpose, though I'd be damned if I could name it.

I gave myself fifty-fifty odds that Kelly would even answer the buzzer. Something in me desperately needed to see her, to see this woman I barely knew, while another, smaller piece wanted to run away and hide in a corner.

To my surprise, the door just buzzed open and I walked in. At the apartment door, Kelly peeked out from behind the security chain. The one eye I could see widened in surprise when it saw me.

"Boo?" She said it in a hushed, curious tone. Like she was expecting someone else.

Maybe she was.

"Yeah. Sorry. Did I wake you?" She had on a pair of light blue pajamas and horn-rimmed granny glasses, so she was obviously in bed. I just didn't have much else to say. I still wasn't sure why I'd shown up.

She shook her head. "Uh, no." She took the security chain off and opened the door. "I had to get up to open my door."

"I'm sorry . . . I'll go . . ."

I turned, but she reached out and tenderly touched my bruised face with her fingertips. "What happened?"

Until she pointed it out, I hadn't realized I still looked as bad as I felt. "There was this pack of dingos, an orphan . . ."

She smirked, rolled her eyes. "Nobody likes a smartass, Boo."

"Really? I've spent my life counting on somebody appreciating that quality in me."

"Never mind. Get in here."

"Were you expecting someone else?" I had to ask.

"Yeah. Occasional booty call. Likes to show up unannounced right about now," she said, smirk widening a touch. She must have seen something in my face that said I wasn't sure whether she was kidding or not. "I'm kidding."

I let out a breath I didn't know I was holding in. "Nobody likes a smartass, Reese."

"Heard that."

"The way you buzzed me in, you're lucky I wasn't some wacko."

"Remains to be seen. Besides, I had Spike at the ready." She held up her left hand. A spectacular pair of modified brass knuckles engulfed her small fist. At the strike point sat four nasty, inch-long spikes. I sure as hell wouldn't want to get hit with them, even if it was by a girl. "Present from Daddy before I moved to the big, scary city," she said as she walked back into her bedroom.

Kelly dropped Spike onto her night table with a thump and jumped into her bed, yawning deeply. "So, what's going on?"

"I . . . um, was in the neighborhood." It was true. Still sounded wicked retarded.

"What time is it, anyway?"

I didn't bother looking at my watch. "It's late. Too late for me to be stopping in. I'm sorry. I'll talk to you tomorrow."

"Don't be stupid. You're already here. I'm already awake, and I'm not mad. I've been trying to reach you again. Got a present for you."

She stood up and leaned over to her purse on her bureau. She pulled out a cell phone. "Here."

"Present from the boss?"

"Present from me. Getting tired of calling all around town looking for you. It's prepaid and all set up. I even programmed a couple numbers for you." She tumbled into bed again and patted the space next to her. "C'mere."

I sat next to her on the bed. She leaned over and kissed me right on the point of the jaw where Sid's fist had nearly removed it from my melon a day earlier. The blood in my veins stopped dead for a second, confused as to where to go. "What was that for?" I asked.

"That was for taking care of me the other night. I'm sorry it was so awkward in the morning." She moved her lips a little higher and softly kissed my busted lip.

"What was that one for?"

"That was because I wanted to." She wrapped herself around me in a warm embrace. "To let you know I still think you're an attractive man, even when I'm sober."

"Hmm," was all I managed banter-wise.

"This isn't, you know, bothering you, is it?"

Bothering me was the last thing it was doing. "No. It's fine." My voice sounded flat in my ears.

She let me go and turned my face to hers. "What's wrong?" she asked firmly. "Is it me?"

"No . . . listen. I . . . I think you're very attractive, but . . ."

I wanted to kiss her, badly. I wanted to lose myself in a simple act of physical intimacy.

Flashing knife.

A touch that wasn't violent. That didn't hurt. That wouldn't make me bleed.

APA PANA

The softness of her pajamas against my fingers.

Clothes torn off.

Hair, smelling of vanilla shampoo.

Cut off.

An inch of smooth white skin, bellybutton underneath her pajama top.

Red.

I stood up, gasping, my breath struggling inside my tightened chest. "I think I should go."

Kelly drew her knees up to her chest and hugged herself. Quietly, she said, "Maybe you should."

I took a step. Stopped and just blurted, "I don't think we're going to find Cassandra." It was the truth. Just not the whole truth. It was the first time I'd vocalized it, and the twinge of accompanying guilt rocked me.

Kelly didn't say anything. I let my last sentence hang in the air. Finally, she said, "Did you get close?"

"Close enough. As close as we're gonna get."

"Don't worry. I'm sure she'll be fine. She's a tough girl. If Mr. Donnelly has to go to the police, he'll go to the police."

"I . . ." I wanted to scream. *She's not fine! I failed! I fucking failed her!* I clamped my jaw tight and put my face in my hands, massaging my temples.

"Hey," she said as she stood up from the bed. She lifted my chin with her fingers. I let her. Her lips curled in a small, sad pout as she looked me in the eyes. "It'll be fine."

Softly, she pressed her lips to my mouth again. Her kisses became firmer as she slid me back onto the bed. I moved my hands down to the small of her back and pulled her to me, pressed her tight against me.

She traced her hands under my shirt, fingers working their way up my stomach to the mass of scar tissue on my chest. I tensed self-consciously. She paused when she reached the lumpy concave over my heart.

I waited, eyes closed.

She didn't ask.

Instead, she kissed me even harder as she pulled my shirt over my head.

My hands explored the soft skin under her clothes. For the first time in days, the rot in my heart and mind was melting away rather than building. The ache in my spirit washing away, overwhelmed by want . . . by my need for her.

No dead girls.

No knives.

No bad things.

The phone on her nightstand rang.

"Don't answer it," I said, hoping it wasn't the booty call she said she was kidding about. When the answering machine clicked on, I almost wished it was.

It was motherfucking Junior.

"Boo? You there? If you're there, pick up the goddamn phone. This is important. Kelly? If he's not there, I apologize. If you're there, *pick up the fucking phone!*"

I cursed and grabbed the phone before he could continue. "*What?*" I hollered into the mouthpiece.

"Ah-ha! Busted!"

I swallowed a big gulp of murderous intent. "Three questions, Junior. One, how did you know I was here?" I'd never said a word to him about the other night or the kiss. And bar gossip (Audrey leapt to mind) would only have taken him so far. "Two, how did you get this number? Three, you're an asshole. And four, what the fuck do you want?"

"You said only three questions."

"Three wasn't a question. It was a declaration."

"Okay, Mr. Grumpypants. One, you must think I'm a moron. Two, you left her card on the desk. Three, you wouldn't have me any other way. And four, we might have the son of a bitch."

Ice water trickled down the back of my neck I spoke very slowly. "What are you talking about?"

"I think we got him, Boo."

"Please tell me he's not at The Cellar."

Kelly put her hand on my shoulder. "What is it? Is everything all right?"

I answered her with a quick thumb-to-forefinger okay, even though I was light-headed, near hyperventilation. "Junior, please, please tell me he's not there right now."

"Wouldn't that be a kick in the nutsack? No, but we got a line, brother."

"What are you talking about?"

"Get back here and find out."

"Tell me, Junior."

"I have to leave some mystery, don't I, player? Stuff your blue balls back in your Dickies and get over here."

Click.

The phone went dead in my hand.

I'm gonna kill that little Irish fucker one day.

All in one blazing series of motions, I called for a cab, apologized to Kelly, then kissed her with a passion and energy I didn't have five minutes before the phone call. After the longest ride of my life, I threw some money at the driver and hustled myself, blue balls and all, into The Cellar.

G.G. stood at the door with Junior. When he spotted me, Junior grinned like the dog that ate the cat that ate the canary. He opened his arms wide. "We got a clue!"

Without breaking stride, I kicked Junior square in the nuts. The top of my sneaker smacked with a *pop* against his crotch.

Junior groaned and flopped over.

"Damn!" G.G. jumped back, reflexively covering his own junk.

Junior rolled back and forth on the ground in a fetal position.

"Help me get him downstairs," I said to G.G. We each hooked an arm under Junior and dragged him down the flight. The bands were done for the night, so we had the space to ourselves.

I went into the walk-in beer cooler and cracked myself a Boddingtons can. I didn't really want to drink, but I was cotton-mouthed from the adrenaline dump. I also hoped the frigid air would bring down my half-erection still clinging to life and repress any urges to kick Junior's package again. G.G. knocked on the door.

"I think he's able to talk now. He stopped dry heaving."

I walked out into night air that felt hotter than before. Junior sat atop the bar, jeans around his ankles and a bar rag filled with ice on his lap. He scowled at me and inhaled deep, slow breaths. "That was low, man."

"You know what's low, Junior? That fucking phone call."

"But I had a clue." He really sounded hurt.

"A clue could have waited until morning. Or at least an hour."

G.G. spat a sunflower shell into a barrel. "Have you hit it yet?"

"That falls under none of your goddamn business, but no."

"Were you about to?" He spat another shell and raised an eyebrow at me.

I shot him a scathing look. "The only fucking I got was from Junior when he called."

The eyebrow went higher.

Junior threw his hands in the air. "So no blood, no foul. Jesus, you've been a sensitive bitch lately."

"How did you even know I was there?"

"What am I, an asshole?" I had an answer, but he went on. "Every time her name comes up, your brain drifts off into Loveland. Doesn't take Spenser to figure that much out, jackass."

G.G. chuckled. "You do get all sparkly-eyed and shit when her name comes up."

"Shut it."

Junior continued. "So when you wasn't nowhere else, I figured I'd give her number a try. And I was right." His smug satisfaction was irritating.

"Yeah. You're a fucking genius."

"You were just about to get a lap dance on the Maloney Pony, weren't ya?"

"I can kick you again, Junior."

G.G. waved his hands in horror. "Aw, hell no. Not booty interruptus. Kick him again."

"Hey!" Junior folded up defensively.

"What is this shit all about? That is if you two clowns are through fucking with me."

Junior held his palms out, setting the moment. "Okay, so I come in and G.G. here is eating his dinner, this thing that looks like some kinda dog-food croissant."

"Hey, man," G.G. said, "that's my culture you're fucking with."

"That wasn't no soul food I've ever seen."

"It's Colombian, you moron."

"Yo, G.G.? I don't want to bust your cultural bubble, but you're black."

"You ignorant little potato-fucker. Ever heard of the Moors?"

"That's like a field in England, right?"

G.G. gave me a "you believe this shit?" face. "In case you didn't know, the second G in G.G. is for Gonzalez."

"*Sorry*," Junior sang sarcastically. He turned back to me. "So anyway, G.G. is munching on this hideous looking thing."

"It's called an empanada."

"I'm getting to that! Christ!" Junior shook his head in exasperation.

"This does go somewhere, right?" I said. "Like somewhere close to a point?"

Junior smiled. "Papa makes 'em."

"What?"

Junior went into the back pocket of his jeans and pulled out a crinkled yellow wrapper. He unfolded the grease-smeared wax paper and held it up for me to see.

My mouth went dry. "How many of these are in the city?"

Junior grinned. "I gave them a call while you were limping down here."

"And?"

"Only one, my brother. Only one."

The wax paper read PAPA'S EMPANADAS in bright red letters. Junior moved his hands over select letters to drive his point home. I didn't need the visual. I already saw the letters in the logo. I recognized them from the neon image that was burned into my mind.

APA and PANA.

Chapter Fifteen

Stakeout #2.

We were better prepared for a long night in the car the second time around. First, we went to Junior's and filled two thermoses with his famous home brew. Coffee is the closest Junior comes to cooking. That said, the man knows how to make a great goddamn cuppa joe. He uses only the finest grounds and, I believe, strains it through old sweat socks.

Once we'd stockpiled the caffeine and picked up a couple grinders at an all-night packie, we chucked it all into a disposable cooler on Miss Kitty's backseat. Junior pulled an empty gas can from the trunk for when the coffee punched its way out of our bladders.

It was close to three in the morning by the time we got to Papa's and got a parking space. As luck would have it, there was a Store 24 right next to the restaurant. I slipped the clerk a twenty and guaranteed myself use of the bathroom. It was better than sticking my dick in a rusty gas can.

Junior chose to continue using the gas can. "Meh," he said, "stuck my dick in worse."

Papa's Empanadas sat on Washington Street, right off Blue Hill Avenue, smack dab between Roxbury and Dorchester. For some people, not the safest place to park and stare. Roxbury is what many of the more polite Bostonians refer to as an "ethnic" neighborhood, while Dorchester is where the working-class Irish migrated generations ago—not the two most compatible cultures. Heaven help any man, woman, or child who accidentally stumbled one block too far. The neighborhood's inhabitants were tough enough on themselves. They were worse if you didn't belong there. Above and beyond our lookout for Snake, we had to keep our urban radar set on high for any roving Irish, Puerto Rican, or Black gangs that might want to test our cultural allegiances.

Using our best guesstimations, we triangulated the angle of the window's view on the DVD and narrowed down the apartment's location to somewhere opposite Papa's Empanadas.

NASA, we're not.

All we knew was that we could eliminate the boarded-up tenement directly across the street. For good measure, I ripped a strip of plywood off a smoke-stained windowsill and peeked inside to make sure our boy wasn't squatting.

So we sat, windows open, listening to the city lullaby of distant traffic.

My eyes flicked from window to window on the apartment buildings, hoping. But creeping doubt began to poke its finger in my brain. Nothing said Snake *lived* where the video was shot. For all we knew, it was a rented space where he shot the videos, only returning when he had a new girl lured in. He might only use the space every few weeks . . . or months.

I kept convincing myself that this wasn't the case, that the apartment in the video had that bachelor lived-in look. A pair of full ashtrays. More than one meal's worth of pizza boxes.

Besides, it was all we had.

Junior loudly munched on a chunk of green pepper that curled up over his lip, almost sticking in his nose. He mumbled something unintelligible through the mouthful of food.

"Swallow first, you goddamn savage," I said, never taking my attention off the empty street, the empty windows, the empty everything.

A little clearer, he said, "I bet you say that to all the boys." He finished swallowing and took a breathy slurp from the coffee. "I said, I talked to Underdog."

"Me, too."

"I talked to him after you did."

I didn't answer him.

"He called me after he left you at the aquarium."

"Yeah. Forgot to tell you. He's out. He doesn't have our backs on this."

"That surprise you?"

"Not really. Probably should have kept my goddamn mouth shut. I don't think he'll turn us in if this thing goes completely to shit, though."

"Yeah. He didn't give me that impression either. He wasn't making threats, but he was worried."

"About what?"

"He was worried we were about to do something royally fucked up. Something that might screw us over. In a forever kind of way."

My heart started to sink. I didn't answer. I didn't like where the discussion seemed to be heading.

Junior took another big bite of his grinder, chewed, and sucked down more coffee before he went on. "I kinda agree with him."

Brutal silence hung in the air between us. I was burning up inside. Junior and I had never backed away from each other. Ever. On anything. The feelings of betrayal slammed me right in the heart.

"You want out? Then go," I said softly, bitterness edging my words. "I'll step out of the car right now, and you can be on your merry fucking way."

"What?" His voice was tinged with hurt. "Fuck you, Boo. I'm not backing off nothing. I got just as much at stake here as you do." He shook his head slowly in disbelief. "Don't even talk to me that way, you fuck."

"What are you trying to say, Junior? Spit it out."

He angrily chucked the rest of his sandwich out the window. "This ain't our fight no more, Boo. The girl? She's dead. We got hired to find her. We didn't. We found out what happened to her, but it's not the same thing. Technically? We're done. We're not getting paid for this, and it's not our fucking responsibility anymore to pull this midnight-avenger shit."

"So that's what this is about now? The paycheck? Fuck what he did to that kid, long as we get paid?"

"Don't be a fucking prick. Open your eyes. What if this thing goes all fubar and we get busted? Is it worth it to spend the rest of our lives in a fucking cage over this? Over a girl we never even knew?"

I opened my mouth to say something. Anything to interrupt him. But nothing came out. The man was making a point—and a righteous one at that, goddamn him.

Junior said, "Well, is it? I've been there, Boo. So have you. We spent most of our lives locked in, and there weren't even bars on The Home. This guy just isn't fucking worth it." Junior motioned vaguely toward the opposite side of the street.

"Maybe he isn't to you." Despite the sound logic in Junior's argument, Snake—whoever he was—mattered to me. I wanted him out of the world I had to live in. I couldn't explain it to Junior in that moment, but damn it, it mattered. My hands started shaking in anger at Junior's sudden turnaround.

"All right. Fine. I'm not saying we don't jack this boy up six ways to Sunday and twice on Monday. I'm not saying we don't find him and beat his ass like a piñata until he tells us what he did with the kid and we get it on tape." He paused. "But we leave him, Boo. We leave the fucker alive. We drop the dime on his now-crippled ass with the video and his confession. All on tape. Then we let the real cops handle this. This just isn't our game anymore. This is bigger than we thought it was going to be, kid."

Junior was right, but I couldn't hear him anymore. I opened the car door and got out. "Go, then," I said. "Step the fuck off."

Junior's tipping point tipped. He kicked his door open and faced me across the car roof. "Goddamn you, Boo! This girl? This fucking little dead girl? It sucks. It sucks worse than anything I've dealt with since The Home. But you know what? It had *nothing* to fucking do with us."

Junior smacked his open palm on the hood of the car. He folded his arms, shook his head, and dropped the bomb. In a quiet voice, he said, "This girl? You gotta realize something, Boo. She's not Emily."

Bang.

All the blood raging in my ears. All the adrenaline pounding in my veins. All of it dropped in a single heartbeat into the pit of my stomach like a mouthful of mercury. Hot tears welled up in my eyes, but I fought them back. I wanted to scream. I wanted to curse and start swinging on him. My best friend. My only family. I wanted to make him hurt like his words did me. But I couldn't. There was something hard and pointy lodged in my throat that made it hard to breathe, harder to speak.

Because he was right.

He threw his hands up in the air. "There. I said it. I was hoping I wouldn't have to, but you're blind to your own goddamn motivations. So you can listen to me and think it over or you can tell me to fuck off again. Your choice. Say the words, and I'm gone."

I stared down at the concrete, trying to fight back the anguish Junior's words had brought up from the bottom of the hole I'd thought I'd buried it in. "You're right." My voice came out in a hollow rasp. "You're right." I lit a cigarette with numbed fingers. I had a hard time looking up at him. "Maybe . . . maybe I've been screwed in the head with this thing all along. But you're right, either way."

"Good. So let's give this shit up for the night, get some sleep, and come back tomorrow. Sound good?" Junior climbed back into the driver's seat.

I followed him into the car. As suddenly as everything had come to a boil—all of the anger, the adrenaline, Junior's coffee—it all rushed out my system just as quickly. My body felt like a full bathtub with the drain pulled. I was exhausted in a place deeper than physical.

We drove in silence. I wanted to apologize again, but it took all the will I had left just to stay awake for the drive home. Junior pulled his car up into the driveway behind the ridiculous hippie van, and I climbed out.

Junior leaned over the seat. "What time you want to get there tomorrow?"

I rubbed at dry eyes with the back of my hand. "Around five, I'm figuring. If the fucker has a jobby-job, maybe we can catch his ass on the way home."

"Sounds good." Junior shifted the car into reverse, but left his foot on the brake. "You okay?"

"Yeah."

"You pissed at me?"

I shook my head. "Nah."

"You sure you're not pissed?"

I nodded.

"Still friends?"

"Yeah," I said, tugging a strained smile onto my face.

"Good, 'cause I owe you this." He flipped his hand across the seat and whacked me on the balls through the open door.

I groaned loudly as my lower equator cramped in pain. Crumpling from the blow, I tumbled backward into the hedges.

Junior peeled out, his spinning tires spraying me with gravel. I could hear him cackling over the engine's roar as he pulled out toward Cambridge Street at a clip.

Luckily for me, his leverage was off and he didn't get off as clean a shot as I had given him. With effort, I got to my feet and stumbled toward my apartment. The hippie was on the steps, looking at me open-mouthed as I approached.

"Hey, dude, you all right?" he asked.

"Yeah," I croaked. "Never better."

"Did that guy just hit you in the nuts?"

"Yup."

"Why?"

"'Cause he's my best friend."

"Oh," he said, as if my answer made all the sense in the world.

I got to the top of the porch, then stopped. "What's your name?"

"Phil."

"Nice to meet you, Phil. I'm Boo."

He mulled it over for a moment, blinking in slo-mo. "Is that like Boo Radley or like Casper, the friendly ghost?"

"Radley."

He smiled and nodded dreamily. "Cool. Good book."

I nodded and went inside my dark, empty apartment. From under the bed, I pulled out my ragged blue hardcover of *The Hardy Boys and the Mark on the Door.* Inside the cover, I found the brittle piece of folded construction paper. My one valuable. I carefully unfolded it and looked once again at the two smiling stick figures standing on a faded field of grass that never existed in front of a house we never lived in, *LovE Emily* scrawled above the smiling yellow sun in a deliberate child's hand. Gently, I folded the paper up and placed it back in its safe place. The Boy lay under my bed, hiding. From what, I didn't know. He took the book from me and held it tightly to his grotesquely scarred little chest.

I held onto the image of the smiling sun as I lay back and closed my eyes.

Day two.

More coffee.

More sandwiches.

No Snake.

The closest we came to activity was around 9 P.M. when a bum started harassing us for change and wouldn't leave.

He stood at the car window, swaying and reeking like sour milk. "C'mon, big guy. Help a vet'rin out. You gotta have some change you kin spare." He redirected his focus to Junior since I refused to give him my attention, much less change. His breath filled the car with the odor of cheap wine and gingivitis.

"You know what I got for you, alkie?" Junior reached under his seat and pulled out what looked like a homemade remote control. He pressed a button on the side, and a burst of electricity crackled across two metal studs attached to the top. "Zappy-zappy. That's what I got for you, you don't start walking."

The bum backed off from the window, palms up. He walked away, slurring his irritated sentiments. When he got halfway down the block, he turned around and flipped us off.

"What the hell was that?"

"I just hate bums," Junior said.

"No, I meant what is that in your hand?"

"What? This?" He held up the thing. It still looked like a big remote, held together with black duct tape. One thin green wire protruded from the bottom of the tape and re-entered the plastic molding just under the metal studs.

"What is that? Is that a stun gun?"

Junior smiled and nodded. "Sweet, isn't she?" He pressed the button again, sending electricity dancing between the electrodes. It made a sound like corn popping. "Twitch made it. He gave it to me on my birthday. I call her Rosie."

Why the hell does everyone name their weaponry?

On my last birthday, Twitch gave me a set of *Reservoir Dogs* action figures. I didn't feel like I'd gotten off easy at the time. At least he hadn't gifted me with something I could electrocute myself with.

We sat until Junior's snoring woke us both up around 11 P.M. Neither of us could figure out exactly when we'd fallen asleep. Needless to say, neither one of us had spotted our man from inside fucking slumberland.

Day three. Pouring rain. And I mean pouring. The rain fell in solid sheets around the car, and gray rivers ran down the gutter. Junior and

I made a game out of guessing what would come bobbing by next, caught in the current. You'd think it would have been a nice relief from the stifling heat, but just an inch of open window and my entire right side would be drenched immediately. With the windows closed, the humidity built up in the car, fogging up the glass and giving us zero visibility.

"This is retarded," Junior said, wiping the condensation off the inside of the windshield with a napkin. "We wouldn't see the guy if he was doing a cha-cha on the hood. Let's do this tomorrow."

We'd only been in our spot for an hour, but Junior was right. I sighed. Day three and zip. Wasn't even noon yet, and the day was in the shitter. "Fine. I'm just going to take a piss and get smokes. You want anything from inside?"

"Cherry Coke."

"Got it." I got out, head down, and ran into the store as fast as I could.

Our bribed counterman pressed the button from behind the counter, opening the lock on the bathroom door. Under the fluorescent lights, my skin had taken on a lovely jaundice, dark bags pooching under my eyes. I sighed at the living dead in the mirror. He sighed right back at me. I took a wonderfully extended piss and walked out. The bell on the door dinged as someone else came into the store. I grabbed Junior's soda and headed to the counter.

"Two packs of Parliaments," I said.

The clerk put the cigarettes on the linoleum counter next to the soda, then he nodded at whoever was standing right behind my shoulder. "Pack of Reds?"

"You got it," came the reply. All the hair on my body shot up straight into the air. I'd heard that voice before.

The clerk passed over a box of Marlboros. Put the pack into a hand. A hand that was on the end of an arm. An arm with a snake tattoo curled around it. The hand dumped a few bills and some change onto the countertop.

Slowly, I turned my head and looked into a pair of blue eyes, drops of rain hanging from his thick eyelashes. His long, too-black-to-be-natural hair hung wetly around his head. Given the time, I probably could have counted each pore on his nose. He had thinner features than I thought he would. He looked about twenty-five. *He's too young*, my mind said. *He looks too . . . normal.*

He flipped me a quick, cursory smile. "How are ya?" he said and walked out. The bell sounded again.

A snapping of fingers next to my ear brought me back. "Yo, bro? You with me here? You paying for the smokes and Coke or what?" I put a bill on the counter, grabbed my items, and walked to the door, numb with disbelief.

Junior was out of the car, standing in the downpour and wearing the same thousand-yard stare I was sporting. I walked over to him and stood at his side. I opened my mouth, but Junior beat me to it. "Please. Please, dear God, tell me that's who I think it is."

"It's him," I said. We watched him walk through the front door to an apartment building that sat at ten o'clock from the front door of Papa's Empanadas. Once he was inside, Junior grabbed the duct tape we'd brought with us off the car seat and the two of us bolted across the street, oblivious to the traffic zipping past us in both directions. A car passed close enough to nip the back of my pants leg.

Snake hadn't used a key to get in the first door. He'd just pushed it open. I hoped it wasn't a double-door foyer with the lock on the second door. It wasn't. It was just one door with a busted lock.

Snake wasn't in the lobby, but the elevator was on its way up. We watched the numbers climb to the fifth floor and stop.

"Gotcha, fucker," I said.

We rode up to the fifth floor. Our original plan was to knock on each door with a pitch for the Church of the Divine Ascension until we got to the right one. I was thankful we didn't need the shtick. Instead, we just followed the wet footprints on the tiled hallway to apartment 506.

"And here we are," said Junior, a bit breathlessly. "You want the honors?"

I knocked on the door and waited, heart pounding like a bass amp. A shadow passed over the peephole in the center of the door and something snapped in my brain. I actually heard a *pop* inside my head.

The world exploded red.

I pressed myself flat against the wall opposite the door in the thin hallway. With the wall bracing my back, I kicked at the lock full-on. The dry wood around the bolt shattered like a Saltine. The sound of the heavy wood bashing onto meat and bone was orgasmic to my ears.

I charged through the open doorway. What I lacked in panache, I made up for in sheer momentum. To his credit, Snake was still standing. It probably would have been better for him if he'd gone down. His eyes were rolled halfway up his skull, and his nose looked like somebody had stuck an M-80 inside a nostril and lit the fuse.

I decked him with every muscle, every pound, focused into the tip of my fist. His wiry body went airborne, launching clear over the couch behind him. When gravity resumed its grip, he crumpled on the hardwood and slid across the floor all the way into the far wall. His trip came to an abrupt end when the back of his head crunched into the scuffed wood molding. I didn't care if it was the molding or his skull that had made the crunch.

I stood over Snake's body, wishing he would stand so I could pop him a couple more times. My fists shook, breath hissing out from between clenched teeth. He wasn't going anywhere.

Junior walked in behind me and gently placed a hand on my shoulder. The muscles bunched under his fingers. "Nice punch."

It was a second before I could answer, snapping out from under the spell of violence as though from hypnosis. I took a deep breath and closed my eyes. I blew out air in a long stream, the violence still under the surface, wanting to do bad things.

Bad things.

"Yeah," I finally said.

Junior nudged Snake with the toe of his boot. "Shit. He dead?"

Snake's chest lifted shallowly.

"Nope." I still wanted blood. I wasn't through hurting him yet.

"You've never been accused of being subtle, have you?"

"Nope. Gimme the duct tape."

While Junior ran out to the car to get the rest of our supplies, I sat in a wooden kitchen chair opposite Snake. I lit a smoke to keep my fingers doing something, anything but what the wild violence wanted them to do.

Looking down at his inert body, I thought it bizarre we had come this far, standing over the guy, and still didn't have any idea what his name was. Who he was.

"The name's Bevilaqua," Junior said, reading my mind as he re-entered. "On the mailbox. What is that? Greek?" He tossed the canvas duffel bag on the couch.

"No idea. Let's get him into the chair." Junior took the arms, and I took the legs.

Dead weight is never easy to maneuver. It's even less easy when you're being careful. We weren't. I hoisted him into the seat by the collar, not caring if I accidentally choked him on the way.

Junior taped his hands together behind the chair, and I taped his ankles to the wooden legs. Snake gurgled a moan as we finished, but he wasn't going to wake up on his own just yet. Blood trickled from his smashed nose onto his chest. Another line ran slowly down the back of his neck from the swollen spot where he'd bonked against the wall.

"So, what do we do now, wait until he wakes up?"

I took a look around the apartment. The walls were painted a dark burgundy, the bathroom door open, another white door next to it. The bedroom. A shiver passed through me, seeing the place as a reality instead of an abstract on a screen. I didn't want to go in. Were the walls still streaked with Cassandra's blood?

For the second time that hour, someone snapped his fingers in front of my eyes, drawing me back. "Yo, Malone! Wake up! Stay with me here. What are we doing?"

"Wake him up."

Junior went to the kitchen. I heard some clatter, then the sink running. He returned with a sloshing saucepan. He dumped the water in one motion on top of Snake's head. Snake slowly held up his head.

"Mnnnnn . . . ow," he murmured, blinking hard. He looked up and squinted at us.

I'm not sure what I expected him to do. I knew I wanted him to cry, to beg. What I didn't expect was him to smirk like he did.

"You're both dead men," he said softly, each word dripping hot acid.

I gave him the back of my hand.

His face snapped around, and came back with a fierce expression. He snarled at me, "You have any idea what's going to happen to you when—"

I cut him off with another backhand. And another. And another. His lips split. His nose began pouring blood again. A thin line of blood creased my middle knuckles.

"Fuck! Stop it! Jesus!" Snake gagged and feebly spit a gob onto his own chest, a white piece of tooth floating in the blood and saliva.

Snake sneered. "Sister or girlfriend?" He huffed a sharp laugh at us.

I looked at Junior, who shrugged. He was as stymied as I was. We both knew there was no intimidating a psychopath.

Snake continued with the abuse. "So, I give one of your girls a good dicking, which she probably wasn't getting from either one of you, and I'm the bad guy?" He was still laughing. "Shit, not my fault you boys can't keep your girls happy."

Junior grabbed my arm, sensing I was a second away from losing it. "My turn?" he asked.

"Go nuts," I mumbled and turned away. I couldn't look at him anymore. I stared at the bedroom door again.

I heard Junior behind me. "Okay, dipshit. Believe it or not, my buddy was the one who was being nice to you. I'm the guy who's actually gonna hurt you." I heard the crackle of Junior's stun gun. "See this? This baby hurts like nobody's business. So, I'm gonna ask you a question, then I'm gonna make with the zap-zap. Thing is? I want to hurt you. Really. I do. I just want to hurt you. You decide whether or not you want to answer. The next one goes on your balls."

"Fuck your mother," Snake said.

"Fair enough. One chance. Where's the body?"

The question stuck in my chest like a barb.

Snake got out one puzzled, "Huh?"

As the stun gun crackled, it suddenly popped into my head just what a bonehead move we—well, Junior—were about to make.

Par for the course, I realized it one second too goddamn late.

"Junior, no! He's—"

I wasn't fast enough. Junior applied an electric charge to a man we'd dumped a pot of water on. Junior was still soaked from the rain. I didn't know the math or physics of it, but I knew that electricity plus water makes bad.

Big bad.

Snake shrieked and convulsed. Junior hollered and flew back as though struck by lightning. Snake slumped into his seat, unconscious. Junior bounced into the wall and came down hard on his ass.

"Ohhhh," Junior groaned and hugged himself. "That sucked so, so bad."

I walked over to Snake and placed my thumb under his ear. He still had a pulse. Good. I wasn't done yet.

The bedroom door clicked. I froze. Junior looked to the door, then at me, then back to the bedroom. The door stuck a little from the humidity and then pulled opened. A girl in sweats walked out, yawning and rubbing her eyes. Freshly dyed black hair hung over a big shiner on her right eye. Her iPod was turned up so loud I could hear the bass line across the room. She hadn't heard a thing.

Cassandra Donnelly stared at the three of us, just as flabbergasted as we were.

I could only imagine how it looked. Snake, unconscious and bloody, taped to a chair and two gawping numbnuts, mouths open wide enough to park a pair of Humvees.

Then, of course, she screamed and ran for the door. "*Help me! Somebody!*"

I roped her around the waist, momentum swinging her halfway around me. Junior was trying hard to stand, but his electrocuted body fought stiffly against him.

"Cassie!" I yelled. "Wait! Wait. Hold it!"

Saying her name had no effect. I lifted her off the ground, and she shrieked right into my ear. Her heels kicked brutally into my shins as I covered her mouth to stifle her caterwauling. Attention was not what we needed. Simultaneously, a tiny heel collided with my hairy beanbag just as Cassandra's teeth found the fleshy part of my thumb. I felt bone crunching just as the air exploded out of my lungs from the nut-shot. My poor, poor balls were having a shitty week. The combo made my knees turn to rubber, and I fell on top of Cassandra with a howl of my own. At least my fat ass landing on her got her to loosen her jaws off my knuckle. My other hand went reflexively to my balls. Cassie saw the opening and scrambled out from under me, heading for the door again.

"Please! Somebod—"

Zap.

Cassandra was on the floor. Junior convulsed, flew back into the wall a second time, then face-planted on the floor next to Cassie. "Fucking ow," he croaked. "I taste smoke in my mouth."

"You think you'd have learned." I pulled him up under his armpits into a seated position. I may have imagined it, but he felt warmer. I slumped back to the floor myself, cradling my abused crotch while I debated the pros and cons of vomiting.

Junior weakly punched me on the chest. "At least I didn't get my ass kicked by two girls this week."

"If I throw up, will you hold my hair?"

"Fuck you."

"There's my hetero life-partner." I remained fetal for a bit, trying to decide which hurt worse: my balls, my hand, or my pride. At the moment, it was a three-way draw.

Always helpful, Junior said, "Bleeding there, Boo."

"Thanks, doc. Hadn't noticed." A deep laceration creased the webbing of my thumb, but I was still able to wiggle my fingers. Small favor, nothing was broken. I've broken both my hands enough times to recognize that particular brand of pain. All in all, I'd have rather had a cookie.

"Little broad's got a strong set of teeth on her, huh?"

"Like wrestling a hundred-pound mastiff." I stood shakily, one knee buckling. I walked toward the bathroom. "Watch them."

"Aye, aye, cap'n." Junior saluted me, then dropped his head back to the hardwood with a thump. Once inside the bathroom, I heard Junior mutter, "I still taste smoke."

Rummaging through Snake's medicine cabinet was like taking a tour through Keith Richard's lunchbox. Dilaudid. Valium. Oxycontin. Hydrocodone. Propoxyphene. All in little prescription bottles, none with the name Bevilaqua on them. Beautiful. Kiddie porn star, pill-popper, and snuff filmmaker. Well, maybe not snuff. At least not with Cassandra. What in sweet fuck-all was going on?

I read a few more labels before I chose one I recognized. I dry swallowed one of the Dilaudids, pocketed the bottle, and went to his bedroom.

The room from the video. I looked around. Blood was still streaked above the bed. I couldn't help myself. I scraped some of the dried residue off with a fingernail and daubed the tip of my tongue, expecting the sweetness of dyed corn syrup. Instead, I got the taste of blood. I gagged and spit onto the floor. Should have fucking known the loony dipshit had been method-acting his fake snuff. A quarter-full bottle of Wild Turkey sat on the floor. I rinsed my mouth and spit it onto the bedsheets.

I slid open one side of the closet door. Ratty looking T-shirts mixed in with high-priced suits with long Italian names on the labels. I ripped the silk lining out of a suit jacket and wrapped my hand tightly. Then I saw that the wardrobe ended sharply at the halfway point in the long closet.

A long mirror faced the bed on the other side of the sliding closet doors. I pushed the clothes all the way over to one side. An expensive-looking camera on a tripod was inside the other half of the closet. The top panel of the door was cut out. The mirror was a two-way.

I took the camera off the tripod and smashed it on the floor. Junior ran to the doorway. "You okay?"

"All good. Just enjoying some smashy-smashy."

Junior looked at the camera pieces. "Nice. Can I piss on it?"

"Who am I to deny you the simple pleasures?"

Junior and I were in agreement that we needed to get our asses in gear and boogie the hell on out. Pronto. We carried Cassandra over to the couch, placing her on the cushions as though she were made of porcelain. After double-wrapping Snake's bonds, we taped his mouth over. Just to be a dick, I wrapped a few rounds over his eyes and ears, making sure I tangled a lot of his hair in the industrial-strength tape.

Junior left to pull the car around front. I was to wait five minutes and hustle Cassandra out the door and into the car.

Four minutes down, and we were going to pull it off. We'd done it, despite the missteps, bullshit, and general lack of having a single clue about what we were walking into. We'd pulled it off, despite every plan blowing up in our faces. I smiled as I looked down at Cassandra's body, every breath she took a bonus.

She was alive.

Gently as I could, I threw Cassandra's arms over my shoulder and lifted her in a fireman's carry. I guessed her weight at about a hundred pounds, maybe a hint over. Even so, it was a hundred pounds of dead weight. And I was five flights of stairs up from making good the escape. I wasn't chancing the elevator and having to explain to other tenants why I was toting an unconscious fourteen-year-old girl over my shoulder. I'm pretty good on my feet, but even I didn't think I could talk my way cleanly through that one.

No matter what, five flights of stairs was just flat-out going to suck. I opened the door and lumbered across the hallway and out the fire door to the stairs.

The first two flights weren't bad.

Three flights down, my shoulder went numb and my fingers were well on their way. I stopped on the landing, breathing heavily, my shirt starting to soak through. Why couldn't Cassie have run away in the goddamn winter? No, she had to go and run away during the hottest summer in twenty years. I cursed myself for not having more cardiovascular in my daily workout. But really, how would I have prepared for this? Gone for a jog with a couple concrete sacks over each shoulder?

By the time I got us down to the second floor, my whole arm was dead and my shoulder felt like a strong breeze would pop it out of socket. Genius that I was, I'd slung Cassandra over the shoulder I'd run into The Cellar's back door. I couldn't figure out any way to shift her to my other arm in the cramped stairwell without smacking her head against the wall. Instead, I gritted my teeth and plodded on.

Finally, we made it to the ground floor just as my lumbar started to cramp up. I propped Cassandra against the wall, holding her up by the hood of her sweatshirt, twisting at the waist to avoid a full blow-out of my back. Pins and needles buzzed painfully down my arm like a swarm of pissed-off bees. I muttered a few curses and looked out the door for Junior's car. He wasn't there yet. I cursed some more. Small blessing that the rain would keep foot traffic to a minimum as we got Cassandra out of the building. Nothing like trying to pull off a half-assed kidnapping in broad daylight.

Then the elevator bell pinged behind me.

My heart seized as I heard the old elevator door scrape open. My mind raced, and I leapt into the one action my panicked brain concocted. I blocked Cassandra with my body and stuck my face in her neck, a pose of lovers mid-makeout.

Tiny feet jumped up and paddled my ass, making my already overtaxed heart bounce around my ribcage like a superball. I jerked and turned to find a hyperactive Boston Terrier in a yellow rain slicker happily playing my backside like bongos.

"Down, Max!" a voice said from the other end of Max's leash. I followed it to an elderly woman in a matching raincoat glowering at me. The dog jumped down and pulled the leash toward the door. "Get a room," the old woman grumbled as she passed.

I turned to block Cassandra from the other side and stuck my face back against her neck. I counted to twenty after the door closed before I chanced another look for Junior. Of course, he was at the door, mouth open in shock.

"Fucking perv," Junior said. Then he cackled softly.

He'd managed to keep his goddamned mouth shut long enough for us to prop Cassandra into the backseat. In the interim, he'd snickered out his nose twice, so I knew it was only a matter of time before the comments came flying.

"Shut it. I mean it. Think about what we just pulled her out of. It's inappropriate."

"It's inappropriate," Junior mocked in a Mary Poppins accent. "Out of the arms of one perv—" His last words got lost in an amused squeak.

"She's fourteen, you sick fuck. Besides, what else could I have done? What would you do?"

"I wouldn't have dry-humped the jailbait against the wall, that's for sure. That's inappropriate," Junior said. Then, softly, "Fucking perv."

"Not another word, Junior." I was trying not to crack up myself. I'd just have to put up with a few years' worth of Junior's mockery. He snorted again, and that was it. We both lost our shit, and I giggled until my ribs ached. All in all, it wasn't funny, but fuck, we needed the laugh.

Cassandra stirred with a grunt, and we quickly stifled ourselves.

"Twenty-five grand!" Junior sang to himself as we drove. Despite the throbbing bite on my hand and great big swollen balls, I felt like belting out a tune myself.

Junior pulled up in front of my apartment and killed the engine. The rain had driven Phil the Hippie off the porch for the day. It looked like, apart from one happy dog up my ass, the kidnapping (The abduction? A forced rescue?) would be brought off hitch-less.

Junior turned to me. "What the hell do we do now? Do we just give Kelly a ring and dump her in daddy's limo when it comes by?"

I shrugged. "I haven't thought that far ahead yet. We're playing this by ear right now." I jerked my thumb at the backseat. "Finding the kid changes things a bit."

"Well, finding her alive sure as shit does." Junior started singing his twenty-five grand song again, and I wanted to stop him before he started dancing. The day had been disturbing enough already. "Well, let's get her inside. Then we'll formulate. I don't want her waking up and—"

Cassandra's shriek just about made the two of us shit ourselves. She'd woken up all volume, swinging fists, and fury.

"Jesus Christ!" Junior yelped as he spun around, catching a flailing elbow to the ear. He fell backward, ass-first under the steering wheel.

"Fuck!" Startled, I jumped high in the seat, whacking my head into the roof hard enough to give myself a sharp pain at the base of my neck. I rolled to the right reflexively, caught the doorknob with my elbow, and tumbled backward out the door.

Abruptly, Cassie cut the screaming and flailing and sat stone still, panting in fright. I held up my hands in a calming gesture from my tactical position, halfway jammed in the rain-soaked gutter. "It's okay! It's all right!" I said. "You're safe. We're not going to hurt you." Well, at least not more than we already had, between crushing her onto Snake's floor and electrocuting her.

She remained still, but the air was thick as freshly poured asphalt. Her short breaths started to hitch. Then she was crying. "My head hurts," she said.

"Uh, Boo?" Junior said softly. "Little help here?" Junior was good and wedged backward under the steering wheel, his upper body bent in a position that seemed unnatural for a guy of Junior's build. I grabbed the seatbelt and pried myself up. Then I went over to Junior's side, opened his door, and pulled him out.

I leaned back into the car. "Cassandra?" I said in a gentle voice.

Cassandra pulled a lock of ebony hair from her eyes and looked at me, her breath coming in short gasps. If I didn't calm her down soon, the kid was going to hyperventilate. Her fear and confusion dug at my heart. The poor kid was doing her best to hold it together, but the trembles in each breath showed the bluff. Her eyes locked into mine with a dim light of recognition.

"Do you recognize me?" I asked.

"Y-you," she said tentatively. "I know you. You work at The Cellar."

I smiled with as much radiant calm as I could muster. "Yeah. That's me."

"You're the guy. You stood up to those jerks for Kevin." Her last words emerged in a choke, and she cleared her throat.

"I'm Boo," I said, cautiously extending my bandaged hand. I was ready to snatch it back in case she decided to bite again rather than shake. "That's Junior." Junior wiggled his fingers at her and smiled.

She looked around, trying to get a bearing on her surroundings. "Where . . . where am I?"

"You're at my place. Your father hired us to find you."

"My dad?" Guilt edged her voice, and she gnawed at her lower lip. "He's gotta be so pissed at me."

I wasn't sure pissed was the word, but I didn't want to blow a load of smoke up the kid's ass. "Probably. But I know he's been worried, too."

"Is he coming here?"

"He doesn't know you're with me yet. I don't see any reason to rush things, but we should let him know that you're safe as soon as we can." Cassandra just sat there, still frozen by the sudden and violent turn of events. "Listen, do you want to come in? We can talk about all this inside."

She thought it over, giving us both a suspicious eye.

"You know, inside? Where it's not raining down the crack of my ass?"

Her mouth trembled, fighting a smile. "Um . . . okay." I offered her my unbandaged hand to help her out of the car. She looked at the blood-soaked silk wrapped around the other hand. "Was that me?"

"Sure was."

"Sorry 'bout that."

"No problem. Happens all the time." And it actually did, in my line of work.

"Boo?"

"Yeah?"

"Why is my hair sticking up?"

Chapter Sixteen

We all needed a change of clothes. The three of us were soaking wet, blood-streaked, and beat the hell up. The cuff of Junior's pant leg also had a hole charred through it.

I switched out of my own ruined clothes and gave Junior one of my T-shirts. It was a size and a half too small for his bulk and made him look like an overstuffed sausage. The pants were the right waist size, but he had to roll up the legs. Cassie changed into an old Bosstones T-shirt and a pair of sweatpants. I figured the drawstring could make up for the massive difference in size. Junior and I waited for her in the kitchen while she changed in the bathroom.

"Going clam digging?" I asked.

"Bite me." Junior sniffed disapprovingly at the coffee I was brewing. "Amateur," he grumbled.

"Sorry. It's all I got."

"Chock Full O'Nuts? Why don't you just drink Folger's instant, ya faggot."

Before I could answer, Cassie shuffled out of the bathroom, her wet clothes wadded up in her arms.

"Feel better?" I took the dirty garments from her.

"Thanks. Dryer, at least," she mumbled. She wouldn't meet my eyes, instead taking in the majesty of my dirty kitchen tile.

"You two chill in the living room. I'll be right with you." The dressing on my bite needed changing. A little disinfecting couldn't hurt either. I went into the bathroom with a bottle of vodka and long strips of cloth I'd cut from another old shirt. I would need to buy new clothes soon at my current rate of ruin. On the other hand, I would easily be able to replace my entire wardrobe as soon as Big Jack's check cleared.

The silk lining I'd used to wrap my hand at Snake's was starting to stick to the wound. Slowly, I peeled away the material clotted to my hand. The bleeding had stopped, but the flesh was badly swollen. I wasn't sure if it looked worse than it felt. The Dilaudid dulled the pain down from sharp and stabbing to dull and throbbing. Once my hand was unwrapped, I wiggled the fingers again slowly. I didn't bother checking my own medicine cabinet for disinfectant or bandages. My rusty can of shaving cream, half box of Q-Tips, and Tom & Jerry juice glass wouldn't do me much good.

Was that a giggle coming from the living room? Go Junior.

To unscrew the bottle of vodka, I had to use my good hand and my teeth. I poured half the bottle over the wound, keeping the cap in my mouth to bite down on. The pain hit hard and fast. I clenched down hard enough to fire the cap out my mouth like a .22 slug, sending it bouncing around the bathtub. Without the cap, my teeth decided to sink into my tongue instead. I cried out in confused pain, not sure which injury to scream about. Taking a few deep breaths, I tied the strips of material together and rewrapped my hand tightly like a boxer's.

As a final precaution, I rolled a mouthful of vodka over my freshly wounded tongue and spit a gob of pink saliva into the sink. I poured myself a cup of (substandard) coffee and went to see what was so funny.

When I walked into the living room, I saw Cassie sitting on my couch and Junior facing her, squatting on a footstool. I froze in the doorway.

Cassie was playing with the stun gun.

Junior was explaining to her how it worked. "When you press that little button right here, BZZZZT!" Junior shook and convulsed to emphasize the results. Cassie giggled at his pantomime.

I said a silent prayer that Junior had the sense to remove the batteries. No way would he be so stupid.

Junior saw me standing there. "Hey, Boo. What was all the hollering about? You yank your plank too hard?"

I never got to answer him.

I learned two things in that moment.

1. Prayers are worthless against Biblical stupidity
   And
2. Junior is beyond that stupid.

Cassie found her window when Junior turned to me in order to bust my balls. She stuck Rosie against Junior's neck and pressed the button—just like the shithead had instructed her to. Junior made a noise like, "Ba-GAAACK," jerked once, and flew backward, tumbling feet over ass over head. His feet stuck straight up in the air for a second before they plopped heavily down to the floor.

"How do *you* like it, fucker?" Cassie yelled. She was on her feet in a flash, holding the stun gun over Junior in two unsteady hands.

I got to take one step before she turned Rosie's business end toward me.

"You stay right there," she said. She jabbed the air with the stun gun, arms shaking. "Give me your phone!"

"Don't have one. It got shut off," I lied.

"Then why do you still carry it?" She pointed the stun gun toward my hip.

Shit. The cell phone. Forgot I owned the stupid thing, much less that I wore it.

Plan B. Nice Guy. I put on my best soft rock DJ voice. "Cassie, put it down. Talk to me. We just want to help you."

"I'll help myself, thank you very much." Her arms shook with the effort of holding up the stun gun. "Now give me the phone!" The kid was running on her last reserves of adrenaline, which also seemed to be all that was holding her up.

"No."

"*Give it to me!*" She took a step forward and pressed the button again to show me she meant business. The electrodes crackled blue arcs.

I slowly bent over and put my coffee on the floor. If push came to shove, I wanted both hands available to me. Her having lost the element of surprise, I was reasonably sure I could disarm her before she got me. What I wasn't so sure of was that I could do it without hurting her. "Who are you going to call?"

"I have people. I have friends."

"Who?"

"I have people I can call." She sounded like she was trying to convince herself.

"Who?" I said a little more harshly. "The piece of shit you've been staying with?"

"Don't call him that. He loves me."

"Guy's got one twisted-ass idea of love. You look at your eye lately?"

She brushed her fingers lightly over her shiner. "I . . . I have other people," she said, all teenage indignance.

"Who? Your dad?" I pulled the cell phone out and opened it. "Shit, I'll call him myself. Remember? He's the one who hired us to find you. The sooner he picks your little bitch-ass up, the better." I held the phone out to her.

She froze, stunned by the rough card I'd just played. Her mouth opened and closed a couple times.

I tuned the aggression up a notch, pushing her back on the defensive. "What do you think we're doing? Babysitting? Kidnapping?"

"I . . . but . . ." Was that a flicker of doubt that played across her eyes? The stun gun went down a notch. If I rushed her now, I'd get zapped right in the testicles instead of the chest.

"We were trying to find you. We thought that you were dead, that the fucker killed you."

Oops.

I regretted saying the words the second they left my mouth.

With that, the flicker of doubt was gone, replaced with fury again. "You're the animal. You didn't have to beat him up so bad!" Then the pieces came together in her head. She realized why we thought she was dead. She shook her head. "No. Nononononono . . ."

Fuck it. I'd already crossed the line. It was time to plant my feet. "Yeah. We saw what he did to you. The guy who says he loves you. He fucking smacked the shit out of you and raped you."

"No! That's not how it happened!" Spittle flew from her lips as she started bawling. She was breaking down, caught between hysteria and denial.

"What happened, then? Was it a practical joke? What am I missing here, Cassie? Tell me!"

"He . . . he said it had to look real. That I had to be really scared. That's why he had to do it that way. So they'd believe it." She was having trouble speaking through the deep jags.

"'They' who?"

"The people who buy those DVDs from him. They pay a lot of money for them. Derek said he could sell just a few of them and make enough money to run away. Just us. So we could be together."

Jesus. One of the oldest lines in the oldest book. "That was a lie, Cassandra. Derek is running a sick freak show, and you were his star attraction." I made a quick mental note. Derek. Derek Bevilaqua. Now I had a full name along with an address to hand to Underdog.

I'd driven the knife into her heart. All I had to was twist it and she'd be broken.

I suck. I know. Fuck you.

"He never loved you. He used you." I let the words hang.

She dropped Rosie and crumpled, wailing. I caught her on the way down and held her as she wept and beat her hands against my chest. I held her tight until she stopped struggling against it. I felt her go slack, all the fight in her evaporated. I put her down gently on the couch and sat to her side. She buried her face in my chest, crying it all out. I didn't know what to do with her. Or my arms, for that matter. For lack of a better place to put them, I held them up over my head. I wasn't comfortable in either my seating position or my role as comforter.

"Um . . . do you mind?" I fumbled for the right words. "Are you gonna bite me again if I put my arms down?"

"No," she said softly into my armpit.

"Promise, Mad Dog?"

Surprisingly, she choked on a laugh. "I promise."

I let my arms down around Cassie's shoulders. We sat there until her sobs trailed off and her breathing evened into an exhausted sleep. My own eyelids grew heavy, and I let the fatigue wash over me. The last thing I heard as I drifted away was a great snore erupting from the floor where Junior lay sprawled.

It was the same snoring that woke me up. Everything hurt. I sat up slowly and stiffly, thinking of Nick Nolte in *North Dallas Forty*. My joints felt like somebody had dug them out with an ice cream scoop and replaced them with month-old taffy.

The sun was going down. Must have been more run-down than I realized. I'd managed to sleep a decent clip with Junior in the room. Most people have trouble sleeping while Junior's in the same zip code. The guy snores like a Rottweiler choking on a bowling ball. I moved my tongue around my mouth and instantly regretted it. Besides tasting horrible, my tongue was still sore from the self-chomping it received.

As was my shoulder from colliding with the door at The Cellar.

And my jaw from where Sid popped me.

And my hand where Cassandra bit me.

Waitaminnit.

No Cassandra.

I jumped off the couch. "Junior!" I yelled.

"Whazza? Wha?" Junior leapt to his feet, fists cocked to ward off potential attackers. "Aaghhh! Mother*charleyfucker*horse!" he screamed and dropped back onto the floor, clutching his calf.

I ran to the bathroom.

No Cassandra.

The bedroom.

No Cassandra.

"Shitfuckgoddamnsonofabitch," I ranted as I tore through my apartment. How could I have been so goddamn stupid? I burst through the kitchen door hard enough to make Cassie jump even with her headphones on. She was rooting inside my fridge and munching on a piece of individually wrapped cheese product she'd found.

Cassie yipped in surprise. "Jeez, Boo. Try some decaf."

I leaned on the stove, gasping and willing my pulse to slow down to "rumba."

Cassie popped another piece of yellow food product into her mouth. "What do you guys have to eat around here?"

"For starters, not the cheese," I said. After all we'd been through, I hoped a piece of ancient cheese product wasn't going to drop Cassie into toxic shock in my kitchen. "How's about we order a pizza or something?"

Junior came hopping into the kitchen. "What the fuck is wrong with you?"

Junior passed on dinner, opting instead to head back to his place to shower and change into clothes a little more dignified. He complained that my shirt was cutting off circulation. Since Cassandra was a vegetarian, we ordered half-pepperoni, half-plain. The pizza arrived and we sat down at my kitchen table and ate in a strange and heavy silence. Cassandra didn't look at me, just stared at a space hovering in the air over the pizza. After half a slice, her eyes started to fill with tears.

"I was so scared," she said.

"Hmmm?" I mumbled, mouth full of hot mozzarella.

"On the video. Derek rigged the knife with a blood pack. He squeezed it, and the blood squirted out." Drops fell from her eyes onto my lucky plate. "Some got into my mouth when I screamed. It tasted like blood. I thought it was my blood."

"It sure as shit looked real."

"I was so scared. I didn't know. I thought it was real."

"We did, too. That's why we freaked out and went to town on Derek." I filled my mouth with pizza so I wouldn't have to talk anymore.

"He lied to me, didn't he?" She was speaking through sniffles. "He didn't . . . he couldn't have loved me."

Jesus. I opened my full mouth but said nothing. I didn't know what I could say.

"Did my dad see the . . . did he?" She didn't have to finish.

"No."

She nodded and stared back into the empty place.

I pulled a piece of pepperoni from my slice and chewed. "Far as I'm concerned, he's never going to."

Her lower lip trembled and tears dropped onto her plate. "What if . . ."

"What if what?"

"What if he finds out?"

"Well, now that me and Junior are done with the job of finding you, we're available for any new gig that might come up."

Her face scrunched up. "I don't know what you're saying."

"You could hire us to get back any DVDs that Derek might have already sold."

"But . . . I don't . . ."

"How much money you got?"

Cassie opened her little purse and pulled out one crumpled ten, three fives, and more crumpled singles. I grabbed the singles and stuffed them in my pocket.

"Done and done," I said and tore off a piece of crust. "You need a receipt for your taxes?"

She sniffled and shook her head. She was smiling, but it looked like she might bawl. She looked up at me with the same eyes that had troubled me a little more than a week ago. There was so much hurt still there. That unsettling maturity remained, but I could see a spark of the kid had survived.

I smiled at her. "Theater camp is your own goddamn problem, though."

Cassie laughed through a mouthful of pizza, almost spitting it onto the table. "God, I hated that crap."

"No shit. Eat your pizza."

It would be over for the kid soon enough. It wasn't over for me and Derek yet. Not by a long shot. He needed to hurt some more. I needed to hurt him some more. I swore to myself, when all was said and done with Cassie, he and I were gonna dance one more time. And I was being paid four dollars for the privilege.

The phone picked up on the third ring. "Kelly Reese."

I pinched my nose and spoke in a high register. "Hi, my name is Fitz Benwalla. I'm calling from the Boston *Phoenix*. We're doing a piece on Boston's sexiest tough guys."

"Excuse me?"

"Rumor has it you've got one of the most eligible, sexiest, smartest, and hunka-hunka burnin' love bachelors in town knocking at your door at all hours. Also that he's super manly. And did I say sexy?"

"Don't believe all the rumors you hear, Boo."

"Okay. That hurt."

She laughed, and I felt a goofy smile play across my face. "Get over it, tough guy."

"Too bad. I was going to ask you out for a very expensive dinner just as soon as the check from your boss cleared."

Silence.

"You still there?" I knew she was, but I was savoring her surprise.

"*Ohmygod!* You found her?"

"Got her."

"Ohmygod!" she said, her voice rising an octave in excitement. I liked the sound of it. The receiver clunked painfully in my ear. I think she dropped the phone. After some quick scrabbling sounds, "Where was she? Is she okay?"

"She's a little banged up emotionally, but otherwise seems okay."

"What happened?"

"You know, guy stuff. She was staying with a guy. He wasn't what she thought he was." And that was the cleanest and most biblically understated way I could put that.

"Aw, poor kid."

"Yeah. We boys sure can suck."

"Maybe I should come over and talk to her? Maybe I could help her, girl to girl."

"Not a bad idea, that. When can you come over?"

"I can get there by nine."

Nine. That would leave me a little over an hour. "Sounds like a plan. Oh, and bring her a change of clothes, if you can."

"No trouble at all. I'll run by The Gap."

"You need her size and stuff?"

"Nope. I'd say she's about a one. I'll get a two, just to be safe. See you at nine."

"See you."

I hung up and started frantically cleaning. I started in the kitchen. Lacking much in the way of cleaning fluids, I just used an old sponge I had in the sink and elbow grease.

When I made it to the living room, Cassandra was watching a talk show. She looked over and watched my half-assed speed cleaning. Finally, her curiosity got the best of her. "What's going on?"

"You know Kelly? Works for your dad?"

"Yeah, she's nice."

"She's gonna swing by, hang with us. Maybe you two can talk. You know, girl talk."

Cassie made a face.

"What?"

"Why can't I talk to another girl without some guy calling it girl talk?" She folded her arms in feminist self-righteousness.

Jesus H . . .

"I don't know. It's just a term. Me and Junior? When we talk, it's guy talk. I was just projecting. Would you mind helping me clean up a bit?"

"Why? Trying to impress your girlfriend?"

My ears went hot. "She's not my girlfriend," I said in a tone more appropriate for denying a cootie infestation.

"Then why are you blushing?"

"I'm not."

"Whatever. It smells funny in here anyway."

"What? Hey!"

The apartment would never get a Good Housekeeping Seal of Approval, but it was as clean as it was going to get by 8:30. I hopped in the shower and gave myself a good scrubbing.

At five minutes past, Kelly was at the door. Since Kelly hadn't had dinner, Cassie had a teenager's bottomless appetite, and I'm a fat fuck in training, we ordered Chinese. The three of us were watching *The Simpsons* in an awkward quiet when the food arrived. I carried the greasy bags into the living room and heard Kelly opening the kitchen cabinets.

"Do you have plates?" she yelled toward the door.

"I have plate."

She walked back into the living room. "Why don't you have plates?"

"Never needed more than one. How many am I supposed to have?"

"Three would be nice."

I went into the bag and pulled out four Styrofoam plates. "Now we have an extra."

She gave Cassandra an exasperated look and stormed back into the kitchen, muttering. I caught the words "bachelor," "unbelievable," and, I think, "zoo." But that could have been "Boo." Then, louder, "Where are your forks?"

"I have fork."

After we ate, I broke out my beat-up poker set. Kelly had obviously played before, and was good enough to make me nervous. This girl was full of surprises. Cassie had a harder time picking up the game. After dropping another hand, she threw her cards on the table.

"Poker? Really?"

"Consider it a life skill I'm teaching you."

Kelly didn't say anything, just gave me a look over her cards.

"I don't suppose you have Grand Theft Auto hidden away anywhere."

"Nope. All I got are these old analog games." I dropped the flop cards.

"He's old school," Kelly said, a barb of sarcasm tipping the words.

Cassie snorted. "You got the old part right."

Kelly snickered behind her cards. I glared.

Cassie snorted another laugh. Then the snort turned into a sniff—which then turned into a stuttering intake of breath.

Uh-oh.

Before I found a new way to look uncomfortable, Kelly whisked Cassie away into the bathroom and closed the door. Why is it always the bathroom with women? Mysteries upon mysteries.

Left to my own devices, I walked out onto the porch to smoke. Hippie Phil was there, as always. I gave him a cigarette, and he nodded thanks. We both sat, puffing away in silence. He spoke first. "Woman trouble?"

I blew out a long breath and chuckled. "Brother, if you only knew."

Three cigarettes later, I went back inside and paced. What was going on in there? I sat at the table, picking at some teriyaki beef, when I heard the bathroom door open and shut again. My watch said it was just past midnight. They'd been in the bathroom for an hour and a half. Good thing I didn't have to piss.

Kelly came into the kitchen and sat opposite me. She talked in a hushed tone. "She's a sweet kid."

"Yeah."

"And she's hurt and confused to beat the band."

I already knew that, but I figured Kelly already knew that I knew. "So, what's going on?"

"It's a girl thing. She just needed another girl to talk to about it."

"So . . . we gonna have a little pajama party tonight?" I asked with my best devilish grin.

"You wish," she said.

My devilish grin deflated into an idiot frown. "Oh. Okay."

"I'll stay a bit longer, but I should be heading home sooner than later."

"Can't you stay here? With her? We have all the modern amenities. Phone. Hot and cold running water. Uh, me?" Until Kelly said she was going to leave, I hadn't realized how terrified I was of being left alone with an emotional teenage girl.

Kelly curled her lip in an evil smirk that made my devilish grin look saintly. Lord, she was cute. "A tempting offer and one that I may take you up on later this week, but it might confuse the issue at hand."

"Meaning?"

"I think that Miss Cassandra has a tiny bit of a crush on you."

I felt the blood gush up from my chest and into my head. "Oh, no."

"Oh, yes." She clearly and smugly enjoyed my discomfort.

"You . . . you can't leave me with her, then. I mean, you can't leave her . . . aw, shit."

"Life is so tough for you hunka-hunkas, isn't it?" she said, pinching my cheek. Not only was she enjoying my embarrassment, but she did Elvis better than I did, too.

"Nobody likes a smartass, Reese."

She laughed evilly as she strolled out of the kitchen.

My only recourse was to stare at her ass once again with all my might. That would show her.

Ten minutes later, Kelly was yawning and ready to go home just as Junior pulled up in front. I was relieved. Any bouncer will tell you, backup is always appreciated.

I walked Kelly out to her car. "So give me a call tomorrow and we'll make the arrangements." I leaned in to give her a kiss goodbye, but she pulled back.

"Un-unh. Cassie might be watching," she said, pressing a hug tightly against me, enjoying the tease. She winked and blew a kiss at me as she drove away.

I needed a cold, cold shower.

Instead, I went back in and sat at the table. Junior had taken Kelly's spot in the poker game. He was rearranging his cards and grumbling about the miserable hand she'd left him. "Jeez, I can't even see what the hell she was aiming for here. Can we start over?"

"The hand's already started. Play what you're dealt," I said.

He grumbled some more, but played on. Cassandra won the hand, but kept quiet. Something was making her uncomfortable. As Junior shuffled the worn cards, she said softly, "I'm sorry I zapped you."

Junior shrugged, but didn't look up from the cards. "S'okay. Besides, I got you first. It was only right that you got me, too." He started dealing the cards. "And I haven't slept that good in a long time."

Cassie smiled and took her cards off the table.

"Does this mean I get to bite you on the hand now?" I asked.

She delicately offered her hand and batted her eyes at me.

Dammit.

I grabbed her wrist and blew a wet raspberry on her knuckles.

"Ewwww!" she squealed as she wiped the spit on my shirtsleeve.

"There. We're even."

After a few more hands, Cassandra looked like she was having trouble focusing on the cards.

"You want to hit the hay?" I asked.

"Yeah," she said drowsily.

"Go ahead," I said. "Me and Junior are gonna play some more cards."

"Mmm. Okay." She yawned wide enough to swallow a football and shuffled into the living room.

"Nice kid," Junior said, as he flipped the cards out of the deck. "But it's over."

I didn't reply.

"You hearing me, Boo?" He stared into his cards as he said it, but the words were weighted with lead. "We hand her over to Pops, hand the address to Dog, and cash our check."

"I wasn't . . ." I couldn't think of a good way to end the sentence, so I just said it again. "I wasn't."

"Yes, you were."

You can't argue with someone who knows you as deeply as Junior knows me, so I didn't bother.

I reached into my pocket and handed him two of the crumpled singles.

"What the fuck is this?"

"Your half of the fee for job number two. Enjoy the riches."

His lips pressed together white. "You lousy fuck."

I lay my cards on the table. "Triple eights. What you got?"

"I hate you."

Junior and I agreed to split shifts on the recliner next to the couch Cassie was sleeping on, still not completely of the belief that Cassie wouldn't make a bolt in the middle of the night. Junior got my bed first. As I quietly stepped into the living room, I looked at Cassandra asleep on the couch. The Boy was on his knees next to her head, running his fingers gently through her hair. The black strands over her forehead didn't stir as his hands softly smoothed them over. With a sad expression, The Boy looked up at me standing in the dim yellow hallway light. His small mouth bowed downward and he shook his head.

"I know," I whispered as I pulled the throw blanket over her thin arms. "I know."

As quietly as I could, I slid the chair into the recline position and tried to read an old *Needle* magazine by the streetlight. Less than half a story in, I'd given myself a massive eyestrain headache. I closed my eyes tight, trying to will the headache away. Instead, I fell right asleep.

It certainly came as no surprise to me that I had a dirty, dirty dream about Kelly. My dream finally nude-ified the body I'd been thinking consistently about for the last week. And for once, my overtaxed and overdisturbed brain didn't disappoint by giving her va-jay-jay fangs or replacing my dick with a dachshund. All was as it was supposed to be and where it was supposed to be.

I had surrendered myself entirely to the dream when just enough reality crept in through the sleep that I realized too goddamn slowly that something was, in fact, manipulating my dick.

I bolted awake, my hands touching skin. Reactively, I pushed it off. Cassie hit the floor with a thump, falling in enough light from the street for me to see she was naked.

I covered myself, my pants unbuttoned, underwear open. "What the fuck?"

Cassie scrambled off the floor and pulled the throw blanket over herself. "I'm sorry. I'm so sorry."

"Jesus, kid. What the *fuck*?"

She pulled herself into the corner of the couch, huddling against herself under the blanket. “I’m sorry. I thought—”

“Thought what? What the fuck could you have been thinking?” I couldn’t suppress the anger in my voice. Some of it reflected my roiling shame at enjoying whatever was happening down there before reality threw a bucket of ice water on my libido.

“I thought . . . I thought you liked me.” She didn’t cry. She just said the words softly, coldly. I was expecting tears. Tears would have been expected. Tears wouldn’t have been as disturbing as the cold.

“Listen, kid—”

“Stop calling me that,” she hissed.

I heard my bedroom door slam open. “Yo, Boo! We okay?”

“All under control, Junior. I— I just rolled off the chair.”

“Dumbass. You want to switch off?”

I looked at Cassie. The kid we’d played poker with, who giggled when I blew a raspberry on her hand, was gone. Fury at my rejection burned through her eyes. She smirked. “Why don’t we do that, Boo? Why don’t you let your friend have a turn?” She let the blanket slip from one shoulder, falling below her breast.

No way in hell was I going to subject Junior to this. “All good, buddy.”

Cassie curled a lip and picked up my pack of smokes, popped one into her mouth. I shouldn’t have been surprised that she smoked, too. “Change your mind?” she whispered, leaning back, letting the blanket slide lower.

I picked her clothes up off the floor, tossed them roughly into her face. “No, I haven’t . . . *kid*. Put your clothes on and stop embarrassing yourself.”

“Fuck you,” she said. But she pulled the shirt over her head. “What’s your use for me?”

“I don’t know what you’re talking about.”

“You said Derek used me. You think my father doesn’t use me? You think he has any other purpose for me in his life than to be his pretty little photo-op? Everybody uses me. What's your use? I don't think I'm going to serve your political career; you don't want to use my pussy—"

"Stop it."

"What is it, Boo? How are you using me?"

I didn't reply, just snatched my smokes away from her and lit my own. She sat in the corner of the couch and glared at me. I sat on the recliner and glared back. I won out. Her eyelids sagged and her head drooped before she even finished the cigarette. I plucked the cigarette from her hands as she nodded off, and ground it out in the ashtray.

"Sorry. Mm . . . sorry," she murmured as she leaned over into sleep. One tear ran from her eye, tracked over her nose. I pulled the blanket over her again.

I didn't sleep any more that night.

"Wow, Boo. Rough night?" Kelly showed up early with a bag of bagels and spreads.

"Just long," I mumbled. I'd taken a quick shower before Kelly showed and still had bags under my eyes that looked like five pounds of shit stuffed into a two-pound sack. Adding to my confusion was the return of Cassandra the fourteen-year-old. When Junior finally woke, she gave him a spritely kiss on the cheek, then giggled the morning away while he showed her how to make a proper cup of coffee. She didn't look at or talk to me all that much.

We ate quietly while waiting for Donnelly to arrive. And, as Cassie happily munched on her sesame bagel, I tried to find the crack in this personality. One of them—the happy kid or the head-case young woman—had to be a façade. But for the life of me, they both felt like the same kid. The right kid. Even the wrong Cassie felt like the right kid.

When the black sedan pulled up in front of the house, I was tired. It was hot, I was feeling beat into dust, and I was ready to get this experience wrapped up.

The car sat there for a minute, engine running. The three of us watched from the window. What now? Was I supposed to walk her out and just drop her in the back seat?

Fuck you, I thought. *Come in and get her.*

Barnes finally got out of the driver's side and opened the back door. I felt bad for my standoffish behavior when I got a good look at Donnelly. It had only been days since I'd last seen him at his condo, but it could have been years. The man looked as tired as I did, worse even. The strain of Cassandra's absence had taken a far greater toll on him than he'd let on.

"Daddy," Cassandra said softly, crying. With a bolt, she was out the door, running to him. His expression when he saw her made my throat lump up. I walked to the doorway and watched the most feared lawman in Boston standing with his daughter in his arms, showering the top of her head with kisses.

Barnes walked over, face set like marble. His eyes were unreadable under his mirrored sunglasses. He held out a thin envelope—too thin to contain both the money and the information that was hinted at. Completely without expression, he said, "Nice job."

I put my fingers around the envelope, but he held on to it for a second longer.

"For a piece of shit bouncer." Barnes took back the envelope and tossed it into my chest. It fluttered to my feet.

I set my jaw.

My eyes never left his face.

Junior picked up the envelope, said, "Does this mean we're not spending Thanksgiving together?" He handed me the envelope, I'm sure in order to have his hands free.

Barnes glared. Then he went back to the car.

Cassie was looking out the window, eyes on the envelope in my hands. Then she looked at me, her eyes radiating hurt and understanding.

She finally knew what my use for her was. I wanted to say something. To tell her she was seeing it all wrong. I didn't say anything, even goodbye.

Was she wrong?

The ride pulled away, taking them back into their own world.

Never even got a goodbye.

"Money!" Junior yelled, shocking me from my guilt.

"I'm going to use the little girl's room and let you boys have your moment," Kelly said with a smirk.

"What kind of moment do you think we're going to have?"

"With that much enthusiasm, I'm not sure," she said, walking into the apartment.

"Lemme see it," Junior said, half-running to the steps.

"Here." I handed him the envelope.

He held the envelope tenderly, as though he couldn't decide whether to tear it open or start tongue-kissing the flap. "I can't open it," he said.

"Give it to me, then."

"No! No. No, I'll do it." He ran the envelope under his nose, breathing it in. "Mmm. Nothing like the smell of Cheddar in the morning. Smells like . . . victory." Carefully, he ran a finger under the fold and pulled it open. With the same care, he pulled two pieces of paper from the envelope. He chucked the one that wasn't a cashier's check to the ground.

"Dude," he said with more than a little awe.

"What?"

"Dude."

"Dude?"

"This is one big check, my friend." He turned the check around. On the paper was the amount of $30,000. Five grand more than agreed upon. More money than we'd ever seen, much less had, in our entire lives.

I picked up the note that Junior had tossed. All it said was:

I hope the extra $5000 covers any expenses.
I am in your debt.
Thank you. You should receive the information
we discussed from my people within two weeks.

Unsigned, of course.

Two weeks. Two more weeks for information I'd waited twenty years for. What was two weeks, right? It felt like a fucking lifetime. Again.

"How soon can we cash this?" Junior asked.

I crumpled up the paper and tried to hide my . . . hell, I didn't know what I was feeling, or why I was trying to hide it. Was it disappointment?

"I'll bring it to the bank tomorrow." Junior didn't have a bank account. Never trusted them. Far as I knew, he kept his money stuffed in a mattress.

"Because, frankly? I want to spread it on the floor, roll around in it nekkid, then rub one out while staring in Ben Franklin's eyes."

"Don't ever ask me to break a hundie for you ever again."

"Brother, from now on twenties are for lighting cigarettes." Junior's eyes flicked to my doorway. "Can't help but notice you got one visitor left."

"And?"

"And I'm going home and going back to bed." Junior clasped my shoulder, looking at me like I imagine a proud father would. "You fuck her, Boo."

I couldn't help but laugh. "Thanks, Junior. But I think she's gotta decide to—"

"Fuck her blue, my friend." He clapped my shoulder and walked backward to Miss Kitty, giving me the double-forefinger gunslinger.

"Dick."

"Fuck her blue," he said one more time in an Irish whisper and climbed back into the car.

When I walked back inside, Kelly was looking at me the way she had at Donnelly the night in the loft. There was admiration there, but there was something breathless on top of it now.

She stood and kissed me hard, pulling me down by the front of my shirt. Our tongues met as she put her hands under my shirt and brushed her fingers along my stomach.

I fumbled with the buttons on her blouse for a moment and couldn't take it anymore. I tore the shirt open, buttons popping off and clattering to the floor.

What the hell, I could buy her a new one.

She pulled back, dug her fingers along the neck of my T-shirt, and ripped it down across my chest, laughing.

I stopped.

She stopped.

Stunned, she looked at the vicious patchwork of scar tissue that made up my torso. The long incision scar that started six inches under my Adam's apple and ran to a point just above my navel. The burns. The smear of ruined flesh that took up a large part of the upper left side of my chest.

Hot shame flooded my cheeks at her touch. She looked me in the eyes, cupped my chin, and kissed me deeper while pushing me toward the bedroom.

Clumsily, I pulled off my jeans and underwear in one quick hopping motion that almost sent me toppling. Laughing, Kelly rolled back on the bed and gracefully slipped out of her skirt and panties. God bless her.

I kneeled at the edge of the bed, and she sat up to draw me on top of her. Our eyes locked. Her lip curled up in that sly smile. "My tough guy," she said. Lying back, she took me in her hand and gently glided me inside. She let out a small purring sound as I started rocking myself into her.

She turned me over and straddled me, forcing me deeper and deeper. I luxuriated in the smell of her, the skin beneath my hands, the tickle of her hair on my nose as I kissed underneath her ear.

It was a close one, but I managed to hang in there and Kelly groaned just before I did. Ain't I a champ?

She wasn't blue by the end, but I still felt pretty damned good about myself.

We lay on top of the sheets. I rested on my back and Kelly had her arms and legs wrapped around me from the side. I couldn't help staring at her naked bone-white skin. Softly, I ran my fingers back and forth over her curves, like lying with a soft marble statue. I realized she didn't have any tattoos on her. She was the first woman I'd ever been with, that I'd seen naked, who had none. The uniform purity of her skin fascinated me.

I inhaled our mingling scents. The day was turning hot and humid again, but there wasn't any discomfort as we lay together, sticky sweat dripping off us. I wouldn't have traded that position for the whole world and half the moon.

She lay her head on my left shoulder, her breath tickling the sparse chest hair that determinedly poked through the thick scar tissue. Her fingers traced the outline of the pink disfigurements.

She didn't ask.

They all asked.

I didn't want to tell any of them before. I didn't feel like telling her yet, either. We both just lay there silently until we dropped into sleep, her hand resting on the scar tissue over my heart.

I awoke with a sharp intake of breath. Kelly was towel-drying her hair in the long mirror suspended on the inside of my bedroom door. I rolled to my side and admired her nudity as she dried herself. She caught my staring in the mirror and smiled. "What?"

"What, what?"

"You're wearing a face."

"I have a face most days. This is mah thinking face."

"Thinking about what?"

"If I told you, you'd have to shower all over again." I wiggled my eyebrows at her.

We showered together the second time.

She was scrubbing my back when she said, "I was thinking about getting a tattoo."

I couldn't explain to her why I laughed so hard.

After the shower, she gathered up her things in a rush. She poked and lifted objects around my room, looking for a missing something or other.

"What's your rush there, Reese?"

"I do have to show up at the campaign office at some point today. Have you seen my shoe?"

I halfheartedly looked around. "Nope." I flopped back onto my bed, the beaded water cooling my skin in the slowly moving air.

Kelly found one shoe under a pillow. "Jeez, now I have to run home and finish my hair."

"What's wrong with it?"

She shot me a look.

"What?" I asked. "Isn't the wet look back?"

"Yeah. And if it dries in this humidity, it'll look like a Brillo pad."

"You girls and your doings, I swear . . ."

"Well, maybe if my shirt still had some buttons on it . . ."

"Don't blame me. Blame your sultry ways. I couldn't control myself."

She chucked the pillow at me as she hopped on one foot, putting her shoe on. "Get up, put on a pair of underwear, and walk me out like a gentleman."

"Wasn't it my roguish devil-may-care demeanor that attracted you to me in the first place?" I said, pulling on a pair of reasonably clean shorts. She just kept muttering to herself as she hustled her way out.

In the doorway, she tried to give me a quick and cursory goodbye kiss, but I held tight and planted a kiss I wanted her to feel in her toes.

She pulled back forcefully. "No! Oh, no you don't. I have to get to work. I'll call you tonight. You can buy me a fabulous dinner with your newfound wealth." One more quick peck and she was off. I watched her car pull around the corner.

With two spectacular sexual exercises lumped on top of my brutal lack of sleep, I felt like I could nap until the Bruins won another Stanley Cup.

I dropped back down on my bed, her smell still in my sheets. I drew in a deep breath of it and smiled. Rolling over, my hand felt something silky under a fold in the comforter. "Well, I'll be damned," I muttered. In her haste and confusion, Ms. Reese had left behind her frilly little blue panties. She said she had to go home to finish her hair. Should I call her and let her know she was air-surfing under her skirt? Could make for an interesting day at the office for her.

I must have drifted off for a little while, because my doorbell chimed, waking me from a wonderful dream about a world without panties.

Dammit.

I opened the door with a smile, expecting to barter for the return of her drawers.

Instead, I got a gun barrel in my face.

I froze in confusion.

The gun slowly lowered from my nose, and I got a brief look at the face at the other end of the arm. Dirty blond hair cut in a flattop. Pale skin and one blue eye. The other was a milky cataract, a bright scar from the corner of the socket worming over the ear like a pink garter snake. He stood a couple inches over me and wore an expensive-looking suit on his wiry frame.

The stranger in my doorway with the gun pointed at me beamed like we were long-lost friends. He was still smiling when he pulled the trigger.

Bang.

Chapter Seventeen

Gravity can be a damned mean bitch.

The gun barked, and my right leg flew back and away. My left foot slipped sideways and I came down hard, smacking the side of my face against the foyer wall as I dropped.

I lay facedown on the hardwood, gritting my teeth so hard a molar snapped like a popcorn kernel. A hot wetness spread underneath me as I lay there, staring at my shooter's expensive shoes. I hoped it was blood. *Please God,* I thought, *if I'm gonna die right here and now, don't let me piss myself.* My whole body shook uncontrollably. I knew I was shot, but it didn't hurt.

Yet.

Then I felt the cool metal of the barrel pressed against my forehead. I closed my eyes tight against the impact I was sure would follow.

Nothing.

A gently brogued voice said, "Be easy, boy. Be easy if this was a kill. You're lucky the word was just to hurt you bad."

A piece of paper being shoved into my hand, dry fingers closing my fingers around it.

I opened my eyes to see the expensive shoes walking away.

Then the pain came.

Boy-motherfucking-howdy.

It sliced through me like somebody had laid me open with a straight razor beginning behind my knee and cutting up into the back of my skull. I screamed with the sudden intensity of it, clutching my leg. When the initial shock of pain subsided, I unclenched my fingers from the blood-smeared paper. An address, mine, handwritten in block letters in black ink. Underneath it, another address.

Kelly's address.

In pure panic and rage, I leapt to my feet, paying instantly for the stupidity. My dead leg buckled, sending me crashing back to the floor, bright new eruptions of pain blinding out the world. I almost passed out right there, but the frenzy overrode everything else. I pushed myself up on shaking rubber muscles and propped myself against the wall, weight balanced on the leg that wasn't shot.

A door opened above me, and Phil trotted down the stairs. "Jeez, man. What was that sound?" He poked his head in my doorway. "What the hell are you—holy shit!"

"H-help me," was all I could say. My wires were scrambled. Too much pain. Too much fear. Too much. Too much.

"Holy shit!" Phil's skin tone went to chalk. "Dude, you need an ambulance."

"No!" I said, louder than I meant. Phil jumped back at the ferocity in my voice. "Does . . . that van drive?"

"Yeah. I think so. But wouldn't an ambulance be better right now?" He took a couple steps toward me, and I grabbed him by the shirt and slammed him into the wall.

"Start the fucking thing. Now!" I threw him toward the door and out. I only had one leg to push off from, but it gave me enough leverage to give him a good launching. I pitched forward with my own momentum and came down on my face again. White lights danced before my eyes. There was no time for clear thought, but I really had to stop falling the fuck down.

As the hippie van's engine coughed over and over, I had a minor epiphany. The cell phone was only a few feet away, charging in the living room. I hopped and dragged myself toward the phone at a frantic clip.

Pulling myself onto the couch, I saw the thick trail of blood zig-zagging in my wake.

Shit, that's a lot, I thought.

I didn't want to look at my knee. I snatched the phone off the side table and hit the autodial for Kelly's cell.

Ringing.

Ringing.

Ringing. Motherf—

Connection!

"Hi, this is Kelly. Sorry I can't answer your call right—"

"Fuck!" I shouted. "Fuck! Fuck!"

Kelly's home number was next in the menu. It rang twice. "Come on . . . come on," I muttered.

It rang a third time and Kelly answered, a bit out of breath. "Hello?"

"Kelly. Call the cops."

"What? Boo?"

"Lock your door and call the cops right now." The words were getting harder and harder to produce. My lips felt shot full of Novocain.

"Boo, what's—"

"Right now, baby. Please."

"Tell me what's happening!" Her voice rose in fear.

"I got shot." Gotta admit: Them's some strange words to hear yourself say.

"Oh my God, Boo! Who shot you? Where are you?"

"I'm on my way. Don't answer the door."

"Boo—"

"Please, Kelly. Just lock your door and call the cops." I hung up before she asked any more questions I really did not have the time for.

I tried Junior's number, but my blood-slicked fingers kept slipping off the small keypad. I took a deep breath and collected myself enough to find the right numbers.

"Wuzzah?" came Junior's sleepy voice.

"Junior, I'm shot. I got shot." It still felt weird saying it. My voice was calm, but it rang in my ears like I was in an echo chamber.

"Huh?"

"Get to 116 Mt. Vernon!"

"Sorry, think I got something crazy stuck in my ear. Did you just say you got shot?"

"Please, Junior. I think he might be going after Kelly." Panic started chewing my gut anew.

"I'm out." Junior hung up. Done and done.

From a distance that seemed too far to be the driveway, the van heaved a mighty cough and started.

Phil came running around the hall into the living room. "She's running. Oh God." He got a good look at my knee and promptly turned eight shades of green. "Oh my god."

I reached out to him. "Help me get up," I said, slurring. I sounded drunk. That couldn't be good. My eyes were getting heavy.

Phil slung my arm around his shoulders and helped me to the van. He put me on my back through the rear doors and ran around to the front. "Where are we going? What hospital? Where is the hospital? Jeez, I don't know where the hospital is!" Phil sounded one notch down the panic meter from where my needle was buried.

"Mt. Vernon. Just . . . just drive to Mt. Vernon Street." The dancing white lights were getting bigger. And they'd brought friends. Not good. I was slipping into shock.

"I know where Mt. Vernon is, but there's no hospital." From my position, the upside-down Phil turned, confused. "And, uh—you're in your underpants."

"Drive, you stupid hippie jackass!" I shouted through clenched teeth.

Phil hit the gas and shot out of the driveway with a screech of tires. He turned a hard left onto Cambridge, centrifugal force flipping me upside down and bouncing my forehead off the van wall. Another explosion of pain shook my nervous system, and I fought back the nausea wringing my stomach.

I looked at the cell phone. Who else could I call?

Twitch. I could call Twitch.

"I don't have a license, man," Phil whined hysterically. "The van doesn't have any plates. What if we get pulled over?"

The van chugged along. Not fast enough. Then I saw Phil had the gas pedal to the floor. We were going as fast as the beat-up van was capable.

I tried to answer him, but somebody had filled my tongue with sand. The lights slow-danced and grouped into one blob—a blob that was spreading over my vision. *Not yet*, I thought. *Not yet, goddammit.* I bit my lower lip hard enough to draw blood, trying to push back the shock. My brain was too disconnected to feel it, like I was biting into somebody else.

I anchored myself, palms flat on either side of me, as the van rocked with each turn. Phil was still yapping protests, but I'd stopped listening. *Stay awake.*

Stay awake.

Flowing, watery black curtains.

Stay awake.

Where is she?

"Where is who?" asked a puzzled Phil.

Don't you hit her!

"Hit who? What are you talking about?"

Was I talking?

Where are my pants?

The van stopped. I reached up, grabbing the seatbelt draped over the passenger seat, and pulled myself into the seat. "Whaz going on," I slurred. "Why'd we stop?"

"Um. Red light." Phil pointed at the traffic light.

The phone rang. I hit the button.

"Boo?" Kelly was panicked. "Somebody's here. Oh God. Somebody's banging on my door!"

My heart convulsed in fear. "Don't answer it. Call the cops."

Kelly screamed. "He's kicking in the door!" I heard wood crunch in the background.

The phone beeped three times. Disconnected.

With the strength I had left, I brought my good leg around the gearshift and stomped on Phil's right foot, flooring the van. Phil screamed as we jumped forward into the intersection. Horns blared and tires squealed as the cars shot around us. We were almost clear when somebody clipped us in the rear and sent the poor, abused van into a spin.

Phil screeched a birdcall in pitch-perfect harmony to the shrieking tires. He held onto the operatic howl until the van came to a stop.

"Dude!" he said. "That was so unfuckingcool."

I didn't know where we were. Blurry. Whole world gone blurry.

Some guy in a Patriots hat smacked Phil's window. "You stupid fuck! Get out of the van!" Must be the guy who hit us.

"Oh God," Phil yelped.

"We facing the right way?" I asked.

"Yeah, but—"

I stomped on the gas again. I saw a Patriots hat go flying up and away in the rearview. Hope we didn't run over the guy's feet.

Phil resumed his screaming. "This is leaving the scene of an accident! *This is leaving the scene of an accident! We can't leave the scene of an accident!*"

For a moment I was afraid he was going to bail, leaving me to drive from the passenger seat.

Two blocks south of Mt. Vernon, sirens ripped the air and two black-and-whites, lights blazing, blew through the intersection ahead of us.

They were heading straight for Kelly's apartment complex.

"We're going too fast!" Phil shrieked.

Phil was right, but I didn't realize it soon enough. When we got to Mt. Vernon, I grabbed the steering wheel and turned hard. I lifted up out of my seat as the van pulled the corner on two wheels.

Then one.

Then none.

Oops.

The van's left panel slammed to the asphalt and skidded, metal howling. I flew backward onto the left side of the van, which was now the floor. Phil screamed in falsetto as we tumbled. Part of the panel tore away against the street, almost sucking me under the van as we flipped over again. We came to a sudden bone-rattling stop, sideways and into a telephone pole. I hit the opposite wall, whacking my head with a bang.

I threw my body against the rear doors and burst out, rolling into the street. The white blobs of light were growing dark. Phil was off like a hippie Usain Bolt, darting between two houses and vaulting a backyard fence. Cops were running at me, guns drawn. I could hear yelling, but they all sounded like Charlie Brown's teacher.

There was Junior. He was on the ground too, facing me, arms handcuffed behind his back. His face was a mask of pain, and I could see blood on his shoulder. He was yelling in the same tongue as the cops.

I tried to move. Tried to crawl. Nothing. Tried to move anything. I was paralyzed. I didn't see Kelly anywhere. I couldn't even scream her name. I was out of time, out of blood, and out of fight. The only thing I was in was my fucking underpants.

So tired.

The white-lights gang-rushed me and drew me down, down, down into a sweet nothing.

Where is she?

Beep. Beep. Beep.

I woke up to that annoying sound. Everything hurt. Everything hurt so bad I didn't want to open my eyes. I wanted to slip back into that nothing.

Kelly.

I opened my lids and found myself staring into a pair of brown-yellow wolf's eyes a foot from my own. The rest of the head came into focus. Ivory blond hair. Pink skin. I blinked to adjust the color levels before I realized who I was looking at.

Twitch.

Chapter Eighteen

And then there was Twitch.

I remember his entrance into St. Gabe's even more vividly than Ollie's spectacular debut. Junior and I were driving mops around the foyer when the batch of newbies got led in. I didn't like looking at the new kids. Their fear, hurt, and loneliness was as solid in the air as the mop in my hands. Their pain reminded me of my own.

Junior had no such problem. I remember his words, too. "Aw shit," he said. "This kid is gonna be meat."

Sure enough, there was the meat. He was twelve years old, but he could pass for younger, he was that small. And lord, was he pink. Twitch looked like he was made out of milk and cotton candy. I felt bad for him, but there was only so much I could do for a kid who had a bull's-eye tattooed on him by natural selection. His natural weaknesses would be noticed. Nobody wanted to be noticed at St. Gabe's.

His left eye fluttered in a spastic twitch, breaking our gaze, and I saw the rest of the newbies. Two of the smaller kids were crying. Some tried to look their hardest, which isn't that hard between the ages of seven and seventeen. All the weaknesses I feared in myself came flooding in.

Then there was Twitch. He looked right at me, *into* me, and Robert Shaw's voice from *Jaws* echoed in my mind. "He's got dead eyes. Like a doll's eyes."

No prerequisite fear. No heartbreak. Just cold, baby, cold.

We absorbed Twitch into our crew. At first, some of the boys thought it was charity for the kid. I knew better. I knew, deep down, that I wanted the kid with the wolf's eyes on my team. Because I never ever wanted him to be an enemy.

All in all, he was safe at St. Gabe's, and the world was safe from Twitch while he was there.

Twitch's pink lips curled in a joyful smile. "So, who am I shooting?"

I tried to get up and fell back to the bed, jabs of pain peppering my whole body. I had more tubes in me than Radio Shack. I sat up again, trying to pull needles and tubes out of my arms, but my body seemed only peripherally under my control.

"Whoa, whoa," Twitch said. His voice hadn't dropped a lick during puberty. He grabbed my shoulders and forced me back down. "Don't want to be pulling those out yet, Boo. Especially not the morphine drip."

"Guhhh," I rasped. My throat was full of cotton balls dipped in lye. "Guhhhh," I repeated, trying to stand again.

Twitch's birdlike hands pressed me flat against the bed. I was so weak I couldn't force off a guy who would lose a wrestling match to a gimpy kitten.

"Kelly," I croaked. It hurt.

"That the brunette?"

I nodded. That hurt, too.

"She's okay. Scared from here to bejeezus, but she's fine." The corner of Twitch's eye spasmed in a wink.

The relief brought tears to my own eyes. "Water."

Twitch handed me a red plastic cup that felt like a barbell in my hands. I emptied it in two huge gulps. The water backflipped a few times in my empty stomach, but stayed down.

I cleared my throat. "Junior. Where's Junior?"

"Cops are talking to him."

"What happened?"

"I only got here in the last act, man. All I know is Junior called me from lockup and told me to get over here."

"He all right? He was bleeding."

"He'll live." Twitch giggled. "He got to the girl's house and heard screaming when he knocked. When he kicked in the door, the psycho broad whacked him with a mace or something."

Kelly must have popped him with Spike. That's my girl. "Where is she?"

"She's in the lobby. Cops won't let her in yet. You gonna eat that?" Twitch pointed to a tray on the bedside with a dried-out turkey sandwich, a mini can of ginger ale, and a deadly looking Jell-O brick.

"Go nuts. Why won't they let her in?"

"They want to talk to you first. Cops already talked to her. She's still pretty spooked." So far, so good. Nobody, including Junior, knew a damned thing to tell the cops. It was going to stay that way. "You even got a patrolman standing outside the door." Twitch held up the patrolman's badge. "See?"

"For chrissakes, Twitch." On top of everything else, Twitch was a master of sleight of hand—pickpocketing and the like. We'd all learned a lot of shady shit at The Home. But while the majority of us fought for the rest of our lives to erase the fucked-up habits The Home carved into us, Twitch continued to hone his long after his release. Then something hit me. "Wait a minute, how did you get in here?

Twitch smiled, and his eye jumped again. "The miracles of technology. Ollie made it in ten minutes." He reached in his pocket and pulled out a perfect Massachusetts license. "I told them I was your twin brother." I looked closer. The name on the license read Marcus Malone. The birth date matched my own.

"And they believed this?"

"The more ridiculous the bullshit, the harder it is to disprove. What were they going to say?"

He had me there. "I'm very disturbed that worked."

Twitch shrugged. "I'm a disturbing guy."

"True that, Marcus."

As Twitch stuck the license back into his pocket, the butt of a pistol peeked out from his waistband.

"Your dick is out," I said.

"Oh, shit." Twitch pulled his shirt back over the gun. "That reminds me, watch your hands."

"Why do I have to watch my hands?" I said, suspicious and weary.

"I got a present for you."

Uh-oh. Twitch and his goddamn presents.

"Look under there." Twitch nodded at the pillow, excited to give me his gift. Twitch only gets that excited about weaponry.

With more than a little dread, I reached underneath. My hands closed around something metal, and I pulled out a snub-nosed .38. I hate guns. I've always hated guns. Twitch knew that.

"You like it?"

I let my glare be my answer.

I held the gun out to him on open palms, barely able to hold it in my quaking hands. "Take it with you."

"Hey, you know the saying. Better to have it and not need it than need it and not have it."

"Yeah, yeah. Didn't you say there was a cop right outside my door?"

"First of all, if a nutjob like me can make my way in, anybody can. Second, how do you know it wasn't a cop who capped you in the first place?"

Good point. Then I remembered the scarred face. "I don't think he was a cop."

Twitch plucked a corner off the green Jell-O brick and sucked it wetly into his mouth. "You ever see the guy before?"

"Never, but I think I know the wheres and the whys." I filled Twitch in, including names. If there are two things Twitch does well, one of them is keeping information to himself. The other is causing havoc. He sat and listened, his only response a rippling eyelid now and then.

Then I got to the point where I got shot. "I opened the door and a guy in a suit has a gun to my face, and he had—"

"Wait a minute. A suit?" He stopped mid-chew on a Jell-O grape.

"Yeah."

"Aw, shit."

"What?"

"Suits aren't good." Double twitch.

"Why?"

"You're planning on shooting somebody, they're going to bleed, right?" He was explaining it to me like I was in kindergarten.

I remembered the serpentine path of blood across my hardwood. "I guess so."

"Well, they are. Why you gonna wear a suit and get blood all over it?"

"I don't know." And I didn't like what he was implying.

"You don't wear a suit unless you know what you're doing, have good aim, and know what's gonna come squirting out where and when you pull the trigger." Twitch made a gun with index finger and fired with his thumb. "In other words, you've probably done it lots of times before."

"I still don't get it." I couldn't imagine Snake having the juice for a pro.

"It's not for you to get. You've been warned. The note was a scare tactic."

Fucking worked. The side effect was that it pissed me off, too. "When I get my hands around that one-eyed fucker, I'm gonna pull out his good eye with my teeth."

Twitch stopped chewing, his eyelid fluttering like a hummingbird on meth. "You say one eye?"

Shit.

"Don't even tell me he had a blind eye."

"Why do I get the distinct impression you're going to make a bad day worse?"

Twitch's baby-pink skin went light pink, which is as close as he gets to going pale. He ran a finger across his temple. "And a long scar along here?"

I nodded. "That's the guy. How did you know that?"

"Holy fuck! Dude, you are one lucky man." Twitch's burst of exuberance sent tiny flecks of Jell-O from his mouth across my legs. He wiped the green mess into the sheet. "Sorry."

"How in sweet fuck-all am I lucky?"

"Lucky that you're not in a meat locker in the basement."

Before I could ask questions, the door handle shifted with a click. Fluidly, instinctively, Twitch slipped behind the opening door. As Barnes came walking in, Twitch slid neatly behind him and out as the door closed. Barnes never even knew he was in the room.

"So," Barnes said.

"So," I croaked.

"You've got some detectives on your ass over this." He clucked his tongue in mock pity. He probably wished the bullet had gone into my face.

"Why?"

"Why?" Barnes huffed a laugh. "Gunshot wound. Always gonna be questions asked where gunshots are concerned. That and a panicked young lady who works for the DA calling the cops, a battalion of cruisers, a smashed van with no driver or plates, and two bleeding jackasses at the scene. You wanna ask me why again?"

"I got shot? No wonder my leg hurts."

"Don't try to pull that shit. I made a couple calls, and the detectives agreed to let me talk to you first. So, what happened?"

"I got shot, apparently." The truth didn't exactly set me free, but it did loosen up some capillaries in Barnes's head.

"You wanna tell me who?"

"I think they were Canadian."

"Canadian?"

"They had French accents. I had a problem with them at the bar. Must've followed me home for some payback." The IV needle was starting to itch.

"And they waited until the next morning?"

"Those Canucks are a patient lot, eh?"

Barnes wiped his eyes in frustration. "So, you expect me to go back to these detectives—who are doing us both a favor here—and tell them a gang of Canadians followed you home, waited all night for you to get up, then shot you."

"Sure."

"And these Canadians went after Kelly because . . ." He held onto the last syllable, waiting for me to answer. I didn't. It was too early in the morning, and I'd been shot. My tank was low on smartass juice. "*Because*?"

"Because of the wonderful things she does?" No, wait. Had a little left.

Barnes grabbed the front of my johnnie and slammed me back onto the bed. I was too weak to offer much resistance. "Play your games, Malone. Play your little fucking games."

"Get your fucking hands off me, Barnes." I grabbed his thumb and twisted it back. The knuckle popped, straining. "You want to dance sometime, we'll dance. You want to get hard on me when I'm too weak to stand? I'll still rip your fucking thumb off." I wrenched the thumb harder, close to the breaking point. Barnes didn't so much as flinch, even though it must have hurt like hell.

"Let's do that sometime." Murderous fires blazed in his eyes. "Soon." With that, he let me go and I released his thumb. He exited, trying to slam the door, but the hydraulics just hissed violently as he stormed out. It was nice to know we were still buds.

My heart was still pounding, hands shaking, five minutes after he'd left. Barnes could have jacked my ass up into the next millennium, if he'd chosen to. Cop right outside the door or not. Shit, the cop probably would have given him a hand.

I figured Donnelly would be worried about damage control. The bullet wasn't an act of God. I'm sure they wished I'd come up with a more plausible line of bullshit to cover their asses, but I was doped up and pissed off. Let them cover their own asses if they needed to. I wasn't lying for them. I was lying for Cassie. Besides, fuck Canada.

The rest was the standard battery of bullshit. Not satisfied with what Barnes told them, another detective came in and tried the threatening approach. I stuck to my story about the rogue gang of gun-toting Canadians. Twitch's theory about disproving an absurd lie seemed to hold true. The second cop didn't seem any happier with my answers than Barnes was, but what were they going to do?

The doctors grudgingly gave me my walking papers. Junior brought me a set of clothes, which was an improvement on the pantsless state I'd arrived in.

Armed with a pair of crutches and a prescription for painkillers, I hobbled out with slightly more strength and muscle control than a rubber chicken. What I needed more than anything was to get back out and rip the world a new asshole. I planned on starting with Snake and Scarface.

Chapter Nineteen

It's funny how sometimes the worst idea can seem like brilliance to a bunch of liberal hippies living as far away as possible from the problem they're trying to help. Camp Freshwood was one of those ideas. Every summer for two weeks, we got trudged deep into western Massachusetts for some fresh air and macramé lessons. Sounds good, don't it?

Two to three different Homes occupied parts of Camp Freshwood at any given time. Still sound good? We were supposed to make friends interacting with others in the same situation as us. Guess what? We hated each other. We weren't peers; we were soldiers all thrown abruptly into one another's company, and we all had something to prove. The only arts and crafts I learned were the art of war and the craft of being crafty.

In the seven years I fought in the wars of Camp Freshwood, three kids mysteriously drowned, countless others got bizarre food poisoning. One kid "fell" off a cliff, and another hung himself with a macramèd noose. I shit you not.

But nothing compared with the summer Twitch vacationed at Camp Freshwood. Incidentally, it was the last summer of that ill-planned social experiment.

We were hardcore kids, but we were still a step behind the Roxbury boys. They were just a little bit bigger, a little bit meaner, and carried weightier chips on their shoulders. They'd also earned themselves quite a rep as a gleeful bunch of ass-rapers. That summer, we got shifted into the camp at the same time.

Twitch caught the first offensive, of course. They found him in the woods. Alone. What he was doing out there alone, I'll never know. I'll never ask, either. I didn't even know he was gone from the group. At mess hall that night, in he limped, wincing each time he brought his left leg around. As he made his way over to our table, I heard chuckling from the Roxbury table. One of the boys made kissy sounds. A thin line of blood dribbled down the back of Twitch's thigh, one sock soaked bright red.

Later that night, the rest of us tossed around ideas for payback. Twitch sat apart from us in the corner, head between his hands like he was trying to hold his skull together. We all went to bed, ready to start the day fresh for blood.

We never got the chance.

All that night, rain beat down on the camp, pounding a wet cadence onto the corrugated metal sheets that passed for roofing. Wet and miserable in our cots, we were woken by a wild-eyed counselor on the edge of full-blown panic. We were herded quickly onto a waiting school bus. The sobbing middle-aged hippie didn't give us an explanation until the bus was tearing down the highway.

Apparently, three of the Roxbury campers snuck out of their cabin during the night. The only thing the staff, the State Police, and the local ME could figure was that they encountered an animal, possibly a bear. What they never figured out was why the bear ripped those kids into chunks but didn't bother eating any.

That morning, Twitch's shoes had an awful lot of mud on them. And his face had an awful lot of smile.

To this day, I believe Twitch gives me far too much credit for his safety at St. Gabe's. I have no doubt of his love for me and Junior; his devotion to us is absolute. Twitch would die for us, if it came to that. So despite him being a sociopath, a borderline psychopath, and pretty much any other path I can think of, his was the safest place I could think of to deposit Kelly until we could get shit cleared up.

⁂

Thank god the teenage Puerto Rican gang that lived on the floor below Twitch wasn't home when we got there. I had Phil haunting the front of my house; Twitch had Boriquas. Nothing had ever escalated into physical conflict, but they got their ya-yas making visitors uncomfortable through stare-downs and low-voiced Spanish threats. Kelly was already at nerves' end, and I didn't need a tête-à-tête with those punks to bring the rest of her roof crashing down.

Twitch jumped out of Junior's car as we pulled up. "Um, could you wait here a sec?"

"What's up?" I asked.

A blush crept up Twitch's pale neck as he cast a nervous glance at Kelly. "It's, um, kinda messy up there, and I want to straighten it up a bit. I wasn't expecting company." Twitch's eyelid had been stuttering nervously for the entire drive.

"No more than five minutes," I said tossing an obvious glance with raised eyebrows to the empty front porch.

When he was out of earshot, Kelly gave me a watery-eyed look so full of tension it broke my heart. "What am I doing here?"

I took her hand in mine, trying to meet her eyes with a hard confidence I wasn't feeling. "Listen, sweetie. Me and Junior need to get this straightened out."

"But the police—"

"No. The police don't give a shit. This is between me and . . ." I didn't have a way to finish that sentence without letting Kelly in on more than I wanted. "I just need you to stay here with Twitch. You'll be safe here." Relatively speaking.

"For how long?"

"I need you to stay with him for a couple days until we can figure out exactly what's going on."

Her eyes glistened, and she hugged me hard. Fear radiated off her skin.

"I'm sorry I got you into this mess," I said. "Until we fix this, I need to know you're protected. You'll be safe here."

Kelly squeezed my hand and nodded. "I'm sure you know what you're doing. I trust you."

Holy Moses on a trampoline, I wished *I* felt like I knew what I was doing.

"Hey," Junior said. "How come nobody's apologized for perforating my fucking arm?"

She laughed through her teary eyes. "Junior, I am heartily sorry for having perforated your arm." Then, mockingly sweet, "You want me to kiss it better?"

"Nah. Probably try to bite it off." Junior turned to cover his smile. He sniffed and rubbed his flattened nose. "Loony broad."

Twitch's apartment was the second floor walk-up of a two-family house. We marched up the thin stairway like a line of ants, with me on point. I was as nervous as Twitch was about the condition of his apartment. At least I could poke my head in first to see if he'd missed anything incriminating. Like a body or two.

Much to my surprise, not only was the apartment in fair order, but it was pretty clean as well.

Spartan would be the best way to describe Twitch's decor. A small color TV on a footlocker stood as his entertainment center. For furniture, he had a leopard print futon and a blue futon mattress rolled up against the wall.

Twitch smiled nervously as Kelly gave his apartment the feminine once over. "Anybody want a soda?" he offered, his tic working so hard it nearly caused a breeze. Poor Twitch. He wasn't exactly a masterful conversationalist and entertainer. Maybe I should have brought Pictionary.

Kelly stared at Twitch's fish tank and the one fish inside. Out of the corner of my eye, I saw the edge of a *Swank* magazine poking out from under a closet door. As smoothly as I could, I stepped over and nudged the corner back under with my cane.

"This fish is beautiful," she said.

Twitch beamed, his face that of a little boy at show-and-tell. "He's a Siamese fighting fish. Named him Roadhouse."

"How do you know he's a he?"

"Got a *huge* cock."

Junior howled a laugh.

I winced so hard, I nearly cramped up.

To my surprise, Kelly guffawed. My respect for the girl kicked up another notch. I suppose I still had some residual filter on her from my first impression.

"Excuse me," Kelly said, "but where's the ladies room?"

"Down the hall on the left," Twitch said, pointing.

I leaned over to him and said under my breath, "You do have TP, right?"

"We're in luck. Just got a fresh roll yesterday."

The last time I'd visited the apartment, I made do with an old *Boston Globe*. The fewer indignities Kelly had to suffer, the better. Wiping with the comics page is a pretty big one, in my book. Unless you're using *Cathy*.

A shriek pierced the air, rising in pitch like an air-raid siren. We all bolted down the hallway to find Kelly waving her hands and dancing a heebie-jeebie in the doorway on the right.

"*Ohmigod, ohmigod, ohmigod,*" she babbled, her face the color of pasta dough.

"Wrong door! Wrong door!" I yelled.

One of my greatest hopes had been that she could spend a day or two without finding the pet room. Instead, she stumbled into it in less than thirty seconds.

In that wrong room, Twitch had two ball pythons and a six-and-a-half-foot long albino boa. Iggy, the iguana, rounded out the zoo.

And then there were the rats.

To feed his babies, Twitch kept a large fish tank full of rats that he bred himself. The tank was brimming with squirming rodentia that day. They all moved in one big, putrid mass of red eyes, oily fur, and teeth. Kelly gasped and made a horrified gurgling sound.

I knew how she felt. My skin crawled just looking at the snakes, never mind the rats. The first time I'd been shown the collection, I let out a scream just one octave down from hers.

"Uh, the bathroom is on the other left," Twitch said.

"Can I tell you how much I hate rats?" Kelly's teeth chattered as she sipped from the tea Junior was kind enough to go get at the packie for her. At least she'd stopped rocking and hugging her knees.

Junior stayed with her when Twitch motioned me into his room.

"Ollie's working research on your shooter," Twitch said.

"What kind of research?"

"He's checking newspaper records, police records. Cross-search kinda stuff. If he is who I think he is, you might want some of this." He lifted his mattress off the box spring. Sandwiched between the two was a selection of armaments that would have made Tom Clancy skeet in his boxers. Besides an assortment of handguns, I recognized an AK-47, a sawed-off Mossberg, a small Uzi, and some type of high-tech sniper rifle, laser sight and all.

"Jesus, Twitch, you expecting an ATF raid or just Armageddon?"

"I expect everything." He waved his hand over the guns like a game show host displaying his fabulous, fabulous prizes. "Take your pick. They're all untraceable."

Against my better judgment, I had the gun Twitch had snuck into the hospital tucked in the back of my pants. "I'm good with the one I got."

Junior walked in and picked up a nasty-looking Ruger revolver. Junior's no better with a gun than I am. Either of us were more likely to shoot ourselves or each other than an attacker.

In an effort to cut down our odds of unintentional murder-suicide, I said, "I already got a gun, Junior," hoping he would the put the damned thing down. Instead, he picked up an automatic, comparing their heft in his hands.

He looked at me, and for the first time, I could see the wear on him. Worry lines creased his face like they'd been etched there with a tattoo needle. He opened the gun. "I don't."

Of course, the gun was already loaded.

Kelly gave me a tight hug like I was leaving for Iraq. As far as I knew, we were going to war. Or starting one. Junior went down to start the car. Twitch looked around the room uncomfortably. Kelly took my face in her hands and gave me a slow, warm kiss. I didn't say anything, but she answered the question she read on my face.

"I'll be fine," she said. "You come back as soon as you can."

As I turned to walk out, I wondered just how fine she would be. The last thing I heard was Twitch clapping his hands together and saying, "So, who wants to feed the snakes?"

It was going to be a long night.

Junior got in the car and reached over to unlock my side. I climbed in and waited for him to start the engine. He just sat behind the wheel, chewing on the filter of his cigarette.

"Before I start this car, you gotta promise me that you will at least attempt to cut the bullshit." He stared out the windshield.

"What shit are we talking about now?"

"The martyr shit. I heard you apologize to Kelly for getting her into this. You need to understand that this isn't your fault. None of this is. We got called into this game way late in the fourth quarter, Boo." Junior popped the dash lighter and lit his cig. "We got the ball when the game was pretty much played."

"Yeah, but we can still kill the spread."

"Okay, too much football. Let's just say, and I'm only saying, as a theory—"

"Yeah?"

"Maybe we did make a bad situation a little worse."

"I like your freewheeling use of the word 'little.'"

"Hey, it's a theory, ass." He jabbed at me with the cigarette. I plucked it from his fingers and jumpstarted my own.

"Can we, in theory, start the car and go?"

"In theory, yes." He didn't start the car. "The point I'm trying to make here is that the situation was already bad, the game was fixed, and we were just playing the game we knew how to play. We got the girl. The rest is prologue."

"Or epilogue."

"Which one is before?"

"That's prologue"

"That one."

"So we're in the epilogue, then?"

"No . . . we're . . . shut the fuck up and listen to me. The main word here is 'we.' I hear one more line about *your* situation and *your* problems, I'm going to hurt you in the groinal area, buddy. A lot."

"I'm sorry."

"Shut the fuck up." He turned the key and Miss Kitty, our war engine, roared. We could have used a better name for our war engine.

There he was. My heartbeat tripled its tempo, breath short in my chest. I'd never had a panic attack before, but I felt close to having one. It wasn't easy looking into the face again. The last time I'd seen it, I thought I was seconds away from a bullet to the skull. The picture was a low-res scan, grainy, but the loose, friendly smile was there, the oyster of a blind eye.

"This the guy?" Ollie asked, looking from the computer screen and back to me. I think my expression was answer enough.

Something spiky had nestled in my throat so I just nodded limply.

"Who is he, and where do we find him?"

Junior was ready to go out and draw some payback. Junior hadn't seen the guy. How coolly he'd pulled the trigger on me. How casual it would have been for him to put another bullet into my skull.

Ollie grimaced. "See, now this is where we may run into some trouble."

"How's that?"

"This is a blowup from a picture I found in the *Herald*'s archives. The guy's name is Louis Blanc."

Louis Blanc. The name scratched at the back of my memory.

"Do I know that name?" asked Junior. "Why do I think I know that name?" He tapped a finger on the glass of the computer screen. "I think I'd remember that face."

"Please don't touch the screen," Ollie said impatiently. He pulled a wipe from a box sitting next to the monitor and rubbed the point of contact until it squeaked.

"The name sounds familiar. Why would I know it?" I asked.

"You would have heard it," Ollie said, matter-of-factly. "Look at the rest of the picture." Ollie tapped a few buttons on the keyboard and double-clicked his mouse to show us the full picture. "You tell me why we have a bigger problem than we may have suspected."

The shot was of a restaurant opening in Southie. An Irish Shebeen called Conor's Publick that got a lot of press when it opened. The restaurant was bought for and operated by one Mr. Conor Cade. In the picture, Louis was standing behind the owners. Conor's son had his arm draped around the old man, smiling. The only other face I recognized in the shot was Conor's son, Francis.

Frankie "the Mick" Cade.

"Aw, fuck me," Junior and I said at the same time.

"His nephew?"

"It's pretty simple, Boo," Ollie said. "Mr. Cade's sister let a guy named Bevilaqua stick his pee-pee in her. They had a bouncing baby Bevilaqua. Named him Derek."

"I was being rhetorical, prick."

"So, Snake is The Mick's nephew?" Junior was having no easier a time than I was processing the information.

"Supposedly, it was a bit of a controversy within the ethnic circles when an Irish lass got herself knocked up and married to an Italian."

I could only imagine. The only people Boston's tried and true Irish hated more than the Italians were . . . well, they hated everybody. "So, we put the rings to the nephew of this town's top organized criminal. That's just peaches."

"And probably I'm next on the hit list," Junior said. A brief flash of pleasure passed over Junior's face. I think he'd always dreamed of making somebody's hit list. Then the blunt rock of reality bounced off his skull. "Aw shit. I don't wanna get shot."

"Guess what, Junior. It wasn't part of my life's ambitions either." I grabbed Ollie's phone and dialed Twitch.

"County Morgue."

"It's Boo. How much do you know about Louis Blanc?"

"Wow! I was right! So it was Lou Blanc. I mean . . . wow!"

Great. I'd been shot by the right-hand man of the local Irish kingpin, and Twitch was star-struck. Too bad I hadn't had time to ask for an autograph. "Yeah, it was a real honor, Twitch. Maybe I'll have the bullet bronzed."

Twitch chuckled. "You have no idea. Blanc is as cold-blooded as they come. Completely heartless son of a bitch. Like I told you earlier, you're one lucky bastard you even got to ID him. There're about three dozen others under construction sites around town who never got the chance. Lou Blanc. Wow."

I gritted my teeth with impatience, sending a bolt of pain into my skull. "Hey, Twitch, you want to go jerk Blanc off or you want to tell me what you know?"

"He's Cade's *numero uno* enforcer. Has been since the late eighties. Nobody knows for sure why, other than Blanc is still standing and so is Cade, which means he does his job well. Pretty much everyone agrees Blanc's got more balls and brains than Cade and the old guard put together."

"Why isn't he boss, then?"

"There are two rumors on that one."

"And they are?"

"One is that Cade's pop saved Blanc's on the islands during Dubya-Dubya Two. You know, the old Irish code of honor bullshit."

"What's the second?"

"The second is the one I'm more inclined to believe. And it's that Blanc just likes doing what he does. Bosses don't get their hands dirty, and that's what Blanc likes to do."

An entire flock of geese and a fair-sized turkey walked over my grave as I remembered the cool gunmetal pressing against my head and the words that followed.

Be easy . . .

"Another popular belief is that the guy's got something seriously wrong with his head."

"No shit."

"Seriously. Urban legend is the bullet that creased his head took out something in him. Like the part of his brain that controls remorse and stuff."

And stuff. Well, wasn't that just ducky. "Thanks, Twitch." I was cold all over.

"There is a silver lining, though."

"What is that?"

"Death is expensive, even for these guys. This was light retribution. They probably just wanted to give you back a taste of what you served the nephew. Because, believe you me, Boo. And if you've ever believed anything I've ever said to you—ever—believe this. If they wanted you out, you'd be wearing a toe tag right now. It's probably over."

The fuck it was.

Junior parked on the opposite side of the street, parallel to the long windows of Conor's Publick. I could clearly see Cade leaning over a plate at a table in the back. I guess when you're the last man standing like Frankie was, you didn't have to worry as much about sitting at dark and secluded tables like the old guard used to. A cherry-colored Caddy was parked in front, a dinosaur in a cheap suit leaning on the hood.

Lou Blanc was nowhere to be seen. I couldn't help but contrast the pair of duos we'd dealt with. Donnelly and Barnes. Cade and Blanc. On one side of the law, the brains ran the show, the muscle performed the errands. From what I knew about Cade's side of the fence, the vulgar strength called the shots. It bothered me to recognize which side I lived on.

We decided it would be just the two of us. Ollie never was much of a tussler, and I couldn't trust Twitch not to pull the trigger on Cade simply because the opportunity arose.

We also decided, much to Junior's dismay, that it would be me who went in. Alone. I'd already been shot. I was walking wounded. If something went horribly wrong and I didn't come back out of Conor's, Junior was more physically able to enact the retaliation that would follow. We may have been understaffed for an all-out street war against the Irish, but my army would at least make sure Cade followed me soon after.

I strolled over to the dinosaur as casually as a man with a hole in his leg relying on a cane could. The dinosaur turned his head on a neck as thick as a telephone pole. "The fuck you want, Gimpy?"

"Nothing with you, Bobo. I want your organ grinder."

A dull film passed behind his big dumb cow eyes. Dim bastard didn't even know I was mocking him. "What?"

Oh, this sweetheart was going to be an absolute pleasure. "I'm here to see Mr. Cade."

"Mr. Cade don't see nobody when he's eating."

"Where you from, *paisan*?" I smeared the last word with the same jackass Italian inflection the dinosaur was affecting.

"Hyde Park."

"Then why the fuck do you talk in that Long Island wiseguy wanna-be *patois*?" I said with a smile.

"Huh?" Again with the stupid.

"I mean, this isn't *The Sopranos*. If you're gonna work for the Irish mob, you should at least affect a brogue or something. The Italian thing just makes you sound like the retard you look like."

A dangerous smile crawled across his lips. "You fucking kidding me, Gimp?"

"If I wanted to kid you, big boy, I'd tell you a knock-knock joke."

He wrinkled his brow, unsure whether to pound me into dust or laugh in my face. He turned his head up a bit, thinking about it. I whipped out the stun gun and jabbed it into his neck.

Nothing.

Batteries were dead.

Fucking great.

"The hell you doing?" he asked, grabbing my wrist. The stun gun dropped out of my hand and smashed on the sidewalk. "What is that, a pager?"

Plan B.

Losing the crutch, I pulled the white and blue striped tube sock out of my leg brace. I brought it down on his skull as I hopped on one leg.

If he hadn't moved, he might have gone down clean. But in his effort to get out of the way, the sock popped him square on the forehead. The skin split wide open, blood immediately gushing over his eyes. He took a groggy step backward, and I took another shot.

The second time, I landed right on the sweet spot. The dinosaur let go of my wrist, bounced once off the hood of the Caddy, and slid down to the sidewalk. A smear of darker red on the Caddy's cherry color marked his descent. The sock tore from the impact and the change from my retirement fund spilled onto the street with a jingle. I dropped the sock on the dinosaur's lap and limped inside.

The air conditioning blasted me as I opened the door. Conor's was empty but for Cade, who barely afforded me a glance when I walked in. Hung over the bar were portraits of the Irish Holy Trinity: JFK, RFK, and Teddy. Only Teddy's had a half-full rocks glass of whiskey in front of him, whether in honest tribute or smartassery, I couldn't tell.

An empty restaurant was the last thing I wanted. The only three sounds in the place were my heart, some Chieftains on the speakers, and the cracking of the lobster claw Frankie was working on.

I sat at his table as casually as I could. Brando in a leg brace.

Caught in the silver lobster cracker in Cade's scarred hands, the claw made a sharp splintering sound, like bone snapping. Cade couldn't have cared less that I'd seated myself. I pressed my hands flat on the table to show that there was nothing in them—and to keep them from shaking.

Looking at him up close was strange. He was as close to a celebrity as I'd ever come. I found it hard not to look at the distinctively wide ears, knobby and cauliflowered, that the crime beat loved to use in descriptives of the man. A thick head with a face like a fist perched on top of his wide body. The wide ears made his head look even bigger. Between the thinning, bone-white hair that was combed sharply back over his pate and the thick white moustache, Cade looked like a polar bear in a light blue, three-hundred-dollar sweat suit. A polar bear that could have me killed just as easily as he ordered his barley pudding.

Something in his face gnawed at my mind. He and his nephew shared no features whatsoever, but something familiar was bugging me about the man.

"You need something?" he said, when it was obvious I wasn't going to go away. As he sat up to give me his attention, I saw the ridiculous bib he was wearing—a white plastic job with a picture of a smiling lobster in a pot of boiling water.

I knew just how the lobster felt.

Before I spoke, I realized that I was staring at his garlic knot ears despite myself. "You had me shot."

A broad smile stretched his thin lips wide. "*Oh.* You're the tough guy who thought it would be a bright idea to smack my nephew around." *Crunch.* He sucked noisily at the claw, letting me know I was as much a threat as the lobster.

"Your nephew is a piece of shit."

That got his attention enough to stop his wet slurping. He leveled his gaze at me over the claw. "Watch your mouth." His eyes threw daggers with the warning.

"You know what he does?"

"I don't fucking care what he does. I care about what you did." He casually pointed a broad finger, greasy with melted butter. "You should care what you do. You should be careful what you're doing right fucking now, kid."

"He makes videos. He rapes girls, and he videos them."

"So what? You a faggot or something? You don't like fucking girls? Maybe you'd like it if there was some nice cocksucking on there? That your thing?" He smirked and lifted his chin. "Huh, big boy? That it?"

"What you should know is that the girls are underage. Not only does he rape them, but he smacks them around first."

"So maybe the little cunts are into that shit. You don't know."

"Vice has a file on him. They'd love to get a name."

Cade rolled his eyes and dropped the lobster cracker on the table from a height where it made a nice thump. "*Oh.* And you know the name? Is that what you're saying?" He laced his fingers in front of him, the index fingers pointing at me like a child's approximation of a gun. "Let me make sure I'm perfectly clear about all this." He cleared his throat and looked me dead in the eye. "You making threats? That right? Hey, Lou? You hearing this?"

"I'm hearing it." Like an apparition separating himself from the shadows, Louis Blanc came walking around the corner. He circled us slowly, one perfectly manicured hand tracing the material of the green-checkered tablecloth. An obscenely large diamond winked at me from his cufflink, like it was letting me in on the joke. "But I'm not sure I'm believing it." He made his way behind me, the hand coming to rest on the back of my chair. He leaned over my shoulder. "That true, kid?" he whispered. "You making threats to Mr. Cade?"

His breath was warm on the hairs behind my ear. His inflection was gentle, almost paternal. Good thing I'd pressed my hands onto the table, since they were starting to tremor. As was my jaw. But since I couldn't press my face onto the table too, I just chomped on my lip to make it a sneer. Unfortunately, I think it made me look like I was pooping.

"You fucking making threats against my family, you little cocksucker?" Frankie's temper was starting to flare. "Who the fuck do you think you are? Do you know who the fuck you're talking to?"

"I know all about you, Mr. Cade. I know you have two daughters—"

Cade stood up, sending his chair backward onto the floor with a bang. "Don't you say another fucking word!"

It was all so absurdist in a way, made more so by the smiling lobster I was now eye to eye with.

"How old was she, Frankie? How old was your daughter when she died last year?"

"Lou! Hold this punk down!" With an animal growl, Cade snatched up the silver lobster crackers.

For the second time that week, I felt the chill of Louis Blanc's gun against my head. His other arm reached around my throat in a headlock, pulling me off-balance in the chair. I had no footing or leverage to resist if I wanted to. So I kept talking instead.

"How old was she, Mr. Cade? She was fourteen, wasn't she? What if it was her, Frankie? What if it was her?"

That caught him for a second. Then, just as fast, the rage overwhelmed his doubt. He grabbed my wrist and went straight for my fingers with the lobster cracker. I made a fist and pulled my hand back. I wasn't going to resist all that strenuously, not with a gun to my temple. Still, I wasn't going to give up my fingers without making it difficult.

"Gimme his goddamn hand, Lou!"

"Uh, Frankie? I only got two hands here. You want me to let him hold the gun for me so I can keep his hand straight?"

"Shoot him in the fucking head, he keeps moving."

I stopped. But then Cade stopped too.

Because I was smiling.

"The fuck you smiling at?"

Suddenly, the grip around my throat loosened. "Well, shit on me," Blanc said.

"What the fuck are *you* smiling at, Lou?"

"Frankie, you might want to look at your lobster," I said.

Cade looked down at the stupid bib. At the tiny red laser dot that danced in the center of the cartoon lobster's forehead. "The fuck?"

Louis whistled through his teeth. "Nicely played," he whispered in my ear as he released his grip around my neck and put all four legs of my chair on the floor. He gently smoothed out the shoulders of my shirt and clapped me on the shoulder as he holstered his gun with the other hand.

"What the fuck is this?" Frankie tried to wipe the laser dot off his bib with a napkin. The light just ran over his hand.

"That, Frankie, is a laser beam. Most commonly used on sniper rifles and the like." I knew Blanc's gun was gone, but I could still feel the ghost of its pressure against my temple.

"Shit," Frankie said.

Feeling a sudden empowerment, I reached across the table and took Frankie's glass of white wine. I swallowed a mouthful to clear my slightly crushed voicebox. "This isn't a threat, Mr. Cade. This is a fucking promise. Now I want you to hear me when I say this."

"Yeah, yeah. You got my fucking attention, kid. Hey, Lou, can you believe this shit?"

Trying to regain my composure, I finished Frankie's wine and placed the glass back on the table. "I understand why you did what you did. But Derek is pulling some sick shit, and he's pulling it publicly. So I'm offering you two things: The first thing is my silence. You talk to him. He stops. Period. I hear of any more movies, and I buy myself a 'get out of jail free' card, courtesy of turning on your nephew." Cade didn't answer me, but I knew he was hearing me. His eyes were down to two slits.

"Second thing is I don't raise my hand right now. If I do, your bib won't save your lovely sweat suit. You proved your point. You got me. You got me good. But don't you ever, ever threaten my friends or anyone I care about again." I let my words hang.

Then they both started laughing. Whooping guffaws of amusement that threw me off the cool hand I thought I was playing. Cade walked around the table and put his arms around me, lifting me up from my chair.

"Jesus H. Christ, Lou! You believe this kid?" Frankie cupped my face in his hands and kissed me on the cheek. I don't think it was a kiss of death, but it wasn't full of passion, either.

"I must admit, Frankie, I'm impressed." Lou leaned against the table, took a pair of cigarettes from a polished gold case, and lit them with a gold lighter. He handed one to me. I was too bewildered to refuse it. I guess state tobacco laws didn't apply in mob-run establishments.

Frankie put his arm around me like we were long-lost family. "I mean, where do you buy pants with balls so big?" There were little tears of laughter in the corners of Frankie's eyes. "C'mere." Frankie hugged me again.

"You're a piece of work, Malone. No doubt." Louis's scar crinkled up when he smiled, the cigarette clenched between his teeth.

Frankie grabbed me by the shoulders. "Listen. You impressed me today. I can't tell you the last time I've been so impressed."

Louis blew a stream of smoke up at the ceiling. "You used to like that Rainey kid in Pittsburgh."

"Before he went and made me have him shot."

"Yeah." Louis looked at me hard. "Before that."

Cade clapped his hands and laughed. "True. But you, Malone. You, I hope, won't make me kill you."

How was I supposed to respond to that?

Frankie continued. "I'll tell you what. You have actually done both me and my nephew a favor today. I'm sure that he don't know about any police file on him. He don't need the grief, and I sure as shit don't. As of today, Derek's production company comes to a halt. I'll see to it myself, okay?"

"Okay." If there was anything else I wanted to say, I couldn't think of it.

Cade chucked me on the cheek and flecks of ice came back into his eyes. "Now, if I ever see you again, I'm gonna personally make sure you eat your own testicles. Got it?"

I got it. He knew I got it. There was no need for me to answer.

"Now, get the hell out of here. I gotta piss, you made me laugh so hard." He dismissed me with a wave and left.

Before I turned to go, Lou gave me one more smile and a wink.

With his dead eye, of course.

Out the door, I hustled quickly past the dinosaur. He'd managed to make it back to his feet with the assistance of the small crowd of rubberneckers that had grown around him. He held his hand to his head, blood streaming between his fingers.

I climbed into the car, and Junior sped off. “We good?”

“We good.”

Junior tossed the laser sight he’d pulled off of Twitch’s rifle onto the backseat. “By the way, what was the backup plan in case they didn’t buy the laser?”

“We don’t need no stinking backup plan.”

“Didn’t have one, did you?”

“Um, no.”

Chapter Twenty

Boo Malone. Had a hell of a week.

It was time for as close to a vacation as I ever got. Kelly took the week off from work to nursemaid me back to health.

That, and we fucked. A lot. One night in bed, a thin trickle of blood smeared down her leg. "Oh, crap," she muttered. "Oh, God, this is embarrassing." It was nearly dark in the room, but I thought I could feel the heat of her blushing.

Before she could get any more embarrassed, I felt the warmth pooling in the sheet under my leg. "I think you're good. I think my leg might have been a little overtaxed."

"Oh, thank the lord."

"Yeah, thank the lord that the bullet hole in my leg is bleeding again."

"You know what I mean."

She turned the bedside light on. In the yellow glow, the blood looked worse than I thought. And now that the endorphins were wearing off, my leg was starting to hurt like a motherfucker again. "Well, looks like somebody needs a bath."

"Looks like we both do."

"I'll get the sponge."

"Let's try something else for a change."

I limped into my kitchen and found an old roll of cling wrap in my junk drawer. After I daubed the blood from my wound and applied a generous dollop of Bacitracin to the stitches, I wrapped my thigh tightly in the plastic.

Kelly poked her head from around the bedroom. "Hmmm, kinky . . ." she said in an inflection I recognized.

"Did you just Hedley Lamarr me?"

"That I did, cowboy."

"Wow. Any woman quoting *Blazing Saddles* is a woman I can fall in love with."

She winked at me. "Feel free." Moments later, I heard water filling the bathtub.

We sat in the hot water, slowly washing each other off, face to face, my legs over hers. Good thing the old claw-foot bathtub was big enough for two.

She squeezed the sponge and the water dribbled down my neck, over my chest, the thick scar parting the water as it ran down my body. She moved the sponge lower and held it, warm and soapy, against my mark. My badge. My ever-present souvenir from a time a loving God could have allowed me to forget but never did.

She never asked. Not once. Maybe that's why I wanted to tell her. Outside of Junior, nobody knew. I'd been asked. I'd never told.

"I was eight years old . . ."

It was a summer of long, humid days and sticky nights. I was spending my summer like all kids did. Playing wiffleball with sugar-sticky hands until dusk settled and mothers started yelling. Chasing the ice cream man. My birthday was coming, and the summer stretched ahead of me with the great promise that only exists until you hit puberty. Maybe I'd get to go to a Red Sox game and see my heroes, Jim Rice and The Yaz. Maybe we'd get to go to Lincoln Park down on Route 6, or make the big trip into Rhode Island to Rocky Point for clam cakes.

Every day had endless possibilities.

Also endless, or so it seemed, was my mother's lineup of boyfriends. That summer, there was the plumber with the rough hands and the musician with the perfectly feathered hair who called me "little man."

I hated that.

I did like the bartender, who always smelled faintly of beer, cigarettes, and maraschino cherries. But, like every summer, the boyfriends came and went.

My mother wasn't a bad person. She was so young. Lonely. That summer, she was younger than I am now. She wasn't a woman who slept around town. If she was, she kept it hidden, and I'd rather not think of her like that. What she was, though, was a poor judge of character.

My mother's name was Annie Malone. I have her last name.

Time hasn't erased her in the slightest, unlike most of my early memories. I remember every kissed scrape. I remember every sacrifice. I remember her love. She was the most beautiful person I ever met. If I'd known who Elizabeth Taylor was then, I might have said my mother looked like her, but with a better smile. My mother had the same black hair. And the eyes. I'll never forget my mother's violet eyes. God's little joke on me, all I got were her cheekbones.

My little sister, now, she was the heartbreaker. Looked just like my mother. She was only five years old, but I remember what a beauty my baby sister Emily was.

I had a week to go before my birthday. I was riding my red, white, and blue Huffy up and down the street, Star Wars toys rattling in my backpack. As I came back up the street, I could see my neighbors milling nervously in front of the house we rented.

Angry voices were pouring through the screen door onto the sidewalk. Again.

Our elderly next-door neighbor, Mrs. MacAllan, was saying to the air and anybody in earshot that she was going to call the police. Mr. Dominguez, the man who lived opposite us, grabbed me by the shoulder. He thought it might be a good idea if I waited outside until "things blew down in there." I shrugged him off and ran inside.

Most of the yelling was coming out of my mother's recent ex-boyfriend, Teddy. Teddy was a mechanic, a tool belt always around his waist. I didn't like Teddy. He didn't take his tool belt off at the dinner table. I thought that was rude. Whenever he shook my hand, he ground my knuckles together until tears welled in my eyes and then smiled when I winced.

I followed the yelling into our kitchen. Teddy had my mother gripped by her shoulders, pinned against the sink with his thick arms. I saw one of Emily's frightened violet eyes and the bright blue marble eye of her stuffed dog, Blackie, looking out through a crack in the yellow kitchen pantry door.

Teddy screamed at my mother, face inches from hers, calling her a lying, cheating slut. My mother was crying. I didn't know what a slut was, but nobody was going to make my mother cry. I grabbed a fork off the kitchen table and drove it right into Teddy's ass cheek. It stuck there, dangling like a silver tail.

Teddy yelped as he plucked the fork out of his khakis. He turned and unloaded a punch to the side of my head that threw me across the room. Blunt pain exploded through my body. I skidded across the kitchen table and crashed to the floor in a heap. I didn't lose consciousness. If I had, maybe things wouldn't have ended the way they did.

My mother roared like an enraged lioness and was on Teddy, fists beating, nails clawing at his face. He got in a punch to her temple and she crumpled to the floor, blood streaming from her head.

I was hurting badly, in ways my eight years on the planet hadn't prepared me for.

Teddy wasn't done with my mother. He pulled a small gun from his waistband and pistol-whipped my mother across the face, saying no man would want her when he was done.

He hit her again.

And again.

Then, for the first time ever, the world turned red.

I shrieked and attacked him, the rage in control, strength flowing through me like nothing I'd ever imagined.

It wasn't close to enough.

I bit a good chunk out of Teddy's bicep, blood warm and salty in my mouth. His scream of pain was sweet music. Then Teddy cracked me across the face with the gun butt, shattering my nose and cheek.

Then he turned his grip around and fired point blank into my chest.

The gunshot slammed me against the wall with a wet smack. I fell to the floor, my body no longer responding to my will. The strength to inhale and exhale, inhale and exhale, was all I had left.

As badly hurt as she was, face battered to pulp, my mother stood on shaking legs. With a howl, she grabbed a butcher's knife from a wooden block and drove it into Teddy's throat. Teddy gurgled, took three steps, and shot my mother twice before he fell backward, dead.

So much blood. I couldn't move. The last thing I remember is my mother reaching out to me as the light left her beautiful violet eyes. I wasn't sure what were sirens and what were Emily's screams.

After that, it all fades in and out. I remember biting a paramedic. I remember doctors yelling. I remember asking for my mother, asking for Emily. I remember asking *where is she* without knowing which one I was asking for.

I never saw either of them again.

"What happened to Emily?" Kelly said softly, a hitch in her breath.

"I don't know. I don't know how long I was in the hospital for. A lot of that time, I spent in one coma or another. The State did what it had to. As far as I know, we had no next of kin."

"You've never looked for her?"

"Nope."

"Why not?"

I had to think about it. I had reasons, lots of them. But I'd never put any of them into words. "I'd like to think that her life has been . . . better. If it hasn't," I shook my head, "I don't want to know."

We sat there until the water went cold.

I got up early the next morning and decided to cook breakfast. I had bread, eggs, and milk, so I tried French toast. What I wound up with was some type of eggy paste with a burned crust that somehow stayed gummy inside. Smelled pretty good, though.

Kelly came out of the bedroom in nothing but a pair of panties and naked morning glory. She scratched at her head and sniffed. "What is that?"

"It's breakfast. I think I invented French toast pudding."

"You are useless in a kitchen, aren't you?" She tiptoed up and placed a tender kiss on my face.

"You've never tasted my Hamburger Helper Almondine."

She made a disgusted face. "I'm not even sure what almondine is," she said.

"You just throw a handful of mixed nuts into Hamburger Helper." I recognized the sharp squeal of brakes from the front of my house and the familiar cough of Miss Kitty's dying engine. "Aw, shit."

"What? What's the matter?" Instinctively, Kelly covered up her boobs.

"It's Junior," I said. I could already hear his boots stomping on the front steps.

"Better get one last good look then, Mr. Malone."

Kelly did a playful pirouette, and I did indeed soak up that one last look. She trotted off to put on some decent clothes for our visitor. A visitor whose ass I planned on sticking a wad of French toast pudding up. I grabbed a handful of goop and headed to the door, stopping dead in my tracks when I opened the door and saw his expression.

Something was wrong. Something was very wrong.

I stood there dumbly with a fistful of raw egg and singed toast. He stared back at me, a heavy weight suspended in the air between us. Yellow goo dribbled down my forearm.

"She's dead, Boo." Junior's voice cracked.

"No." I shook my head. "Don't even kid—"

"She's dead."

Chapter Twenty-One

Junior's words struck Kelly like an open-handed slap. She ran to the bathroom, and I could hear her crying behind the door. Junior kept clearing his throat and stalking back and forth in the room.

I wondered where my anger was. It should have been there, coursing through me. Empowering me. It was there for Seven. It was there for Derek. Hell, it was even there for Underdog. Why wasn't it there for Cassie?

A demon whispered in my ear. *You're used to losing women.*

Of course. Of course, she's dead.

You were supposed to be her hero, Boo.

Could you ever have been her hero? Anyone's?

No, my demon said. *You never saved anyone. You never could.*

And you never will.

"What happened?" I finally asked.

"She ran away again. Two kids found her in the Dutch House. A step let loose or something and she fell. She must have broke her neck."

"Did anyone see her?" My voice was as flat as a machine's.

"See her what?"

"Did anyone see her fall?" I stared past Junior, to my front door, to the street.

Junior gave me a look. "No, Boo."

"So if nobody saw—"

"Don't do this. There's nothing to figure. It's a big rotting squat. You know that. Who the fuck knows if anybody saw anything? If they did, you can get yourself a nice list of junkies and degenerates as witnesses. Fucking place has been condemned as long as we've been in Boston."

"Witnesses to what?" I turned away from the street.

Junior flopped down on my couch, slouched over. He stopped massaging his hands and paused. "What?"

"You said I could make a list of witnesses. Witnesses to what?"

"I was just saying—"

"Don't bullshit me, Junior. You wouldn't have said it if you didn't think there might be witnesses to something."

"To what? Witnesses to anything! To her falling! To somebody finding her. Shit, at the Dutch House, you're probably likely to find more than a couple witnesses to alien abductions."

"Try to find Paul. Ask him if he knows the kids who found her."

"Boo, the cops already looked into this. Don't make it into something it's not. She's the daughter of the goddamn DA. You think they didn't look into every fucking detail?" There was no anger in his reprimand, just pity. Telling Ahab that there was no white whale.

"They didn't know every detail. We do. We just yanked that kid away from a kiddie porn—no, a *snuff* porn—freak who's the nephew of the most dangerous man on the Eastern Seaboard. We don't know who had a copy of that movie. We don't know what kind of maniac watched it and jerked off in his mother's panties every time she died. Maybe . . . maybe one of them saw her walking down the street and . . . and . . ." I was reaching, and I knew it.

Junior knew it too. "You listening to yourself?"

"I don't believe in three things, Junior: the Easter Bunny, a loving God, and coincidences. Just call Paul." My failed breakfast experiment was drying into glue on my hand. In my numbness, I'd forgotten to wash it off. I nearly tore off the faucet head turning the water on.

Defeated or just too worn out to argue, Junior said, "Fine. We'll look into this. But I'm only giving it a week, Boo. Our answering machine at the office is flooded. We've spent enough time with this. Curtis is pissed that you never called him back about last weekend, so we lost our Drop Bar account to Ironclad Security."

I soaped up my hands and ignored him.

"We've got a dozen more waiting to hear back from us. I'm not losing 4DC over this. Our job ended when we handed her over. This is business I'm talking now, Boo. It's a fucking tragedy and I'm sorry she's gone but we have a goddamn business to run. One week." With that, he marched out the door and drove off.

I drove Kelly back to her apartment in a heavy silence. We parted with the quiet intact, sorrow stripping us of our words.

Junior gave me one week. It only took two days.

I went alone that night to the Dutch House. A decade and a half ago, fire had gutted most of the old house. Not too long after, a local assemblage of homeless addicts, nutcase bums, and runaway teens moved right in. Some kids would just hang out there and get high, away from the street. A place they could call their own, burned, rat infested, moldy, and dangerous as it was. Since day one, Mr. Dutch always had a motley assortment of stragglers coming and going.

I knew the place all too well. I bunked there for a spell when I first came to Boston, jobless and homeless.

Mr. Dutch had probably moved himself in before the place stopped smoldering. Nobody knew Dutch's full story. Since he lived at the house that bore his name, I guess he wasn't technically homeless. Nobody knew how old he was or where he'd come from.

I found him across the street from the house, nervously twisting on his lanky, graying dreadlocks. For a vagrant, Dutch was always well-groomed and articulate. He spotted me as I walked down Brattle Street.

"That you, Boo?" Dutch cupped a hand to his mouth and blew out a long stream of marijuana smoke.

"It's me, Dutch."

"Well, hell's bells, white boy. What you doing in this neck of the woods? You lose your lease?" He cackled and offered me his joint.

"No thanks," I said, my eyes locked on the house across the street.

"Make your leg feel better." He pointed the joint at the brace on my leg. "Help heal that shit up fast." Dutch would tell you marijuana could cure everything from hepatitis to Republicans.

"No thanks. Got my own pills for it."

"Got any more?"

"Sorry."

"Whatever. Might at least help knock off that ugly gorilla face you wearing. Good for the heart and the mind." He tapped a finger off his chest, then head. Dutch practiced what he preached. A lot. But he never seemed stoned. "Whatever did you do to yourself?"

"I got shot."

"Mm-hmm." He didn't seem surprised at all, which bothered me. "You sure do know how to piss off the wrong people, dontcha?"

"Guess I do." It was hard not to smile for Dutch, but I wasn't feeling anywhere close to the humor he usually brought. "What can you tell me about the girl?"

He didn't have to ask which girl. He knew.

"Aw, don't tell me she was a friend of yours. That poor thing was just a baby." Dutch shook his head and comforted himself with another toke.

"I knew her, yeah."

"I'm so sorry for that, Boo. I guess the old stairwell just couldn't hold no more." Dutch shook his head sadly for his poor house falling down around his ears.

"Did you find her?"

"Nah. By the time I got here, there was cops and lights and shit all over the place. Thank God. Thing like that'll stay with a man. Wish I could've been here to help her, but I sure am glad I didn't find that poor child."

"Was anybody there at the time?"

"Shit, if they was, they got themselves the hell gone when they saw the police coming."

"Anybody say anything when they came back?"

"Nobody came back but me. Damn police scared away all my tenants."

And odds were, those former tenants would be impossible to find even if I knew who they were. Finding a girl was one thing. Tracking homeless nomads in a city like Boston was another problem entirely.

"I need to see the house."

Dutch pressed his lips together and shook his head. "I wouldn't go in there right now."

"Why not?"

"I got a double-crack in there right now, losing his got-damn mind. That's why I'm out here."

"What's a double-crack?"

Dutch smiled, a little embarrassed. "A cracker crackhead. No offense."

"How long has he been in there?"

"He just showed up today, looking for Louisa. Louisa ain't been here for months. He's flipping out, saying he won't leave till she gets here."

"I'll be right back," I said, crossing the street. From my backpack, I pulled out a thick Maglite flashlight and lit up the front of the house.

The front porch gave an ominous creak as I walked up the steps. Yellow police tape fluttered, broken in the breeze. I pulled a short piece off the rusted iron rail and stuck it in my pocket. I don't know why I wanted it, I just did. The air wafting out the missing front door was heavy with dark odors of rot and waste. The smells brought with them overpowering memories of the time I'd lived here as one of Dutch's tenants.

I moved aside the blue nylon tarp that covered the doorway and walked through. A plastic mop bucket that had been used for a latrine sat by the door. I gagged as I passed by and pulled my shirtfront over my mouth and nose.

"Louisa?" A gruff voice called out from the darkness toward the back of the house. My dealings with the chronically fucked-up have given me an ear for the difference between drinkers and brain-damaged lifetime addicts. The guy's voice sounded like he'd made a career out of huffing any chemical he could soak in a sweat sock.

"Time to go, man. Louisa ain't coming back," I called out as I turned my flashlight his way. Roaches scurried away from the sharp glare cast on the floor.

"The fuck're you?" the voice asked as my eyes detected a flicker of motion in what was once the kitchen.

I held the light low, so as not to blind the double-crack and freak him out further. He was wearing a grimy T-shirt reading Baby On Board and filthy cutoffs with sandals. His skin was so crusted with muck that it was difficult to tell where the dirt ended and the man began.

"I'm the fella who's kicking your ass out of here. Now move it." I flicked the flashlight toward the door, in case he'd forgotten how to get there. I hoped my no-bullshit tone would pierce his addled brain.

"I ain't doing nothing until Louisa comes back." He emphasized his point by waving a short piece of rebar menacingly in the air.

My thin patience snapped, and I brought the bright flashlight beam straight into his face. "Hey!" he yelled. He defensively brought the metal post up over his head. In one motion, I flipped my hold on the flashlight and brought the handle down hard on the knobby bone in his wrist. The junkie howled in pain as the rebar clunked onto the floor.

From behind, I slipped the flashlight between his legs, turned it flat against his thighs, and pulled back. I grabbed a handful of his slimy hair and pushed his upper body forward. Trick of the trade. A ten-year-old could pull off the move against an NFL linebacker. I had no trouble maneuvering a skinny crackhead. He was like a smelly marionette in my grip.

As I scooted him toward the door, he lurched sideways to escape. Not only didn't it break my grip, but his aim was terrible. Using his own momentum, I dunked him head-first into the shit bucket. His screams quickly gurgled out as I held his face down in it.

"Oh, God! Lemme go! Please! I'll leave!" he begged when I let him up for air.

"How long you been here, you fuck?" I snarled.

"I—I just got here this morning, man. I just wanted—"

I cut him off with another dunking. His screams gurgled up through the viscous fluid.

"Were you in here on Saturday, you dirty fuck? You like to put the hurt on little girls? Huh? Answer me, shitbird."

Thick bubbles rimmed around his submerged head as he screamed. His arms and legs whipped around wildly, clawing for any purchase. He grabbed at my pants legs, my arm, my shirt. I held him down harder.

I stopped when I heard Mr. Dutch pleading, "Boo, let him go! He wasn't here. He really did just show up today. He was in lockup."

I let the crackhead go and he scrabbled into the corner by the door, turtling himself up, whimpering like a child waiting for the next blow. "I just want my Louisa," he blubbered. "I just wanted to find my Louisa." He rocked back and forth, clutching his knees close to his chest.

Dutch stared at me, horrified. There was only one crazy nutcase covered in shit in that room right then. Nobody needed to point fingers to figure out who it was.

Dutch led me out back, where a spigot and hose still gave water despite clanking a protest. I washed off the mess best as I could, but there was no amount of cleaning that would save my clothes. I was going to be walking around in a potato sack if I lost any more of my wardrobe.

"I'm sorry, Dutch," I said, sick with myself.

"S'okay, Boo. You feeling a lot of hurt right now. I can see that. Jest don't think poor George deserved to suffer from it."

Knowing the crackhead's name made me feel worse. "I just lost it, Dutch. I thought . . . I don't know what I thought," I said, turning the faucet off with a squeak.

"Like I said, it's okay. At least you got George to hit the bricks. Probably don't have to worry about him coming back, neither."

Dutch led me back to the wide stairwell at the south end of the house. I remembered going up those stairs to the room I'd kept my sleeping bag in. The stairs supported me just fine back then. But ten years was a long time in a house that should have been demolished in the early 1990s. Stringy wisps of carpet remained tacked onto the edges of the stairs, fibers black from the flames that burned through the house. A wide hole opened like a gaping mouth three steps from the top.

Carefully, I walked up the first four steps. Cassandra couldn't have weighed more than an even buck with all her clothes on and wearing wrist weights. The stairs creaked, but gave only a little under my two-thirty.

"Be careful, Boo," Dutch said nervously. "No offense to you or that little girl, but the last thing I need is another dead whitey in my house. The damn police already put me through their suspicious-nigger line of questioning."

"I'm all right," I said as I made my way higher. One step below the hole and the stairs still held me. I was only eight feet off the ground floor, but I knew falls from lesser heights could kill, especially if you weren't expecting the drop. I ran my fingers along the edges of the broken planks. The wood grains were swollen with moisture, but didn't appear to be suffering any excessive rot.

That wasn't what I was looking for. I was there to see if someone had marked his territory. Made it look like a collapse when it wasn't anything. Maybe he'd dropped his wallet or carved "I killed Cassandra Donnelly" on the wall and signed it.

As one last test, I gave the wood on the side of the broken stairs a good stomp. The impact boomed an echo through the lonely hallways.

"Oh, sweet Jesus," Dutch complained. "Please don't do that. No more dead whiteys, Boo! Please?"

I stared down into the hole. The cavity that swallowed Cassie's short life. How long did she lie down there? Was she knocked out? Killed instantly? Or was she down there dying, alone, for hours? I couldn't see through the darkness to determine what lay at the bottom. Basement? Closet? Was there blood? The hole just stared back at me, unconcerned with my opinion of it.

The wood held. I stomped three more times.

Bang bang bang.

Nothing. If it held me and withstood by best stompings, then—

Creak.

"Oh, Boo. Get offa there, *please*."

With an earsplitting screech, the banister tore away from the wall, the entire stairwell collapsing under me. I was lucky enough to land on my good leg and roll when I hit. I bounced off the floor once, and Dutch screamed. I got the wind knocked out of me, but I was okay.

The same drop had been much worse for Cassie.

"Boo!" Plaster and ash floated thickly in the air, making Dutch wheeze.

"I'm over here, Dutch." I called back, coughing in the chalky dust coating the inside of my mouth and lungs. I pulled the front of my shirt over my nose again as I ran for the door. Dutch was right behind me, gasping.

So the stairs weren't up to code. So what? They stood long enough with my fat ass on them. They should have been able to take Cassandra's weight without a squeak.

But they did collapse, what was left of my rational mind said.

But they should have held her, the irrational majority said.

But they didn't.

But.

Ifs and buts.

I put on my one suit. My funeral blacks. It seemed death was the only occasion I had to put on decent clothes. It took me a long time to get the necktie knotted, since it had been about seven years since I'd last had to tie one. That, and I couldn't use a mirror. When I caught my own eyes in the reflection, I saw the surfacing ghosts. A grief I hadn't seen in many years. A grief I still couldn't afford.

Junior and I waited at the New Cavalry Cemetery gates for the procession to arrive from the church. For reasons neither of us could touch upon, we didn't feel it would be appropriate for us to attend the funeral mass, but we both wanted to be there for the graveside service.

I sat on Miss Kitty's hood, leafing through the *Sunday Globe*. The story of Cassandra's death had made the front page for a couple days, then been bumped to page three by the end of the week. Today's article was about the funeral and Big Jack's sudden spike in the polls. Sympathy made for a lot of votes, apparently. I doubted Mr. Donnelly felt the value of those votes versus what they had cost him.

"Here they come," Junior said, spitting an empty sunflower seed into the street.

A long progression of black cars crept up the street, headlights on.

Cassandra's casket was laid into the ground under a large willow tree, next to her mother. A good number of people were in attendance. Cassandra's friends huddled together on one side, their pubescent emotions unchecked and on display. Two girls wailed their way through the entire service, the cries of kids who just got a sucker-punch of a reminder that they weren't immortal. Their grief was a palpable presence, like currents of ozone before a thunderstorm.

Our sadness was for a recent loss. We'd barely known the kid. Our contact with her could be broken down into a matter of hours. So why was I hurting so bad?

Junior and I kept to the back. We didn't belong, standing there in our cheap suits, barely knowing anyone there. I could feel the class line right there and then. Death may level all playing fields, but only for the dead. At one point, Kelly spotted us and lifted her fingers. I could see streaks of wetness underneath her sunglasses. I just nodded at her.

Jack Donnelly wasn't so big that day. In fact, he was the smallest man I've ever seen, as though a sinkhole had opened in his chest and was pulling him inside out as the service progressed. His eyes never strayed from the copper-colored casket and the open grave underneath. At his side stood Barnes, looking like he was ready to take control if any control needed taking.

From our isolated spot, we couldn't hear the priest's words, but as he finished and the casket was lowered, the cries reached a crescendo and I saw Jack sway. In a heartbeat, Barnes curled his arm around his old friend for support. As the crowd parted, people cried on each other's shoulders, held one another, shook hands, and went their ways.

I wanted to make my way over to Mr. Donnelly. I wanted to look him straight and say . . .

I don't know.

That I was sorry.

A small procession of people before me were doing just that as Barnes led Donnelly back to his limousine. By the time Barnes got him there, I was a step away and found no words to say. I started to extend my hand when the levee of Donnelly's grief broke. He bayed softly, crumpling onto the side of his car.

"Jack . . . Jack . . ." Barnes said in a calm voice to his friend.

"I killed her," Donnelly wept. "I killed my little girl. I pushed her away from me, Danny. I pushed her, and she's dead. She's gone. Oh, God—"

"Jack, get in the car, please." I heard Barnes' voice crack as he opened the car door and placed Donnelly inside.

The mass of mourners looked away uncomfortably or cried harder for their friend's daughter.

I just felt sick. I was physically ill at my own selfishness. I'd made Cassie's death about me, my world. I'd placed my own bullshit existence into Cassandra's death when I had no reason. No right. I realized that as I watched the collapse of Jack Donnelly, and I felt sick to my core about it. For him.

We went back to The Cellar after the funeral to drink death away.

"That sucked," Junior said as he swallowed another mouthful of wine.

That pretty much summed it up.

Ginny was waitressing and came over to us. "What's with the monkey suits boys? Somebody die?"

I gave her my eyes, and she realized her question wasn't as rhetorical as she'd thought.

"Oh shit," she said and put her hand on my shoulder. "I'm so sorry. I didn't know."

"S'okay," I mumbled. I patted her hand.

"Let me get you guys another round," she said, and she quickly sauntered off.

"It's done, Junior," I said.

"Thank God." Junior sighed with relief.

I gulped the rest of my bourbon. "You were right. I don't know what I was thinking. She was the goddamn district attorney's daughter—"

"You wanted to be sure, brother. I understand that much."

"I know you do. Seeing Donnelly like that, I dunno, made me rethink where we stand in all this. For crissakes, the guy is the top cop in town. I don't know what made me think I could do any better than he could."

Junior shrugged. "What can I say? You're an egotistical narcissistical motherfucker."

I glared at him, and he laughed. Then I started. We laughed in the only way friends can when they're at their worst. Ginny was all the more confused when she brought our drinks over.

When we stopped laughing, I said, "There is one more thing I'd like to do." I cleared my throat. "For Cassie."

Junior raised his wine. "For Cassie."

"I wasn't toasting, you fucktard."

He lowered the glass. "Oh. What's that, then?"

"What do you say we finish the job, get all those DVDs back? We find out who bought the videos from Sid, and we burn the DVDs in a big-ass bonfire?"

"Only if I can hurt the pervs. Lots."

"Oh, lots and lots."

"Joy."

Junior went home, and I continued my search for God. I closed the bar and extended my search for The Almighty all the way into the bottom of a Beam bottle. I might have seen Moses in the peanut bowl, but I might just as easily have been fucked up. A jingle of keys at the front door stirred me from my religious questings.

"Mr. Boo," Luke said with his usual reserved cheer. "You look nice tonight. What you get all dressed up for? You have yourself a date?"

"Had a funeral, Luke. Friend of mine died."

"Oh, I'm sorry to hear that, Mr. Boo. It wasn't that young girl, was it? The daughter of Mr. Donnelly?"

"As a matter of fact, it was. How did you know?"

"Saw a picture on your desk a while back. Saw her picture in the newspaper. Just made a guess." Luke clucked his tongue and shook his head sadly, leaning on the ratty mop he'd pulled out of the utility closet. "Shame a young girl like that goes when there's so many people who've lived their lives and wait, sick, for their turn to meet Jesus." He said it like he was waiting on that day himself.

I nodded. "I just can't figure out the whys of it anymore, Luke. I mean, I don't know. I just can't figure out the why."

Luke sighed and looked off into a distance beyond the peeling lead paint on the walls. "Sometimes life goes wrong, Mr. Boo. Pure and simple. God has a plan. It don't always feel right to us. Most of the time it downright hurts so bad you just wants to scream and curse His name, but that ain't right neither. Sometimes, life just goes wrong." He strolled off to the kitchen and turned on his radio, the same fire-and-brimstone preacher shouting out salvation into the night.

I didn't find God that night, but I felt Luke's words were as close as I was going to get. I said goodnight and went home.

The next day, Junior and I were ready to start back at the beginning. Junior would find Paul, I would go to Seven's to smack any and all remaining information out of him.

When I got to Seven's, I found an unlocked door and the apartment stripped to the walls. Seven had skipped.

I was back at The Cellar when Junior called my cell phone.

"What's up?"

"I'm in Harvard Square. I haven't found Paul yet, but some of the kids told me he was around. I'm gonna wait another hour to see if he turns up. And Boo?"

"Yeah?"

"A couple kids asked me if I was you."

"What? Why?"

"They said Paul has been looking for you the last couple days and told the other kids to look out for you."

"Why?"

"I dunno. I'll catch you in an hour."

I sat in the office and finished my pack of smokes, waiting for the phone to ring. When it didn't and the nic fits started, I decided to check in downstairs with Audrey.

Audrey smiled when I walked in, but her eyes never left her solitaire game laid out on the bar. "What's up, Willie?"

"Have there been any kids coming in?"

Audrey's attention lifted from the cards, her smile turned to indignation. "You know me better than that, Boo. I card everyone who walks in that door."

"No, no. Have there been any kids coming in and asking for me? Skinny white kid? About fourteen? Dredlocks? Maybe smelled of weed?"

"Oh, yeah. Kid came in yesterday looking for you."

"Did he say where I could reach him?"

"No, I told him to beat it." Audrey winced. "I thought he was some kid dropping your name so I wouldn't ID him. I didn't know he was a friend of yours."

"It's okay, but listen—if he comes back, hold him here and call me right away." I scribbled the cell number on a bar napkin.

Junior came walking in as I was heading out.

"You find Paul?" I asked.

"Not yet. Some new scrubs hit the Square and said he was gone for the night. I'll run by tomorrow."

"He was looking for me here, too."

"What the hell for?"

"Yeah, exactly."

Then it hit both of us.

"You don't think he was at—"

"Maybe he was at—" Junior said simultaneously.

Neither of us finished our sentence. We both knew the last words were going to be "Dutch House."

Junior shook his head. "Are we getting paranoid, Boo?"

"Even paranoid people have real enemies."

"Where to now?"

"I was going to head over to Derek's. See if he's got a list of buyers."

Junior was hurt. "You wouldn't have gone back there without me, would ya?"

"Wouldn't consider it."

Derek's apartment had a new door and new molding. I knocked hard, figuring it would make a nice change of pace from kicking in the door on his face. "Derek. Open up!" Considering our last visit, we still flanked the door. Just in case Derek had armed himself and would choose to shoot first, ask later.

"We're not gonna kick your ass this time. Scout's honor," Junior yelled. Since Junior wasn't ever a scout, the promise wasn't worth shit.

I leaned over and pressed my ear against the unfinished wood. Nothing. "It's quiet in there. Maybe he's not home," I whispered.

"*Too* quiet," Junior responded, wiggling his fingers at me like a vaudevillian hypnotist.

I tried the knob anyway. It was locked, but the new door didn't have a deadbolt installed yet. Junior took out his laminated Blockbuster card and slipped it in the poorly fit space between the door and molding. With a flick of the wrist, Junior popped the lock.

"That was easy," I said.

"*Too* easy," Junior said, wiggling his fingers in my face. I smacked his hands away.

The room was silent, and the air was thick with the smell of alcohol and dirty laundry. The plasma television sat shattered in one corner of the room, a number of smashed Wild Turkey bottles on the floor. The sink was full of dirty dishes, a cluster of flies buzzing over them.

"Jeez," Junior said, pinching his nostrils. "Looks like he and Sid been trading housekeeping tips."

I lifted my chin toward a closed door. Quietly as we could, we stepped over the glass and debris to the bedroom. I turned the knob and slowly pushed open the door. The hinges creaked like in an old Hammer film, sending chills down my back.

Derek sat on the edge of his mattress in a pair of dirty boxer shorts. Another half-full bottle of Wild Turkey was in his hand. He looked up woozily as we stood there.

"Wazzup?" he asked, like we were expected company. "You guys here to finish the job? You guys gonna kill me now?" He burped a wet one and scratched his privates. His face was swollen, splotched with purple bruises, his chest still sporting an angry red burn mark from Junior's stun gun.

"We're not here to kill you, Derek," I said softly. "We just want some information."

He swiveled his head back at us. "You can kill me—you know? I wouldn't mind. I don't care. I don't fucking care no more." He trailed off as he put the bottle back to his lips. Most of the slug dribbled down his concave chest, into his boxers.

I pulled the bottle out of his hand. "Hey!"

"Hey!" he protested back.

"Who buys the movies you make, Derek?"

He blinked his glazed eyes at me and shrugged. "I dunno. Buncha people." He reached for the bourbon. I pulled it back. He was off by a foot but snapped his fingers like he'd just missed.

"I want names. We're going to get the DVDs you sold. We're going to get rid of them." I wasn't sure why I was telling him our agenda, but I felt he might care.

"Thas good. She deserves that at least." He turned his head and something pinged inside my brain as I looked at his profile. Same as when I'd seen his uncle. Some resemblance that itched at me.

I pushed the thought aside. "Do you have a list of any kind? A list of buyers?"

He shook his head like it was resting on a pile of ball bearings. "Nah. Sid does all that distribution stuff. I just made 'em."

It looked like another visit with Sid was going to be unavoidable. We turned to go.

"I really, really loved her, you know?" he said to our backs, his voice crumbling.

I felt the old warm violence creeping through me again. I felt the urge to beat him into a puddle again and ask him if it was love. *Is it Derek? Is this the love you gave those girls?* Instead I took a deep breath.

Derek barked a humorless laugh. "The only reason I made that other movie was so we could make some money." He tried to stand and fell back to the mattress. "We were gonna run away together. I loved her. I really did." His self-justification cut off as he started bawling.

I couldn't help but realize that if I'd never found her, if Derek and Cassie had run away together, as fucked-up and flat-out wrong as it would have been . . .

She would still be alive.

Junior had no problem splitting our search. He went off to look for Paul again, and I went to Sid's. Truth be told, I think Junior was a bit afraid of the woman.

I found Sid's Vids closed two hours ahead of schedule. Suspecting another run for the border, I peered through the greasy windows. Everything was there. Then I heard the barking of the fat chihuahua. Sid must have closed up shop early to get a head start on dinner.

I walked around back to the residential entrance and found luck in the form of an already popped lock. As I inspected the busted deadbolt, rumbling thunder sounded above me in the clear blue sky. I fucking hate omens.

The dog's shrill barking sounded frightened and alarmed. My nerves jangled further when I got to Sid's door. The locks were splintered in five places, and the door was slightly ajar.

Not good.

Definitely not good.

Somebody wanted in before me. And wanted it in a hurry.

"Sid?" I whispered. No answer. I feared Sid would come leaping out of the shadows to attack—okay, maybe not leaping, and it would have to be one hell of a shadow—but I couldn't hear Sid's raspy wheeze. All I heard was the dog and the television.

Gently, I pushed open her door. My heart froze when I heard the clatter of tiny feet on linoleum. The fat dog jumped on my braced leg, licking at my fingers. The apartment still stank to high heaven, but there was something else. A primal smell. I closed the door behind me.

"Sid!"

Still no answer.

Still no wheezing.

Then I saw the foot sticking out.

I followed the mammoth foot around the corner to its leg. And then on to Sid herself . . .

. . . and the two neat holes where her nose and left eye used to be.

Blood spread out under her head along with chunks of skull and brain. A pathetically small, two-shot derringer was on the floor a couple inches from Sid's outstretched hand.

Not part of the plan.

I had to call Junior. I needed him to pick me up and get me the hell out of here. There was no way I was going to hail a cab from the apartment of the murdered. My cell phone rang as soon as my hand touched it. Stifling a yelp, I juggled the phone, catching it before it dropped into Sid's pooling blood, which seeped toward my shoe.

"Yeah," I whispered hoarsely, "who's this?"

Galloping through my brain was the thought that maybe I shouldn't have answered. Could the cops peg where the cell phone was calling from? Was I marking myself as a suspect by putting myself at the scene of the crime?

Paranoid? Absofuckinglutely. It wasn't the first dead body I'd seen, but it was the first one I'd found.

"Boo!" Junior's frantic voice sounded in the tiny earpiece. "Where the fuck are you?"

What was *he* so frantic about? I was the one next to four hundred pounds of dead Sid. With a shudder, I took a step back so the blood wouldn't touch my foot. Sid's curtains blew in on a strong gust of air. I leaned to breathe in the breeze rather than the sickly odor of bodily evacuation that flooded the room.

"I'm in Sid's."

"I'm right out front. I've got Paul with me."

"Listen to me, Junior, Sid's—"

"He came to The Cellar. He saw somebody at the squat. Cassie didn't get there on her own. You were right."

The room spun like I was in a centrifuge when the callused hand of reality suddenly squeezed my nuts.

"Junior, wait a sec—"

Why was Sid's blood still pooling?

A tiny wisp of gray smoke curled up from Sid's brand-new nose hole.

That wasn't a rumbling of thunder I'd heard; it was Sid hitting the floor.

The open window.

A hand reached around the open sill and started firing in my direction. I heard the *fup-fup-fup* of a silencer as chips of paint and concrete flew around my head. I dove for the kitchen and landed right on my bad leg. I screamed as the stitches tore, blood immediately seeping through the bandages, soaking my pants leg. A cloud of plaster dust filled the room, and the dog started yipping in fright again. I covered my head and stayed low.

The gunshots stopped, and the dust settled around me. The fire escape rattled as the shooter made his escape. Hobbling, I scooped up Sid's pistol and got to the window just in time to see the door shut on a dark green four-door. I fired the pistol's two bullets at the car.

Being the shot that I am, I managed to miss an entire car with the first bullet. The second one chipped off the windshield. The gun didn't even have enough firepower to get through glass at that distance.

The engine roared to life as I grabbed onto the fire escape ladder and slid the floor and a half down. Jagged pieces of rusted iron sliced my palms.

I hit pavement just as the car sped toward the alleyway to the street. When my newly re-opened leg hit the ground, my nervous system short-circuited. Nothing but pure adrenaline got me back to my feet through the blinding pain.

I turned the corner just in time to see the taillights whipping away.

Paul stood at the end of the alley, waving his outstretched arms to stop the car.

"Paul! No!" I yelled. "Get the fuck out of the way!"

The car wasn't going to stop.

Junior came out of nowhere and open-field tackled Paul. The two of them flew sideways across the mouth of the alley.

A second too late.

With a thumping crunch, the car plowed into them, launching them both into the air and out of my line of sight. The car screeched left, and I heard a second terrible crunch of shattering glass.

As fast as my gushing leg could carry me, I bolted down the alley. People were screaming. Tires screeched—the driver of the car blowing through a red light, missing the honking cross traffic by inches, then gone. In the melee, I couldn't find Junior or Paul. In a panic, I ran to the closest assemblage of witnesses.

Junior lay in a crumpled heap against Miss Kitty, a huge dent in the driver's side door where he'd hit. Paul had been launched through the window of the candy shop where Junior and I bought our Sno-Caps and jellybeans the night of our stakeout. A cascade of bright candy poured out around Paul's mangled body.

Groaning, Junior pushed himself up with his left arm, his right arm bending at the bicep in an unnatural angle.

I ran to Paul.

All of Paul seemed to be pointing in wrong directions. His eyes were wild with fear and pain as I kneeled next to him, glass cutting into my knees. Red, green, and purple jellybeans ran onto the sidewalk, mixing into the small river of Paul's blood.

Paul's eyes locked into mine. "B-B-Boo?" His jaw hung awkwardly in his mouth. Wet gurgles stuttered every breath he struggled to take.

Then I saw the shards of glass sticking out of the kid.

"Oh God. Oh fuck," I babbled. "Stay calm, kiddo. An ambulance . . . Somebody call a fucking *ambulance*!" I screamed to the rapidly building crowd, panic breaking my voice.

Too much blood.

"I . . . I shaw him, Boo."

So much blood.

"Shh," I said, my voice shaking. "Hold on to it, Paul. You can tell me later. Just keep cool."

Paul began to squeal in pain.

The kid was dying right in front of me. In my arms.

I'll never forgive myself for asking him, but I had to know. I couldn't look at him when I asked, "Who, Paul? Who did you see?"

The kid was starting to arrest. Convulsions wracked his skinny body. "G-g-g-g-*GAHP*!" he screamed.

He gasped.

He gasped again.

He gasped once more and went limp.

"Oh no. Oh fuck me, no," Junior said, stumbling, fighting his way through the crowd.

Junior placed a hand against his left ear, fingers coming away red. "Shit, that ain't good." The blood drip-dripped twice onto his shoulder before his eyes rolled up white and he collapsed hard onto the sidewalk.

The sirens sounded so far away.

Chapter Twenty-Two

Fourteen hours. Paul died.

Twice.

Twice they brought him back by the skin of his teeth.

Junior hadn't woken up yet.

We got to the hospital, and I waited. I got another batch of stitches to keep my blood where it belonged, and I waited, numb. I don't know if I dozed or not. I sat and stared at the pattern on the worn carpet for long stretches.

I didn't take my lies too far from the truth when I talked to the cops. I told them we were going to ask about some movies when the car shot out of the alley. Sooner or later, the police were going to cross-check some names and see that I'd just been shot a week earlier. But for the moment, my answers seemed to satisfy the bored-looking detective.

Every few decades, I'd get a report on Junior.

In and out, they'd say.

He's still on the operating table, they'd say.

They were doing everything they could, they'd say.

I stared at the name on the triage paperwork.

Darrell McCullough.

Junior.

It was a name I knew but didn't recognize. It was a name for someone who hadn't existed for nearly twenty years. He'd disappeared into the same place that took Billy Malone.

An older man in green scrubs came up to me. "Are you the gentleman who came in with the hit and run?"

"Yeah," I said, waiting with my guts in my shoes for *I'm sorry*.

"Your friend is in critical condition. I'm afraid he suffered a lot of internal injuries." He read from a clipboard like he was going over a grocery list. It was a long grocery list. "Five of his ribs are broken. One lung collapsed, and the other is severely bruised. On top of his arm and leg, both of which are broken in a couple places, he's suffered a fairly serious head trauma."

Suddenly, I realized I didn't know who he was talking about, Paul or Junior. "Wait a minute. I came in with two people."

With a sigh, he flipped back a couple of pages. "This chart is Mr. McCullough's."

"Can you tell me about the kid?"

"Far as I know, he's still in surgery. His family has arrived, so I'm afraid that any information about him will have to come through them first."

I nodded. "So, give me the shorthand. What's happening with Jun—Mr. McCullough?"

"I'm afraid he's in a coma."

Seemed the doctor was afraid of an awful lot.

I was afraid, too.

Finally, I tore myself from the waiting area. I needed something to eat. I needed sleep even more.

I went home to my empty apartment. For the first time in twenty-three years, alone was a presence in my life. Alone was a noun.

The Boy was sitting coiled on my kitchen floor, holding himself tightly. Fire and hell burned in that little boy's eyes.

I trudged into my bathroom to change my dressing. For the briefest of glimpses, I thought I saw the ghost of Billy Malone in the mirror, but I was wrong.

It was only Boo.

ꝏ

The next morning, I was bedside with Junior.

Lost.

I took his rough, bandaged hand in my own. "I'm with you, buddy," I said. The only response was the beeping of his heart monitor and the asthmatic wheeze of the respirator.

ꝏ

I was ten. I hadn't spoken a word in two years.

The other boys at The Home took easy potshots at me, seeing my trauma for the weakness it was. I took a lot of beatings, daily humiliations. They called me retarded, even though I spent most days alone in The Home's meager library, spending hour after hour lost in the worlds of Asimov's robots, roaming the streets of Metropolis, having dinner with the Hardy Boys. My most vivid memories about the adventures of Frank and Joe Hardy involve the luxurious meals described in the books. It made for one hell of a fantasy for a boy forced to eat state-subsidized food three meals a day.

I devoured the fiction, making a different world inside my mind. I was detached from their world, their cruelty. I was detached from my own. I was the boy at the bottom of the well.

And I liked the well just fine.

But sometimes the abuses just wouldn't be ignored. One afternoon, some of the bigger kids dragged me into the bathroom. While two held my arms, a third would piss on my head and laugh. I hardly reacted, just tried to keep my head up and my mouth closed. With two down and the third opening his fly, the bathroom door crashed open. I remember imagining the whole population of The Home was in line outside, waiting for the opportunity to piss on the back of my neck.

"Yo! The fuck is this? You fags having a circle jerk in here?" The new voice sounded younger than my attackers. The voice was fearless.

"Get out of here, fucko," one said.

"Fuck off," the new voice said. I turned my head to see one of the newer residents of The Home standing at the door. The new kid was a little red-haired hellion who'd already caused himself a lifetime's worth of trouble at St. Gabe's. The administrators had taken something of a gentle touch with him. Word around the concrete schoolyard was that his family had been wiped out in a fire.

Even from the position I was in, with my urine-soaked head in the urinal, I could feel the charge in the room, the older kids' uncertainty. They were accustomed to having their age and size advantages being enough to bully the younger kids. They sure as shit weren't prepared for a challenge.

"Why don't you leave him alone?" the new kid asked.

"Why don't you mind your Ps and Qs?" the boy holding my right arm said.

"Well, I gotta take a whiz and you got his head in the urinal."

The third kid laughed. "Just piss on the retard."

The new kid paused. "Who is that? That the mute? Boo?"

"Yeah. He won't say nothing even if you—" The kid behind me had his words cut short with a thump. A squealing wheeze of pain followed.

"Hey!" the kid on my right said. Another thump and a guttural groan. My right arm was free.

"Hit 'em, Boo!" the new kid said.

I threw an uppercut with my freed arm into the sternum of the third, right under the ribcage. With a pained explosion of breath, my left arm was released, too.

"In the nuts! Hit him in the nuts!" my new coach yelled.

I lowered my aim and brought my right fist up into the boy's crotch. Hard. Another yelp. Another moaning body on the floor. The other two were in identical positions, rocking on the ground and clutching their assaulted balls.

I felt a flush of victory as the new kid stepped over them and started pissing in the urinal where my head used to be. "Little trick, Boo. The bigger they are, the bigger their nutsacks." He finished and zipped up his fly. "Why do you let them do that to you?" he asked as he stepped back over them. He held the door open. Did he want me to follow him? Nobody ever wanted to talk to me, much less hang out.

I had no answer, so I shrugged.

"Are you really retarded?"

I shook my head.

"Then how come you don't talk?" He was leaving. I followed him out. "You're not deaf, 'cause you answer my questions. Kinda." He looked at my face thoughtfully. "Unless you're reading my lips. Is that it?" He held his hand over his mouth to test the theory. "You a lip reader?"

I shook my head again.

"My name's Junior." He stuck his hand out, then pulled it back. "Never mind. You got pee all over. Your name really Boo Radley?"

I shook my head once more.

"That all you can do? Shrug and nod?"

I shrugged. "W . . . whu . . ."

Junior's eyes bugged out. "What? Say it."

"What's the Junior for? What's before Junior?" My voice, unused for so long, sounded more like Froggy from the Little Rascals than the falsettos of the other boys my age.

"Wow! You can talk!" He laughed and clapped his hands. "It's short. Short for Junior Mints. One time, we went to the movies and I ate so many that I threw up." He smiled at the memory. Then the smile caught on something and faded away. "My brothers, they used to call me Junior Mints after that." A deep ache shadowed his face at the mention of his brothers. He's never mentioned them since.

The rest is my life. Boo Radley and Junior Mints. My first words in two years were to Junior. Maybe I never would have talked if I hadn't met him. I don't know. I didn't want to talk to him as he lay on the hospital bed. I wanted, needed the next words passed between us to be his. I didn't know what to say, anyway. Instead, I just held my brother's hand.

And remembered the last word Paul said.

"Gahp," he'd shrieked. The word mangled in his broken mouth.

An accusation.

Cop.

Chapter Twenty-Three

"It doesn't make any sense," Underdog said. "The guy is a hard-ass, but he's a cop, for chrissakes. He couldn't."

"*You* couldn't," I said.

I'd called in Underdog and Twitch. We sat in the office, and I told them the full story.

"So where is he?" Twitch asked. "We roll on the fucker, and I unload into him." Blood was the only retribution he knew. I knew there were worse things.

"It does, Dog. It does make sense. When Junior and me were at Donnelly's house, he said it himself. He said his own stock goes up if Donnelly gets elected mayor. He said that little bitch wasn't going to get in his way."

"But to kill her? That's nuts. How much could his stock go up? Enough for that?" Underdog was still thinking like an honorable officer of the law. He was making the assumption that all cops followed his code.

"It's Murder 101, Dog. Who benefits?"

"Barnes would," Dog said. "So would Derek. He'd lose all cred as a snuff maker if anyone found out his victim was alive. So would Cade. What would Donnelly do to him if he found out about that movie? So would—"

"Paul said 'cop.' He didn't say anything else."

"You don't know what he was saying," Underdog said, matching my tone. "The kid was hurt. He was dying. He was in shock." Dog counted the reasons one by one off his fingers. "Maybe he was calling for one. He might have been calling for help."

"Pshhh," said Twitch. "I say we just torture the fuck until he admits it. Hacksaws and Drano work better than sodium pentothal any day." I could see the bloody fantasies running through Twitch's mind. His lips twisted into a tight smile at the daydream.

"Not yet, Twitch."

"Not *yet*, not *now*, not *fucking ever*!" Underdog yelled, bewildered at our words.

"That's why I need you, Dog. That's why I'm not doing it Twitch's way." Not immediately, at least. "The setup is sound. It's a mousetrap, Dog. He doesn't go for the cheese? I walk away. But if he does . . ."

Dog plopped into the yellow chair and held his hands over his face. "Why, Boo? Because of what the kid said?"

"He said cop."

"You *think* he might have said that! What you're working with, this . . . this suspicion—" Underdog ran his fingers through his hair. "It's not enough."

"It is for me." Twitch pulled a chrome nine-millimeter out of his pants.

"What the—What the fuck is that, Boo?" Underdog's pitch rose near hysteria. He pointed at the gun in Twitch's hand. "You! Do you have a license for that?"

Twitch cackled; his eye twitch-twitched. "For this?" He held up the gun. "You need licenses for these now?"

"I don't believe this. I don't believe this." Underdog stood and paced the room frenetically, fingers pulling nervously at the ends of his hair.

"Dog," I said in as calming a voice as I could, "I've been shot once, and shot at a second time. Junior is in a fucking coma right now. Two kids whose ages don't add up to mine, one is in her cold, fucking grave and the other might be well on his fucking way. And I don't have anything else."

Dog looked at me.

"Help me, Dog. If I'm wrong, I'm fucking wrong. That's it. But I need you if I'm right."

Underdog sighed and put his face in his hands again. “Make the call.”

The call went as planned. I rang up Donnelly’s office. Barnes fielded the call. I expected him to.

“What do you want, Malone?” He sounded tired.

“I need to talk to Mr. Donnelly.” I worked to keep my voice level. I wanted to reach through the phone and close my fingers around Barnes’s throat.

“About what? Anything you need to talk about can be talked about with Ms. Reese.”

“This I need to talk to him about. Personally.”

“Listen to me, asshole, in case you hadn’t noticed or aren’t listening—”

“I found a witness.”

A pause.

“A witness to what?” He tried to make it sound snide.

“I got someone who was at the squat. They saw someone else there.”

“Who?”

“I can’t tell you that. He wants to talk to Mr. Donnelly personally.”

“No, I mean who did he see? Where did he see this person?”

Barnes was asking all the right questions. Not giving anything away. “He didn’t give me the full story. Meet me at The Cellar tonight at eight if Mr. Donnelly has any interest in this information.”

“I swear to God, if you’re screwing around—”

“I’m not. This sounds like the real deal.”

“I’ll be there at eight.” Click.

Let the games begin.

Like any recon worth his salt, Barnes showed up early. He was wearing his coat again. He came over to me at the bar, looking mighty pissed. And nervous.

"What the hell is going on? Where is this guy?"

"He's waiting by a phone. Did you talk to Mr. Donnelly?"

"Yeah. He's at a phone, too. He wants to know what's going on." Barnes got bumped drunkenly from behind. "Hey, watch it, asshole."

"S'cuse me, man."

Barnes gave him a hard look.

"You remember the loft on Atlantic Avenue? Where you first brought me to meet with Donnelly?"

"Yeah."

"Call him. Tell him to meet us there in half an hour."

"What is this? A shakedown? This guy wants money?"

Bingo. The slip. "Why do you think that?"

"Nobody gives up info for free. If this douchebag is sniffing around for some kind of reward, he better think twice."

Goddamn it, he did it again. He didn't slip a damned inch. "I dunno. That's going to have to be between him and Donnelly."

Barnes chewed his lower lip, mulling it over. He came to a decision. "Shit," he said. He opened his cell phone. Halfway through dialing, he got bumped again. He spun and grabbed a handful of his nuisance's shirtfront. "Listen to me closely, Pinky," he said through clenched teeth. "You bump me one more fucking time and I'm gonna knock two more inches off you. You got it, midget?"

"Yeah, man," Twitch slurred. "Jeez. Take a chill pill."

"Fucking assholes," Barnes said and released him with a shove. "Nice joint you run here, Malone." He resumed dialing. I walked out of earshot and dialed a number of my own. Underdog picked up on the first ring. "Half an hour."

I made Barnes drive us both to the loft. I didn't want him out of my sight for a second. We left the bar right after the phone calls were made and got there fifteen minutes later.

Barnes had a set of keys to the loft, and he let us in. As he turned on the work lights, the door opened behind us. In walked Big Jack, looking like both feet were in the grave and he was just waiting for someone to close the lid. I realized it was the first time I'd seen him out of a suit. He looked like a normal human being in his jeans and T-shirt. A normal human being in inhuman pain.

"What is this all about, Mr. Malone?" When he looked at me, I realized how bad this was going to get. I was getting ready to drop the boom on his best friend. The best friend who had killed his only daughter.

Where the hell was Underdog?

"One of my contacts might have seen someone. Somebody at the squat the night Cassandra died." Dammit. I'd had the dialogue all mapped out in my head, but nobody was following the script. Not even me.

"What? Who?" Donnelly reacted like my words were ripping out his lower intestines.

The shrill bleat of the intercom cut the question short. I watched Barnes. He looked like he could crack any second, shoulders bunched up tight, jaw clenched.

I slid my hand down toward my hip. Waiting for it. Sid's Derringer fit perfectly in the seam between my thigh and my leg brace. Twitch had reloaded the gun with hollow points. No way would those just bounce off, he said.

Cop-killer bullets, he called them.

Underdog walked in the door looking scared shitless.

I looked back at Barnes a second too late.

"No!" he yelled, his gun halfway up before I could even process how badly I'd fucked it all up.

Two eardrum-cracking gunshots.

Two big holes exploded onto Underdog's ratty denim jacket, the impact sending him sprawling.

Barnes had his gun up and aimed. Aimed right at Big Jack.

Big Jack Donnelly gripped a smoking revolver in his hand.

And had it pointed right at my face.

Barnes was supposed to crack under the pressure. I was counting on it. He would lose his shit and draw his gun and the truth would set us free. In front of the DA and an undercover cop, no less.

Now the only thing standing between me and a trigger-happy, lost-his-fucking-mind Big Jack was Barnes.

Barnes, who was pointing an empty gun in my defense.

At the bar, Twitch had pulled a bait and switch. Twitch bumped into Barnes and switched his gun with one of his own, for weight. Twitch then unloaded the gun and returned it to Barnes's holster with a second drunken bump. There was no way I was going to let the scene go down with live ammo in Barnes's gun.

Real fucking clever, ain't I?

"Jack, please. I'm begging you. Put the gun down." Barnes had his empty gun trained on Donnelly's chest. He extended his other hand gently toward his friend. Slowly, Barnes was putting himself between Donnelly and me as I carefully moved my left foot back and hit wall. On one side were the windows, and on the other were the tall bolts of canvas. "Jack, listen to me," he pleaded.

Unfortunately, Jack wasn't home anymore. His face was the death mask of a lost soul. The skin around his eyes and the corners of his mouth hung slack, as though he no longer possessed the strength to hold them in place. His eyes looked past the gun in his hand, through me, and into a deep nowhere. Tears streaked down his face, his nose running.

"I killed her, Danny," he said in a soft detached voice. "I killed my little girl."

Aw, hell no.

"Jack, it was an accident."

If Donnelly noticed the gun Barnes was pointing at him, he didn't seem to care about it any more than he did his running nose.

"I pushed her. I pushed her away, and now she's dead." He turned his face to Barnes but kept the gun square on me. "How could I do such a thing, Danny? How could I hurt my little girl like that?"

Fuck me.

It wasn't the grieved ravings of a father's conscience that I'd overheard at the cemetery that day.

It was a confession.

"It was a mistake. A horrible accident. You lost your temper. You're under a lot of stress, Jack. Please, don't make this worse than it already is."

Instinctively, I'd put my hands up when the guns were pulled and the shots were fired. Other than Donnelly, I held the only loaded gun in play. But there was no way I could get to it without giving Big Jack ample time to blow Big Holes through me.

When Donnelly's eyes finally focused, they drew on me with a dry fury. I instantly wished he'd stayed in La-La land. "Did you know?"

"Know what?" As soon as I asked, I knew what he was talking about.

Donnelly nodded his head loosely and shuddered a pitiful sigh. "You did, didn't you. You knew about the disc. You knew, and you didn't *tell* me." He jabbed the air in front of me with the gun.

"I didn't think you knowing about it was necessary." All I could do was keep him talking, anything to keep his mind off pulling the trigger.

Barnes cut in again, his desperation intensifying. "It was an accident, Jack. She fell. Nobody knew."

"Somebody did." Donnelly waved toward Underdog's body with the gun. Then his hands were at his side. My gun might as well have been in Malaysia.

But Barnes saw his chance. "Goddamn it, Jack. This shit is deep enough. I'm not going to jail for you! I'm sorry, Jack."

He pulled his trigger on empty chambers. He dry-clicked it three more times in disbelief. "What the fuck?" Then he looked right at me, his face a snarl of rage. "You stupid mother—"

"I'm sorry too, Danny," Donnelly said, and he shot Barnes in the face. Blood and brains sprayed across me. Barnes dropped face-down to the hardwood with a wet thump, jerked twice, and then was still.

In the fraction of time between Barnes's blood spattering me and his hitting the floor, it all flashed through my mind in a rush.

I'd been shot over this already.

Kelly's life had been threatened.

Junior was in a coma.

Underdog was on the floor.

Paul might be dead already.

Barnes sure as fuck was.

And Cassandra.

Even Sid's gorilla mug passed through in that wisp of a second.

I saw my mother's face.

My sister.

They had all died.

They were all dead.

Enough, my mind screamed.

Enough, enough, enough, enough.

ENOUGH!

In that same splinter of a second, the room exploded crimson.

My hand reached for the peashooter in my brace as Donnelly turned and fired at me. Slugs drove into the bolts of canvas with dull thumps, toppling them behind me. More bullets detonated into the wall at my back. Focusing my rage into as tiny a pinpoint as I could, I raised my pistol just as a heavy bolt of canvas slammed me on the back of the neck. As I fell, I fired my only two shots in the direction I hoped Donnelly stood.

Another bolt came down sideways and popped me in the face. My nose burst and I dropped onto my back, stunned. My ears rang, and the room flickered as I lay there. I could taste the blood from my nose running through my sinuses and down the back of my throat. Panic fueled me to scramble up off the floor. For what purpose, I didn't know. On my maimed leg I wouldn't have gotten far before Donnelly dropped me.

Donnelly was on his knees. His gun hand was pointed at the floor, and the other clutched at his neck. Bright arterial blood gushed from between his fingers. He looked around the room, as though wondering how he'd gotten there.

Then he noticed me and blinked some more. "Nice shot," he gurgled. His head lolled as he looked at the gun in his hand. "Got one left." With all he had remaining, he put the barrel under his chin and pulled the trigger.

Bang.

But for my own ragged breathing, the room was silent with death.

Then Underdog groaned miserably.

I scrambled on the floor over to him.

"Aw God," he moaned. "This sucks so much." A trickle of blood seeped from a hole in his collarbone. From his chest—from the shot that would have killed him, should have killed him—there was nothing. Dry.

"Dog!" I yelled with hysterical happiness. "You wore a vest?"

Dog smiled crookedly at me. "You . . . think . . . I'm a fucking idiot?" He grimaced in pain. "One got through. The other one knocked me down. Ow. I think I might have a broken collarbone. Hand me your phone so I can call myself an ambulance, would you?"

I gave him the phone. "How much did you hear?"

"All of it. Give me that stupid fucking gun in your hand and get the hell gone. You were never here, got it?"

I got it, and I was gone.

I exited the building as casually as I could and walked away fast. I was only three blocks away when I heard the platoon of sirens.

Chapter Twenty-Four

I waited for the hammer to fall. It never did. The news shows were reporting an undercover police officer had seen Danny Barnes the night of Cassandra's death and went to inform the district attorney when the shit hit the fan. The officer was in stable condition. Underdog would get himself a medal out of the ordeal. Shit, he deserved it.

I added to my battery of injuries a nose that looked like a ripe plum about to burst and a quarter-sized piece of ear that was missing. I'm still not sure how that happened.

Depression started to blanket me. I'd gotten Barnes killed. I'd possibly gotten Paul killed. My actions, my self-inflated obsessions, put Junior in a coma. If justice was served, it sure hadn't been my responsibility to serve it. I'd fucked up, and the people around me paid the price.

But I still wasn't done.

First, I returned to Sid's. Nobody had reported her AWOL yet. I kept an eye out for any yellow tape or unmarked cars. I didn't see any.

Carefully, I made my way into her apartment. The smell must have been more horrific than usual, but my broken nose kept me from having to experience it. Blessings in disguise. I found what I was looking for fairly easily. In her desk, sitting right in the top drawer, was a ledger. On the front, in big, bold magic marker, was Red Dot Customers. The information on the inside was complete with payments, amounts, and . . .

Addresses.

I stuck the ledger under one arm, the fat chihuahua under the other, and left.

I named him Burrito.

During my flicker of lucidity right before I pulled the trigger on Donnelly, I realized what had been bothering me about my meeting with Cade, what had lurked in the recesses of my mind the second time I saw Derek Bevilaqua.

Ollie confirmed my suspicion with a few clicks on the computer when he hacked into the Boston Public School records.

I called ahead to Conor's Publick this time. The dinosaur glared at me from under the thick bandage wrapped around his head but let me pass.

Without saying a word, I walked over to Cade's table and placed the disc on the checkered cloth, then turned and left. I had nothing to say. The disc would tell all. Cade would recognize his daughter. I did. I would have never made the connection had she not inherited her father's tragic ears. The poor kid who looked like the scared mouse on the first video we'd seen. The video where Derek beat and raped Angela Cade.

Frankie's daughter.

Around the time of her death, there were rumors it was a suicide. She couldn't have done it long after the video had been shot. She was thirteen at the time she died.

Five days later, the depression decided to stop dicking around and sucked me in completely. I spent a lot of time drinking with my whispering demons. 4DC lost two more security accounts. I had to let six of our guys go. I was still fucking up, still bringing grief into the lives of those around me. I found it hard to care. My mind flooded with questions. No answers.

What now?

Who gives a shit, the demons answered, and toasted me another round.

The media was still going apeshit. Forensics pulled up traces of blood on the floor of the DA's bathroom. They found more in the trunk of Danny Barnes's car. They'd pieced together that Cassandra died in the apartment and Barnes helped Donnelly cover it up, leaving the poor kid's body in the squat.

I got no comfort from Barnes's involvement. I'd still cost him his life. I wasn't so sure he deserved what he got. When I'd walked a mile in his shoes, would I have done the same for Junior? Would he have done the same for me?

I didn't like what I thought the answer might be.

Right behind the Donnelly story was a report on a severed arm found wrapped in a black plastic bag in a Dumpster in Providence. The report included an artist's rendition of the snake tattoo wrapped around the dismembered limb.

Rhode Island police would appreciate any information.

A week and a half after that, I started to feel a little better. I managed to stay sober for a whole twenty-four hours.

I repossessed the last of the DVDs. In my recoveries, I only had to break a total of six fingers, one wrist, five noses, and three or four ribs.

I enjoyed each and every one so, so much.

Then I anonymously mailed the ledger with a note of explanation to the Boston Police.

ꝏ

The bounty we'd collected was almost depleted between the hospital bills from both my trips and Junior's care. I didn't give a fuck. The money was tainted, and I couldn't get it out of my life fast enough.

Trying to buy a little bit of redemption, I bought a '68 VW Van. After parking it in the driveway next to the house, I dropped the keys in an envelope and taped the envelope to Phil's door. I think he'd been in hiding ever since he ran from the crash. I knew he was still up there, though. The clouds of pot smoke hadn't diminished one bit.

ꝏ

I ended the day by paying a visit to Cassie's grave as the setting sun painted the horizon the same pink as her room. I knelt to say a prayer before I remembered that I didn't know any. Somehow, I'd managed to spend ten years of my life in a place named Saint Gabriel's without memorizing one prayer. Not that I believed in it, but I thought Cassandra might have liked to hear me say one.

"I'm sorry, kid," I said softly. "I wanted to be your hero. I couldn't. I'm sorry."

Then I placed the bouquet of yellow and white daisies under the long shadow of her grave marker and listened to the wind for a while.

ꝏ

I got another message from Kelly. She sounded like she'd been crying when she asked why I wasn't answering my cell or my phone at home or calling her back. As I listened, a gnawing ache dug through me. I wanted to talk to her. I wanted to see her.

I also wanted her to do better than me. She deserved better. She deserved better than a thug who was good for nothing but playing tough guy. I tried to think objectively about the events, about what had happened.

Only one fact was carved in my mind as though set in marble.

The people I loved died.

She was kind enough never to come by The Cellar.

That's not to say I didn't look for her every night.

She deserved better.

I was sitting at Junior's bedside, reading him some Eddie Bunker, when the nurse came in. "Hey, Boo," she said.

I looked at her, vaguely recognizing her. "Hey," I said.

"My name's Patti. You remember me?"

Suddenly, I remembered the girl. She bartended at The Cellar while she was in school. For nursing, I could only assume. "Hey," I said again. "You look different."

She ran her fingers through her chestnut brown hair. "Yeah, they kinda frown on platinum mohawks on the nursing staff. Had to grow up a little."

"Glad one of us did."

"Just thought you'd want to know. The kid who came in with Junior?"

"Yeah?"

"He's gonna make it. He's out of the woods and out of the ICU."

Relief flooded my chest so violently I couldn't even breathe in for a couple seconds. "Thank you. I hadn't heard."

She lifted her chin at Junior. "How's he doing?"

"Fucking thirsty," Junior said.

"I'll get you some ginger-ale," Patti said, unaware of how big the moment was.

"Hey," I said.

Junior squinted and took in a long breath through his nose. "Was that Patti?" he mouthed in a dry whisper.

"Yup."

"Always did want to fuck her."

Junior was going to be fine.

I walked into The Cellar to work out the weekly schedules. Since Junior wouldn't be able to work for at least a couple months and I wasn't exactly at my fighting best, I decided to hire in a couple of the guys I'd just given their walking papers at the other bars. It was as close to redemption as I could get.

When I walked in, Audrey was leaning at the end of the bar nearest the door, concentrating on a hand of solitaire with her well-worn deck of Jack Daniels cards. There was only one customer, sitting alone in the darkest corner of the bar.

"Hey, Willie," she said in a bored and lonely monotone.

"How's it going, cupcake?"

"You seen Brendan around?" she asked, ignoring my attempt at idle chitchat.

"Nope. Guess he's taking a break." I hadn't seen him since the night at the loft. I hoped he was doing well. A week ago, I'd considered paying him a visit, but I thought it might unnecessarily complicate things.

"I got nobody to play cards with no more," she said.

"When I come down from the office, we'll go a few hands of gin."

Her round face lit up. "You promise?"

"Promise." I put up two fingers and held them together.

I got two steps away from the bar when I saw who the lone customer was.

Louis Blanc sat in an immaculate gray suit, sipping a bottle of Coke. He stared straight ahead at the liquor bottles behind the bar. His blind eye faced me, the long scar creasing the side of his head like a second mouth, frowning at me.

His lips made a soft popping sound when he brought the bottle away from his mouth. "Got a minute, Mr. Malone?" he said toward the bottles in that eerily paternal brogue of his.

I quickly calculated motive versus opportunity divided by common sense and decided he'd either come for the buffalo wings or to kill me. I took the barstool to his left, where he could at least see me. He didn't look over. He wasn't even watching me in the mirror. He seemed content to keep his eye on the bottles.

"Mr. Cade sent me here," he said.

I didn't answer. With gaping depression comes comfortable fatalism. It was a perk, in a way.

"He doesn't want to thank you, exactly, for what happened. But he wants you to know that he's in your debt. For opening his eyes."

I didn't want that unholy cocksucker to be in my debt for a goddamn thing, but I kept that to myself. I just nodded and stood up to leave.

"And I wanted to apologize," he said.

Blanc saw that I didn't understand.

"Not for your leg. You earned that one. I wanted to apologize about your friend. And the boy."

"It was you at Sid's that night," I said with numb lips.

"Yes, it—"

Before I processed the consequences, my body was in motion. With a roar, I grabbed the collar of his perfect suit with my left hand and my right snatched the thick Coke bottle, smashing it into his temple in one vicious motion. His head snapped to the side as the glass exploded against his skull. As momentum and surprise took him backward over the barstool, I ran with him, off-balance myself, and drove him into the jukebox with my full weight. The glass on the jukebox shattered and we fell to the floor, my body on top.

Audrey screamed as we hit the floor. "Willie! What are you doing?"

Blanc's good eye rolled up, and he groaned as I knelt over him. Two thin trickles of blood ran from the spot where the bottle burst on his head, one from the corner of his blind eye like a teardrop.

I still grasped the jagged neck of the bottle in my fist. I pressed the splintered glass against his pulsing throat. "Motherfucker," I screamed in his face, spittle flying. I was foaming at the mouth like a mad dog. "Why?" I pulled him off the floor and slammed him back down. His head knocked loudly off the wood. "Why?"

"Willie, stop!" Audrey cried, doing a frantic dance from foot to foot behind us.

"Get back, Audrey," I yelled over my shoulder. "He's got a gun." *C'mon*, my mind screamed. I leaned close and whispered. "Reach for that fucking piece. Do it. Just try, and I'll push this bottle through your fucking neck until I hit the floor."

Audrey gasped and Blanc, the cold bastard, smiled. "Actually," he said calmly, "I don't have a gun." Bleeding, assaulted, and on the floor with a broken bottle pressed to his neck, he might as well have been on a cruise.

"Answer me why, you fuck! I swear to God, I'll do you right fucking here!"

Blanc cleared his throat and spoke gently. "It truly was an accident. Sid pulled a gun on me, and I killed that pig. But I don't kill children."

His eyes locked with my own, never blinking as he said his confession.

And Lord help me, I believed him.

I climbed off him, panting harshly. "You . . . you're a fucking killer," I said, my voice ragged.

"This is true," he said, gingerly applying his fingers to his wounds. He rubbed the light smear of blood between his thumb and forefinger. "But I'm not a murderer, and I think you know the difference." The trickle of blood ran down his neck, seeping into his shirt collar. "Excuse me, do you have a napkin?"

"Get out of here. Now."

Blanc helped himself to a few napkins off the bar. Dabbing at his head, he said, "Derek was told only to make one disc. He wasn't supposed to make the second—the fake."

Derek had said something about "making the other movie." Another hint I'd missed.

"What disc? Who's Derek?" Audrey was still way in the dark and confused to tears. "Who's got a gun?"

Blanc took Audrey's pudgy hand and smoothly kissed the knuckles. "I apologize, Audrey. It was a poor joke on my part, and Boo misunderstood me. Everything is fine."

Hardly. But Audrey seemed satisfied with his answer and, so help me, blushed like a virgin on prom night. "That right, Willie?"

"Yeah. Misunderstanding."

Satisfied, Audrey poured me a whiskey and cracked Lou a fresh Coke. "You two drink and make up, or I'm kicking both your asses." With that, Audrey sauntered back behind the bar and resumed her solitaire game.

"*Slainte*," said Blanc, holding his bottle to me with that smile.

"Fuck your mother," I offered back, and I downed my shot.

"May I continue?"

When Audrey was out of earshot, I lowered my voice. "Cade . . ."

"Mr. Cade wanted his nephew to capture the girl in an inappropriate situation. A situation he could use for leverage, were Mr. Donnelly to be elected mayor."

"And you don't see where that's fucked up?"

"I'm not justifying it. I'm just telling you what happened."

I swallowed a swelling lump of disgust. "She was fourteen. Fourteen fucking years old."

"Fourteen-year-olds have sex every day, Mr. Malone. I'm not here to debate the proper age for sexual activity to start. But that was all the DVD was supposed to be. Unfortunately, Derek was a weak and confused young man, and he made a second DVD to sell. I was at Sid's for the same reason you were. Mr. Cade wanted me to recover the other discs, but you interrupted my recovery."

"And you shot at me."

Blanc smiled at me again. "I shot around you. I had no reason to kill you. I didn't have to miss."

"Gee, thanks. You're a fucking prince. We done?"

"You feel bad, don't you? About the cop?"

That stopped me. I felt like a fly caught in a web as it was built around me.

"You shouldn't. Barnes is no loss to this world."

"How do you know?" I was the only person left alive from the loft except Underdog, and I couldn't see him relating the story to Blanc.

"Knowledge is power." Opening his gold cigarette case, he took out a long, dark cigarette and tapped it on the case. "Don't worry. I won't light it in here."

"Thanks," I mumbled.

"I received a phone call," he said, matter-of-factly. "I had been keeping tabs on Barnes all week. He was working both sides, as you may or may not have known. We weren't sure how much we could trust him anymore, recent circumstances being what they were." He paused when he saw me fighting to process the new information he'd tossed on my lap. "He thought you were stringing them for more money. If at all possible, he wanted to avoid more deaths. At least, deaths he would have to dirty his hands with. You played it well, Mr. Malone. The only reason he didn't kill you himself was your aggression. With you putting him on defense, he couldn't take you out, not knowing fully all that you had on them."

"He wanted you to do it," I said, stunned.

"I told him to clean up his own messes. Either way."

"Donnelly wasn't going to be a problem for you or Cade anymore."

"Smart boy," he said, tapping his finger on the tip of his nose. "How do you think Mr. Cade has remained so untouchable for all these years?

Who do you think led us to Cassandra, so that Derek could make his little movie?"

A chill ran through me. "You telling me it was Barnes? Barnes set the whole thing up?"

A nod.

"Why?"

"Mr. Barnes had his own weaknesses, or shall we say tastes? Mr. Cade makes these tastes his business. As I said, knowledge is power."

Nearly the same words Donnelly had dropped on me the first time we met.

Blanc went on. "Let me ask you a question." He leaned in and looked me straight, eye to eyes. "Assuming you watched them? The DVDs."

"Yeah. I saw them."

"Did you notice anything about the cinematography, so to speak?"

Then it hit me like a thunderclap between the ears. Why hadn't I noticed it? How the hell could I have missed something so simple? It was literally right in front of my face on the screen.

The camera panned.

Somebody else had to be in the room, in the closet behind the two-way, moving the camera.

Blanc saw understanding dawn on my face. "Bright lad," he said. He opened his black leather billfold, placed a twenty on the bar, and stood to leave. "Be seeing you," he said, crisply pulling the creases from his coat sleeves. As he walked out, he lit his smoke with the lighter that would have cost me two weeks' wages. Over the flame, he gave me a warm parting smile and a wink.

With his dead eye, of course.

Coda

I opened the door to the office one Saturday afternoon. On the floor sat a folder with my name on it, slid under the door. No other markings on the front.

I knew what it was.

Still wasn't sure that I wanted to see what was inside.

I opened it . . .

. . . just a bit . . .

. . . just a peek.

There was a picture of a woman on the lower left side. I forced my eyes to not look at it directly, squeezed them shut and looked up as I closed the folder.

She was a woman now. She'd made it that far. I swallowed hard. The lump that had swelled there didn't want me to.

Sliding my thumb under the fold, I pushed the top page up just a bit.

Just a bit . . .

There was the name at the top.

Last name: Malone.

First name: Emily.

Middle name: Madeline.

I took a deep and shuddering breath as I realized that I'd forgotten her middle name.

I didn't know her anymore.

She didn't know me.

And for the life of me, I couldn't come up with a good goddamn reason why she would want to.

I wiped moisture from under my eyes as I touched the flame of the Zippo under the corner of the folder. I watched it burn away, felt the flames touching my fingertips. I let the fire burn me, I let it hurt . . .

. . . just a bit . . .

. . . before I dropped it in the metal wastebasket.

Goodbye, Emily. Hope your life's as good as I imagined—as good as I hope it has been. Shit, I hope it's been even better than that.

Better than mine, baby girl.

Then the fucking fire alarm went off.

Acknowledgments

OR, you can blame the following people I'm about to thank for the book you just read. Your choice.

First and foremost, thanks go to my agent, Stacia Decker. It took a long time to get this book into hands that cared for it, and she stuck with it and busted her ass to make it so. Ben LeRoy and the staff at Tyrus Books—you're the good hands. Thanks for that.

My family—you *support* what I do, even when you don't necessarily *get* what I do. Sorry, Ma. Love ya.

To my wife Allison—you're the strongest woman I've ever met, and you've been strong enough to stick by my ass. I love you. To my little man Sam—you're not going to be reading this for a long time, but I hope daddy makes you proud when you do.

To those readers who made it this far—hope you dug it, and I appreciate the time you chose to spend with this book. Deep thanks go to you, since *without* you, I'd be screaming stories to the air and that would just make me a crazy person. Thanks for being a reader.